"How did you entertain yourself for the whole afternoon?" Michael asked.

"Did you get a tour of the gardens?"

"Yes, and the house, too. I saw everything, even the kitchens. Ashby Hall is wonderful, Michael. I've fallen in love. Quite desperately, I'm afraid."

He shot Julia a quizzical glance.

"With the house," she explained.

"Lucky house." There was no reason for him to have said something so suggestive. Why was it that with Julia his tongue always seemed to be racing two beats ahead of his common sense?

"Or lucky me." She gave him a rueful smile. "I've a suspicion that love affairs with houses tend to work out a lot better than love affairs with people."

"I'm sure you're right," he agreed, straight-faced. "Of course, the sexual aspect of the relationship can be a bit challenging."

Weddings by De Wilde™

Weddings by DeWilde™

PREVIOUSLY AT DeWILDES

Jeffrey DeWilde never would have guessed a quiet California vineyard held the keys to his family mystery.

- Marguerite Kauffman knew more about Derrick DeWilde than anyone, it seemed. And she'd developed a yen to come clean—to Grace DeWilde, of all people—just as Nick Santos was about to beat a path to her door!

- Falling in love with Kate DeWilde, however, was putting a considerable crimp in the detective's plans for recovering the stolen DeWilde jewelry.

- Then Dr. Kate is seriously injured in a shooting incident that causes her to question her career choice...permanently. Nick is the only one who can make a difference in her outlook, and in her life.

Once recovered, the jewels need to get back to their proper home in London, and Grace DeWilde has very definite plans about how the delivery of the precious cargo should be accomplished. Grace and Jeffrey, one on one. At last.

To Grace Allison, so glad you're here!

Jasmine Cresswell is acknowledged as the author of this work.

ISBN 0-373-82548-X

I DO, AGAIN

I Do, Again
JASMINE CRESSWELL

Harlequin Books

TORONTO • NEW YORK • LONDON
AMSTERDAM • PARIS • SYDNEY • HAMBURG
STOCKHOLM • ATHENS • TOKYO • MILAN
MADRID • WARSAW • BUDAPEST • AUCKLAND

DeWildes™

To: Lianne
From: Gabe

Lianne, honey—

I've been trying to reach you all afternoon, but I keep getting the answering machine. Just wanted to let you know that Michael Forrest is arriving at London Airport tomorrow morning. I invited him to spend some time with us at Briarwood Cottage, and he's accepted. Try to arrange a dinner party for Saturday night— and be sure to include Julia Dutton. One of these days, those two are going to realize they were meant for each other! I'll call you tonight from the flat.

Love you.

Gabe

P.S. When you invite Julia, make it seem as if we're trying to fix her up with Edward Hillyard. She'll refuse to come if she has the faintest clue that Michael's the man we're aiming for!

CHAPTER ONE

THE FAMOUS GROUND FLOOR of DeWilde's London store was silent, the lights dim, the glittering trays of jewels covered, the daily throng of customers dispersed. Jeffrey DeWilde prowled among the deserted displays, noting the changes that had been made during the past week and wondering if they were improvements. He admired an elegant arrangement of Spanish leather handbags and Italian silk scarves, raised an eyebrow at the decision to present sterling silver hairbrushes on a bed of purple satin underwear, and paused for a moment in front of the eye-catching booth that now housed the gift registry. Was it really a good idea to bring the registry down from its traditional cramped quarters on the fourth floor and set it up in a prominent position here on the ground floor by the lifts? Jeffrey had no idea, but Gabe seemed to think so, and over the past months, Jeffrey had learned to trust his son's judgment on matters of merchandising.

Until their separation little more than a year ago, Jeffrey and his wife had always made this ritual Friday-night tour together. With Grace at his side, explaining the practical significance of each innovation, Jeffrey had thoroughly enjoyed the hour it took to complete the tour. He'd treated their stroll through the quiet store as a prelude to the weekend, a way for Grace and him to unwind after the frenetic intensity of their work week. Sometimes, he'd even been able to contribute something useful by tying in what Grace showed him with the overall financial status of the

DeWilde retail empire—which included branches in Paris, Sydney, New York and Monaco. Sales figures, wholesale costs, interest charges, overhead and profit margins were always crystal clear in his brain. But without Grace to help him translate that financial picture into more concrete terms of day-to-day retailing, he had nothing to offer when it came to decisions about the choice of merchandise and the way it was displayed.

For the past fifteen months, his Friday-night tour had been little more than an act of defiance—a gesture to prove to himself that everything in his entire world hadn't changed for the worse just because Grace had left him and they were now divorced.

Divorced. As far as Jeffrey was concerned, the word still sounded nonsensical when applied to himself and Grace, although his solicitors had assured him in one of their typically pompous letters that after thirty-two years of marriage and a year of separation, he was once again a bachelor. He'd wanted the divorce from Grace. Five months ago, when she took up residence in Nevada in order to file for divorce, he'd positively craved an end to their marriage, yearning for a surcease of the pain they were causing each other.

He'd been officially footloose and fancy-free since April, and now it was almost August. Fifteen weeks of glorious liberation from the chains of matrimony. Jeffrey let out a crack of harsh laughter. Ah, yes, he was experiencing all the joys of freedom from his miserably failed marriage. He hoped—he really hoped—that in another year or so, the mere mention of the words *divorce* and *bachelor* wouldn't have the power to make him feel suicidally depressed.

"Is everything all right, sir?" One of the uniformed security guards stepped out of the shadows into Jeffrey's line of vision.

"Yes, everything's quite all right, thank you." If you

didn't count the frequent desire to throw punches at the nearest wall, everything was just wonderful. Jeffrey swung away, reluctant to submit to the guard's barely concealed curiosity. He would never get used to the fact that his most intimate concerns were a matter for interested gossip by his employees. Not to mention the prurient articles in the tabloids. The gossip magazines seemed determined to treat him as a sex icon for any readers too mature to go into raptures over John F. Kennedy, Jr., an idea that Jeffrey would have found hilariously funny if it hadn't been so embarrassingly wide of the mark.

They were standing next to the octagonal glass case that housed the Empress Eugénie tiara, and his movement away from the guard brought him face-to-face with the dazzling coronet of diamonds and pearls, displayed on an artfully rumpled cloth of scarlet velvet. The cascade of seemingly casual folds formed a perfect contrast to the formal rigidity of the tiara, the rich color adding a voluptuous contrast to the icy brilliance of the jewels. The display setting had recently been redesigned by Lianne Beecham, Jeffrey's daughter-in-law, and its exotic flair carried the unmistakable stamp of her talents.

The tiara was the genuine article, a multimillion-pound piece of history, a costly tribute from Emperor Louis-Napoléon to his much-loved wife, and Jeffrey felt a brief surge of emotion each time he passed the display case and registered the flamboyant sparkle of the diamond clusters and the warm luster of the priceless pearls. The genuine tiara, missing for almost fifty years, had finally been returned to its rightful home almost a fortnight after Grace had left England for San Francisco. The timing, Jeffrey reflected, had been quite spectacularly ironic. He'd regained one of his family's lost heirlooms at virtually the same moment as he'd lost his wife. A hell of a price to pay for a few jewels, however historic.

He pulled himself together, refusing to let his thoughts

ramble down that well-worn path of useless regret. "Did you know I'm expecting a courier to deliver something important tonight?" he asked the guard, whose nametag identified him as Bill Babb. "I spoke with your supervisor yesterday to arrange an after-hours security clearance."

Bill nodded. "Yes, sir, everything's been taken care of. Keith is at the security desk, and he's planning to give you a ring as soon as the messenger arrives. I'll escort the visitor up to your office, or wherever it is you want to meet with him."

"My office will be fine." Jeffrey glanced at his watch. "I expect the courier to arrive before seven, which means some time in the next fifteen minutes or so. Let Keith know I've gone up to the sixth floor, will you?"

"Yes, sir. I'll pass the message on right away. Good night, sir."

Back in his office, Jeffrey shuffled through the stack of papers and spread sheets waiting for his attention, then gave up pretending that he was doing any work. He walked across to the bar concealed behind the mahogany doors of a wall cabinet and poured himself a whisky, not bothering to find ice or soda. He let the mellow single-malt Scotch rest on his tongue for a moment before swallowing. He cradled the glass between his hands, but resisted the urge to keep sipping. He'd managed to control the heavy drinking he'd indulged in right after Grace left for San Francisco, but he knew he still depended too much on alcohol to take the edge off his loneliness. Slowly, painfully, in the months since Grace left him, he'd come to realize that it was better to acknowledge what you were feeling, even if it was unpleasant. If you buried your feelings too deeply, eventually the pressure built up until something exploded. In his case, what had exploded had been his marriage.

The debris from that giant explosion still littered his personal landscape, blighting positive emotions and intensifying the negatives. His lack of excitement over the return of the DeWilde jewels was a perfect example of his problem. For the past year, he'd focused with almost desperate intensity on the mystery of the missing jewels and the fate of his long-lost uncle, Dirk DeWilde, who had disappeared at the same time. With the help of Nick Santos, his private investigator, all the mysteries had been solved and the jewels recovered. He'd had the pleasure of meeting two sets of previously unknown DeWilde cousins in Australia, seen a long-standing feud with the Villeneuve family laid to rest, and discovered the reasons behind Dirk's disappearance. Tonight, as icing on the cake, the last of the missing jewels would be returned to him. An occasion for major celebration—except Jeffrey could barely remember why their return had once seemed so vitally important.

The phone rang, providing a welcome interruption to his gloomy thoughts. He picked up the receiver. "Yes?"

"Mr. DeWilde, this is Keith Jones at the security desk."

"Yes."

"The courier you were expecting from San Francisco has arrived, sir."

"Good. Send him up right away, please."

"Er...yes, sir. Bill is escorting the...courier upstairs now."

The pause before the guard replied had been so slight that in the old days Jeffrey would never have noticed it. But, if nothing else, his separation from Grace had taught him to be more alert to the subtle nuances of people's conversation. "Keith, is there a problem?"

"Er...no. No problem, sir. The courier's papers are all in order. Signed by Nick Santos, like you said." The guard made an odd noise, which he tried to disguise as a cough. "I've released the lock on the lift controls, sir. Bill and the courier are on their way up to the corporate offices. Shouldn't be more than a couple of minutes until they're on the sixth floor. I'm sure you'll find everything in order, sir.''

"All right. Thank you.'' Jeffrey set his unfinished whisky down on his desk and walked across the room to open his office door. Halfway to the door, he realized he was still bothered by the hesitation he'd heard in the guard's voice.

Damn it, something was wrong. The guard had said the proper things, but his tone of voice had hinted at a problem. Far more than hinted, in fact. Toward the end, he'd as good as announced that he was hiding something.

Nick Santos should have made this important delivery in person. Jeffrey had protested when Nick informed him that another courier had been found to bring the jewels from San Francisco to London, and now it seemed as if his sense of foreboding had been right on the mark. The courier was bringing some sort of trouble with him, Jeffrey could smell it.

With heirloom jewels worth millions of pounds about to be transferred into his keeping, he was in no mood to take chances. What if Keith had unlocked the lifts with a gun held to his head? The only way Jeffrey could find out was to go down to the ground floor and personally inspect the lobby, but he was unarmed and untrained, and although he'd once been a bruising tackle on the rugger field, these days he was prone to arthritis in his left knee. Any attempt on his part to play the hero might well precipitate a tragedy. Or a humiliating farce.

He needed professional help. Securicorps had been warned of the imminent return of the DeWilde jewels, so they wouldn't be altogether surprised to get an emergency summons to the store.

Jeffrey strode back to his desk and activated the silent alarm that connected directly to Securicorp's headquarters, feeling better for the knowledge that armed guards would be dispatched immediately to check into any problems. He might be overreacting, but there was no point in waiting for Nick's courier to arrive in his office—trailing armed robbers—before deciding there was trouble brewing. By the time he had proof of what instinct was telling him, it might be too late to sound the alarm.

Jeffrey heard the lift doors open and he tensed, bracing himself for trouble. The thick pile of the carpet muffled the sounds of approaching footsteps, and neither the courier nor his security escort seemed to be talking. A bad sign. Bill Babb had struck him as the garrulous type.

His office door stood slightly open, but Bill knocked, anyway, simultaneously poking his head around the door. "Your...er...your courier has arrived from San Francisco, Mr. DeWilde."

The guard was visibly ill at ease. Jeffrey gripped the edge of his desk. "Send him in, Bill."

"Yes, sir." Bill sighed with evident relief and sidestepped as if to hold the door open for the person accompanying him.

Jeffrey frowned. "Come in," he said sharply, tired of being played for a fool. "I don't know how you expect to get away with this, whatever you're planning. We have state-of-the-art security...." His voice died away as a woman walked into his office. He realized his mouth was hanging open and snapped it shut.

"Hello, Jeffrey."

He swallowed twice before he could reply. "Grace," he said thickly. "Grace, what are you doing here?"

"Nick allowed me to act as the courier for the return of the DeWilde jewels," she said. The familiar huskiness of her voice curled around him, squeezing all the breath out of his lungs. She lifted a slender aluminum briefcase onto his desk and stood directly across from him, close enough for him to see the flush of color that ebbed and flowed in her cheeks. Close enough to smell the light fragrance of her perfume. She pointed to the briefcase. "I have all four pieces here, waiting for your inspection."

"You've cut your hair." He hadn't meant to say something so irrelevant—so personal—but he was hypnotized by the changes in her appearance. He had seen her only a few weeks earlier, at their daughter Kate's wedding in San Francisco, but tonight she seemed a different person. After a lifetime of styling her hair in a smooth, heavy twist at the nape of her neck, she'd had it all cut off. She now wore it brushed back from her face, except for one thick blond strand that swept forward over her forehead and skimmed the side of her cheek. He felt unsettled at this visible sign of the fact that she'd moved on to a new stage of her life. Leaving him behind in the old rut.

"Kate decided it was time I updated my image." She gave a slight smile. "If Kate noticed a problem, I knew my hairstyle had to be at least ten years overdue for a change." She tucked the wayward strand of hair behind her ear and fiddled for a moment with her sapphire-and-gold stud earring. "Do you like it?"

He stared with hypnotized fascination as her fingers massaged her earlobe. He'd never before realized that earlobes were a part of the female body with major erotic potential. "It's very...nice." He cleared his throat and tried again. "It suits you. Very flattering and modern."

Her voice was low, huskier than ever. "I'm glad you think so."

How was he supposed to respond to that? he wondered. Jeffrey looked away, clenching his fists helplessly. In a business setting, he could command an audience of hundreds, field hostile questions, toss witty asides into the conversation and quell hot tempers with calm reason and good judgment. But with the people he cared about, when he really needed to be fluent, his tongue seemed to stick to the roof of his mouth, too thick and clumsy even to mumble acceptable platitudes.

This was the first time Grace had been in his office since the day she left him. That had been a Friday, too. A Friday in early May, over a year ago. It was disorienting to see her in such a familiar setting—looking so different. How odd it was that after a lifetime of marriage and more than a year of separation what he felt at this precise moment was neither nostalgia nor regret—not even anger. What he felt was pure desire, the sort of straightforward and consuming physical lust he couldn't remember experiencing since he was in his twenties. He conquered a primitive urge to toss his ex-wife onto the couch and make mad, passionate love to her. Quite apart from any other considerations, he had just enough sense of the ridiculous left to wonder if he'd be able to put his fantasy into practice without his arthritic knee giving out on him.

As always when he was at a loss for words, Jeffrey took refuge in the practical and nonemotional. "Nick shouldn't have allowed you to cross the Atlantic with millions of pounds' worth of jewels in your custody. That's not a job for a..." He'd been about to say for a woman, but he caught himself just in time. Megan, Kate and Lianne had managed to raise his consciousness at least to the point that he no longer gave voice to his prejudices. "That's a job for a trained professional," he amended. "I hope you didn't run into problems with Customs?"

"No, none. I had wanted to fly out the night of Kate's wedding, but I realized the logistics were impossible. Nick arranged for an experienced courier to make the flight with me. He took care of all the paperwork, shepherded me through the maze of Customs regulations and drove me here tonight. But I wanted to have the pleasure of being the person who actually returned the missing DeWilde jewels to you."

He wondered why that had been important to her but was afraid to ask. Ever since that fateful New Year's Day nineteen months ago when Grace had confessed she had

married him without being in love with him, Jeffrey had
realized it was dangerous to ask personal questions unless
you were absolutely sure of the answer. Still, he couldn't
help but be cheered by the knowledge that Grace had deliberately sought him out. She'd spent most of the past
year protesting that she needed "space"—an American
euphemism that seemed to mean she wanted to be anywhere that her husband wasn't.

Jeffrey recovered enough equanimity to smile with false
heartiness. "Well, I suppose I'd better open the briefcase
and take a look at the jewels...make sure they've survived
the journey."

Grace held up her hand and he saw that the case was
fastened to her wrist with a faceted stainless steel chain
welded to an engraved and polished manacle. The manacle
was lined with padded black velvet and clasped her wrist
like a kinky sex toy. He wondered if she'd commissioned
the handcuff specially or gone shopping in one of San
Francisco's sex boutiques. Neither possibility did anything
to lessen his smoldering sexual tension.

"Here's the key to the handcuffs," Grace said, reaching
inside the neckline of her navy blue linen suit and pulling
out a chain of interwoven threads of gold and silver. She
slipped the chain over her head and held out a little silver
key toward Jeffrey. "This will open the padlock and the
handcuff. Nick told me you already know the numbers for
the combination lock on the case itself."

"Yes, I do." Jeffrey took the key, which was still warm
from being nestled between her breasts. "Could you...
could you hold out your hand? The lock on that handcuff
looks quite tricky to unfasten."

"Certainly." She held out her hand, palm upward, and
he unlocked the clasp. The manacle around her wrist
opened, falling to the desk with a clatter that sounded ex-
plosively loud in the oppressive quiet of his office.

Jeffrey stuck his fingers inside his starched collar, tugging to loosen his tie. His office seemed to be suffering from a severe ventilation problem. Grace massaged the inner flesh of her wrist, and he turned away abruptly, keying in the combination that would open the jewel case. Some crucial synapse must have been disconnecting between his brain and his fingers, because it took him four attempts before the locks sprang open. When he finally succeeded, he raised the lid slowly, actually forgetting about Grace's nearness for a second or two when he saw the four exquisite pieces nestled in their custom-designed compartments.

"Thank goodness," Grace said, bending down to examine the jewels. "They don't seem to have moved in transit. Some of the settings are so fragile I was worried there might be some damage."

"No, they were very well protected. Whoever designed the carrying case did a good job."

"Nick and I worked on the specifications together."

Jeffrey lifted out a pair of earrings and held them up to the light. They were almost too heavy to wear, set with priceless Burmese rubies and diamonds. The brooch was a mixture of rubies, diamonds and emeralds, mounted against an unusual background of stark black onyx. Even more stunning was the Dancing Waters necklace, a cascade of diamonds scattered with bursts of sapphires that looked like the blue depths of a mountain river, glimpsed through foaming white water. And last was the Empress Catherine tiara, an exquisite circlet of diamonds, rubies and emeralds, once owned by the Russian empress.

Jeffrey picked up the shimmering necklace and turned it slowly so that the diamonds caught fire in the refracted light. Grace exclaimed in delight and, acting on impulse, he fastened the necklace around the slim column of her throat. "Jewels always look better when they're worn," he said.

Her laugh was soft and breathy as she bent down to

catch her reflection in the narrow strip of mirror behind the bar. "True, but I don't think navy blue linen does justice to a necklace like this. Jewels this spectacular need satin and rare Mechlin lace at the very least."

"No," he said. "All they need is the bare shoulders of a beautiful woman like you."

Grace's gaze locked for a moment with his. "Sometimes, Jeffrey, you pay the most astounding compliments."

He smiled wryly. "No, I don't. That was a case of speaking the simple truth and sounding eloquent."

"Perhaps we should test your theory," she said, reaching for the row of tiny buttons that fastened her suit jacket. "I say satin and lace, you say bare skin. Let's see who's right."

She was going to take off her jacket. Jeffrey reminded himself to breathe. She was his wife...his ex-wife...and her body was entirely familiar to him. He must have held her naked in his arms a thousand times.

That mundane fact seemed to have no impact on his pounding pulse and racing heartbeat. Afraid to speak in case he stuttered, he watched her unfasten the buttons of her jacket one by one. She slowly drew the lapels apart and shrugged out of it, letting it drop from her hand onto his desk with casual abandon. Underneath her suit jacket she wore only a confection of translucent peach silk. A camisole, Jeffrey thought dazedly. He remembered that type of wispy top was called a camisole.

Grace pivoted slowly beneath the light, so that the necklace sparked with pinpoints of white flame against the creamy smoothness of her skin. She smiled at him. "Well, who was right?"

With considerable effort, Jeffrey recalled what they'd been talking about. "I was," he said, relieved to discover that the power of speech hadn't entirely deserted him. "Satin and lace would be complete overkill when you have such perfect shoulders."

She laughed and turned a little pink. "Thank you—I think. I'll concede the lace, maybe, but I'm sure I could make a compelling case for midnight blue satin. A low-cut dress, absolutely plain, with a long straight skirt, split at the side to mid-thigh."

Not only could he visualize the dress, he could imagine exactly how Grace would look wearing it. Jeffrey was swept by a wave of longing so intense it hurt. To hell with minor problems like the fact that they were divorced and he was supposed to be rebuilding his life without her. He covered the space between them in a single swift stride and pulled her into his arms.

"God, Gracie, I've missed you so much. It feels like two lifetimes since we were last together."

She spoke against his chest, her voice muffled. "We were together in San Francisco just a few weeks ago—at Kate's wedding."

He shook his head. "We weren't together. We were just in the same place at the same time. That's different."

She didn't reply, but she didn't move away, either. "Gracie..." he murmured, and then gave up on the hopeless task of finding words to express the turmoil of what he was feeling. He bent his head and kissed her passionately, all the pent-up frustrations of the past weeks and months somehow transforming themselves into an urgent need to show her how glad he was to have her here again in DeWilde's flagship store. In his arms, where she belonged.

Their kiss was as warm and familiar as his favorite armchair, as fresh and intoxicating as the return of spring after a cold and dreary winter. She was pliant in his arms, soft and yielding against his body. Her warmth seemed to pour into his veins, renewing his spirit and doubling his energy level.

For a few wonderful moments she returned his kiss with such eagerness that he was disoriented when she suddenly

jerked away from him and grabbed for her discarded
jacket. "Jeffrey," she muttered. "Look behind you. There
are two men standing at your office door. They've got
guns."

Guns? He swung around, stepping in front of Grace and
wondering frantically how he was going to protect her
from a pair of armed robbers. "There are security person-
nel and cameras throughout the store," he said to the in-
truders, his voice cold and clipped. "You have no hope of
getting out of here with any jewels, and even less chance
of escaping from the police."

The two men exchanged glances, and one of them
stepped forward, his gun still aimed with unnerving firm-
ness at Jeffrey's middle. "We're not burglars. There seems
to be a misunderstanding here. I'm Ron Bradley, with the
Securicorps Quick Response Team. This is my partner,
Alan Hicks. Identify yourself, please."

Jeffrey glared at the two men who claimed to be security
guards. What the hell did they mean by bursting into his
office like that? He'd never seen them before and didn't
recognize their names, but they were wearing the khaki
Securicorps uniform—and then he remembered. Good
God, the silent alarm! Grace's unexpected arrival had so
scrambled his brains that he'd forgotten all about his emergency summons to Securicorps. How in the world had he
managed to forget something so important?

"I'm Jeffrey DeWilde," he said, trying not to sound as
idiotic as he felt. Behind him he was aware of Grace scrab-
bling to fasten the buttons on her jacket, and he heard her
smother a tiny gurgle of laughter. He suddenly saw the
humor of the situation himself. Hiding a grin, he wondered
how many years had passed since he was last caught neck-
ing. He turned back to the guards, using his body to shield
Grace from their view. "If you'd like to see some identi-
fication, I'll have to get my wallet, which is inside my
jacket."

"You're claiming to be Mr. DeWilde?" The security guard looked confused, as well he might. "Reach inside your jacket very slowly, sir, and hold out your wallet at arm's length."

Jeffrey held out the wallet. "As you can see, I am indeed Jeffrey DeWilde. I was waiting for the delivery of some valuable jewelry this evening and I had reason to believe there was a security problem. However, I realized within moments of activating the silent alarm that I'd been mistaken. There was no problem."

"But you didn't deactivate the alarm? Or call in to headquarters?"

"No." Jeffrey decided against inventing some plausible excuse to explain that oversight. This was an occasion, he decided ruefully, when his reputation for aloof inscrutability came in useful.

The guard scanned the contents of Jeffrey's wallet. "Everything seems to be in order, sir, but to confirm that there hasn't been any breach of our security systems, would you key in the code that deactivates the alarm signal? Nobody knows that except Mr. DeWilde."

Jeffrey punched in the six-number code and the guard examined a small beeper, watching as an indicator light flashed from red to green. "Thank you, sir. That's the correct code. The alarm has been deactivated."

"Then I won't keep you," Jeffrey said. "Check in with your colleagues at the security desk on your way out. Let them know that my wife and I will be another twenty minutes or so and then we'll be leaving, too."

The guard's eyes narrowed with renewed suspicion. "Your wife?" he queried.

"He means me, I expect." Grace stepped forward and smiled warmly at the two guards. "I'm Grace DeWilde, Jeffrey's former wife. We were married to each other for so long, we sometimes forget that we're divorced now."

Jeffrey was furious with himself for making the mistake

of calling Grace his wife, and even more furious with her for the ease with which she glossed over his mistake. The guards, however, seemed reassured by her friendliness. Grace explained that she'd just arrived from San Francisco for a brief vacation in London, and one of the guards immediately started to recount the details of his holiday trip to America the year before.

Typical, Jeffrey thought, deciding to be annoyed. *I have to give the guards a wallet full of proof before they'll accept I'm who I say I am. Grace just smiles, and they're her instant pals.*

"You can report to your supervisor that I was disappointed to discover that it took Securicorps fifteen minutes to respond to my emergency alarm signal," Jeffrey said when a pause finally opened up in the exchange of chatter between Grace and the guards. "I trust that Securicorps will work on improving that response time. If there'd been a genuine robbery in progress, the thieves would be halfway to Land's End by now."

"Yes, sir." The guards stopped smiling and visibly reverted to their stiff, professional selves. "We had problems with heavy traffic, sir."

"We'll talk about it on Monday," Jeffrey said, already regretting that he'd snapped at the guards for no better reason than because he was annoyed with Grace. No, he amended. Because he was annoyed with himself. He waited until the guards had left before speaking to her directly.

"Am I to conclude from your conversation with the security guards that you're planning to spend some time in London?" he asked, inwardly wincing at the stuffiness of his words and the chill of his tone.

In the old days, Grace would have grinned, rolled her eyes and answered his question just as if he hadn't asked it like a pompous ass. In their uncertain new relationship, she hesitated for a moment, then replied in a voice carefully devoid of color. "I plan to spend a few days in England, and then go on to Paris and see Megan and Phillip."

"Would you..." He cleared his throat. "That is, I wondered if you would have time to join me for dinner one night?"

Grace, it seemed, was not in the mood to make things easy for him. "Why do you want to have dinner with me, Jeffrey?"

Damned if he knew the answer to that simple question. Hadn't he wanted the divorce precisely so that there would be nothing left to discuss, no issues that needed to be confronted, no cause to lacerate his soul by sitting across the table from her, feeling their love erode molecule by molecule, heartbeat by heartbeat?

"We were husband and wife for over thirty years," he said stiffly. "We have three children, all of whom got married in the past year. Surely we could find something to talk about?"

"I'm sure we could," Grace acknowledged gently. "But why should we? We're no longer married and the children all seem to be doing just splendidly."

She was quite right. There was no reason for them to get together to discuss three adult, happily married children. Jeffrey spread his hands helplessly. When all else fails, he reflected wryly, try telling the truth. "I don't know why I want to have dinner with you, Gracie, but I do. Very much."

She didn't say anything for a moment or two. Then she reached up and unfastened the clasp of the Dancing Waters necklace and held it out to him. "When you can think why it is that you want to spend time in my company, Jeffrey, give me a call. I'm staying at that new hotel in Knightsbridge, the Goreham. Good night."

She left the room so quickly he didn't have time to say anything more. Jeffrey was left alone in his office with nothing to keep him company except several million pounds' worth of fabulous jewels and the haunting fragrance of Grace's perfume.

CHAPTER TWO

OVER THE PAST YEAR, Julia Dutton had discovered that working herself to the point of bone-deep, mind-numbing fatigue was a pretty good way to disguise the fact that her heart was broken. Unfortunately, living in a state of permanent exhaustion hadn't done a whole lot for her appearance. Adjusting the position of the swivel light over the bathroom mirror, she scowled at her reflection. Not a pretty sight, Julia concluded gloomily. She looked like an escapee from a Casper the Ghost movie, all mournful eyes, scrawny arms and pallid skin.

There was no way she could face Lianne and Gabe looking like this. For them, of all people, she needed to present the illusion of Miss Vitality. Adjusting the light didn't help much; she looked dreadful from all angles. What she needed right at this moment was a fairy godmother willing to wave her wand and bestow instant glamour.

Fairy godmothers being conspicuous by their absence, Julia rummaged around the bathroom cabinet and came up with a year-old pack of rejuvenating facial mask. Not exactly the magic she'd been looking for, but for some months now, magic had been seriously missing from her life.

Piercing the tube, she slathered on the gritty goop, which the packaging blurb promised would transform her pallid complexion into one of pink, glowing beauty. Ten minutes seemed rather a short time to achieve such a miracle, but Julia was willing to believe. While she waited,

she plugged in her curling iron and considered hairstyle
options. She couldn't remember the last time she'd felt the
urge to dress up for an occasion, and the curling iron felt
heavy and awkward in her hands.

She shook her hair loose from the clip that had held it
up on top of her head while she bathed. At least she wasn't
having a bad hair day. Bad everything else, perhaps, but
her hair had always been her one redeeming feature. Long
and thick, it bounced with health and had a natural shine
like polished rosewood, even when the rest of her felt limp
and frazzled.

To her surprise, Julia realized that tonight she didn't feel
limp or frazzled, despite a tough week at school teaching
an intensive summer course in French, and long evenings
at home sewing a quilt copied from a 1920s photograph
for her niece's third birthday. In a burst of renewed opti-
mism, she got busy with the curling iron, gave herself a
few extra curls, and persuaded her fringe to flick away
from her face instead of flopping over her forehead.

She squinted dubiously at the result, and hoped she
wasn't deluding herself that the effect of the backward flip
was slightly wanton. Tonight she was definitely aiming for
wanton. She would see Gabe again for the first time in
almost four months, and she wanted to look like a woman
who had a life. An interesting life, crammed full of exciting, sexy men. She'd be damned if she was going to be
on the receiving end of his silent pity anymore. She'd had
enough of that to last several lifetimes.

The mere thought of Gabriel DeWilde was enough to
make her cheeks turn hot beneath the clay mask, and she
quickly cut off memories that remained too vivid and
much too painful. Gabe and Lianne were happily married
and expecting their first child next month, and it was
time—past time—that Julia got her stupid feelings for
Gabe under control. Unplugging the curling iron, she wondered why the Victorians had considered unrequited love

so romantic. Personally, she felt there was something ridiculous about a woman whose love life was so pathetic that she couldn't conquer her feelings for a man who'd dumped her more than a year ago.

Being dumped by the love of your life in favor of another woman was not an experience Julia would recommend as enriching. Being dumped in favor of your best friend was an experience she wouldn't wish on her worst enemy. It was a testimony to how close she and Lianne had been in the past that they were still good friends despite Gabe. They saw each other whenever they could get their busy work schedules to coincide, and phoned each other at least once a week. When they met, to overcome the awkward truth that Lianne was married to the man Julia loved, they'd developed a system whereby they tossed casual references to Gabe into the conversation and pretended they didn't notice each other's strain. It was a necessary pretense since they both wanted to save their friendship.

For the past few weeks, though, Julia hadn't needed to pretend very often, because she'd seen little of Lianne and nothing of Gabe. With their baby due in late August, they had been spending most of their weekends in the country, trying to speed up the workmen who were adding a new kitchen and an extra bathroom to the eighteenth-century stone cottage they'd bought soon after their marriage. The previous owners had been a pair of elderly sisters, recently deceased, and the place had been long on charm and short on convenience. The existing bathroom had a wonderful Edwardian claw-foot tub but no hot water. The bedrooms had pretty casement windows but plaster ceilings moldy with damp. As for the kitchen, it had a two-hundred-year-old oak floor—along with a cooking stove that had been the latest word in modernity around the time that Queen Victoria celebrated her Diamond Jubilee.

Julia's fingers had positively itched to get busy working

on the interior decoration when Lianne had shown her over the cottage. Interior design had always been an obsession with her, even when she was a child, although she realized her parents were quite right when they told her it was far too unreliable and competitive a field in which to earn a living. Since the debacle of her affair with Gabe, she'd filled her empty weekends touring National Trust houses, enlarging her knowledge of antique furniture and becoming something of an expert on the fabrics and linens used to decorate English country homes over the past three centuries. Her trips had started out as a ploy to avoid brooding, but at some point along the way, Julia realized she'd developed a genuine fascination with the techniques of antique fabric preservation and restoration.

In renovating the cottage, Lianne had frequently asked Julia's advice about patterns and color schemes, since she and Gabe wanted to achieve a workable compromise between comfort and an authentic period look to their house. Then, last week, Lianne had phoned to say that the workmen were finally finished.

"They're gone, they're out of here!" she crowed. "I think I'm ecstatic, but I'm too tired to know for sure! We have a house in which every room has four solid walls and a dry ceiling."

Julia laughed. "That's not only wonderful, it's truly amazing. But how many of the solid walls are painted?"

"All of them. Every last one. You can't imagine how gorgeous the house looks, Jules. And can you hear the blissful quiet? I'd forgotten what it was like to spend a day without listening to a bunch of workmen all hammering at once and yelling at the top of their lungs so they could hear each other over the noise of their radios."

"You must be thrilled to have the cottage to yourselves. Did Liberty's finish the curtains for the drawing room? I'm dying to see how they look."

"Yes, they're finished and they look wonderful. You

were absolutely right that I needed the rose chintz, not that dreary moss green I was looking at. And the Wedgwood-blue wall panels in the dining room are perfect as a contrast to the ivory plaster moldings. I don't know what's happened to my color sense recently. It all seems to have dissolved in prenatal hormones. Thank God most brides still wear white, or DeWilde's would have fired me months ago.''

Julia grinned. "I seriously doubt it. It would be tough for them to fire the woman who was voted Designer of the Year by *Brides Magazine*."

"How did you hear about that?" Lianne asked, sounding embarrassed. "Did Gabe tell you? Honestly, he was impossible when the magazine called us with the news. I barely managed to restrain him from putting up a billboard in Trafalgar Square."

Julia kept her voice light. "No, I haven't spoken to Gabe recently. Megan told me the news. We had lunch together when I was in Paris at the end of last month."

"You were in Paris? You never said anything." Lianne laughed. "I hope you were doing something scandalous."

"Nothing even remotely scandalous, unfortunately." Julia repressed a sigh. "I was escorting a group of sixth-form students on a tour of the city's cultural highlights. The closest I came to scandal was when I caught two of the girls drinking in the hotel bar at two in the morning."

"That isn't scandalous, Jules, that's just annoying. Damn! I was hoping you'd met some gorgeous man who'd whisked you off to Paris for a weekend of hot sex."

"I don't think I'm the sort of person who inspires men to rush off to Paris for hot sex," Julia said, then immediately wished she hadn't sounded so sorry for herself.

"You're one of the prettiest women I know," Lianne said. "And you have a great body. Fabulous legs. You could attract any man you wanted."

Not Gabe. And she didn't want anyone else. "Thanks

for the compliment," Julia said. "But pretty isn't the same thing as sexy, is it?"

"I'd say how sexy a woman is to a man depends more on how she thinks about herself than anything else. Your family has you so convinced you're a domesticated homebody, Jules, that you can't see the truth. In my opinion, you're a package of dynamite, waiting to be ignited by some lucky man."

Julia laughed, albeit a touch wistfully. "The package must be wet, or the fuse went dead or something. You're a wonderful friend, Lianne, but honesty compels me to admit that I have never in my whole life inspired a man with passionate thoughts about hot sex and sinful weekends in Paris."

"How do you know what the men around you are thinking?" Lianne asked. "Are you a mind reader?"

"I don't think a woman needs psychic powers to know when a man is lusting for her body," Julia replied with a touch of irony. "Aren't there supposed to be a couple of more obvious clues?"

"Do you want to inspire men with lust?" Lianne asked, her voice turning alarmingly thoughtful. "I always assumed you were only interested in dating men who were already tamed and domesticated."

"I am," Julia said quickly. And it was true, of course. She wanted to find a decent, honorable man to marry, so that they could settle down to have children and live a nice quiet life together. Some people might find that wish old-fashioned and boring, but it was what she'd always planned for herself. Even if she'd suddenly been endowed with enough sex appeal to rival Sharon Stone—even if she weren't still in love with Gabe—wild affairs wouldn't be on her agenda.

Julia spoke firmly to quash any crazy ideas Lianne might be getting. "We've been friends for a long time now, Lianne, and I know exactly what it means when your voice takes on that thoughtful note. You're mentally reviewing your list of bachelor friends as we speak, trying to decide which one would be most likely to rush me off somewhere exotic for a night of sex and sin—''

"No, no, Jules, of course I'm not." Lianne changed the subject with incriminating speed. "Actually, the reason I'm calling is to invite you down to the cottage this weekend. We're having a few friends join us to celebrate the fact that Gabe and I are no longer sleeping with buckets in our bedroom to catch the rain. Say you'll come. We have to move back to town on Monday so that I can get ready for the baby's arrival, and we're dying to show off the house before we're knee-deep in diapers and midnight feedings. If you need any more persuading, they're forecasting sunshine all weekend, and the countryside's gorgeous right now."

"I don't need any persuasion at all," Julia said. "I'd love to come. I can take a train to Winchester if somebody could pick me up at the station—''

"There's no need to take a train—Edward Hillyard can drive you," Lianne said quickly. Far too quickly. Edward was an old schoolfriend of Gabe's, recently divorced, and this was the third time Lianne had roped him in as an escort for Julia. Obviously, he was the bachelor Lianne had decided to pair her off with, Julia decided, trying to be grateful that her friend had picked on such a solid and respectable citizen. Edward was exactly the sort of man any sensible woman would want to marry. Except his ex-wife, of course. Julia sometimes found herself wondering exactly why Edward's marriage had lasted less than two years.

Lianne rushed on before Julia could say anything. "Edward's already accepted our invitation to come for dinner on Saturday evening. He plans to return to London on Sunday after lunch, so he could take you back with him, too. Why don't I ask him to pick you up about four on Saturday?''

"That's fine with me, but shouldn't you ask Edward first? Are you sure he won't mind giving me a lift?''

Lianne gave an exaggerated sigh. ''Honestly, Jules, you're hopeless. And you're the woman who claims to know what the men around you are thinking! Edward is positively dying for excuses to spend time with you, and you ask a question like that. I'll have him call you so that he can tell you in his own words just how thrilled and happy he is to drive you down here.''

Julia quite liked Edward, so she had thanked him politely when he called to repeat Lianne's offer to drive her down to the cottage. Edward was a barrister, fast making a name for himself in legal circles, and he'd seemed both kind and intelligent on the two other occasions Julia had gone out with him. He was also good-looking, and she was hopeful that, with a little effort, she could persuade herself that she found him sexually attractive. Surely to goodness there had to be a few men in the world, other than Gabriel DeWilde, who had the power to make her heart beat faster? With any luck and a little hard work on her part, Edward Hillyard might turn out to be the man who made her forget all about her abortive love for Gabe.

Julia splashed cold water on her face and washed off the mask, which—amazingly—seemed to have left her complexion pink and glowing as advertised. Glancing at her watch on the bathroom counter, she saw that she had only fifteen minutes left before Edward was due to pick her up, and Edward was never late. Unfailing punctuality was just one more of his many admirable characteristics. Julia wondered why she suddenly felt depressed.

Twelve minutes later, makeup done, hair brushed into artful casualness, and skin spritzed with perfume, she stepped into the dress she'd bought specially for this weekend. It hadn't been easy to find an outfit that made the statement, *I'm really glad you and Lianne are happy, but look what you missed out on, Gabriel DeWilde,* but she'd been rather pleased when she discovered this one.

Turning slowly so that she could view the short, tight skirt—well, okay, the very short and very tight skirt—from all angles, Julia realized she might have gone a little overboard with her subliminal messages for Gabe. Given the skimpy dimensions of the skirt, perhaps she hadn't needed quite such a low neckline. Or maybe she should have chosen a more subtle color than in-your-face yellow. Working in a private girls' school, and having grown up with two older brothers who for years had checked her appearance before every date, she tended to buy clothes that were conservative, even for special occasions. The outfit she was wearing tonight could be called many things, she decided, but conservative wasn't one of them.

Slipping into high-heeled black shoes and stepping back to view the final effect, Julia was assailed by the awful suspicion that the dress wasn't sexy and intriguing but simply vulgar. Panicked, she decided to change into her standby outfit, a sober suit in beige linen. If only Edward could be a couple of minutes late for once, she'd have time to make the switch.

She had her new yellow dress half on and half off when the doorbell rang. Edward—inevitably—was right on time. Muttering words her brothers would have been horrified to realize she knew, she shoved her arms back into the sleeves and pulled up the zipper. Naturally, it stuck. And of course the dress was too tight to get on or off unless the zipper was open all the way.

Julia reminded herself that she was not a woman who believed in omens. The weekend wasn't doomed simply because she had to face Edward Hillyard with a half-open zipper. She walked briskly to the door, holding the front of the dress up to her chest. Glancing through the peephole, she confirmed it was Edward and unlocked the door to her flat, greeting him with a friendly smile and inviting her heart to beat just a little faster at the sight of him. Her heart refused.

Julia tried not to be discouraged. She'd introduced Edward to her parents when they met by chance at the theater, and they thought he was wonderful. Her mother had managed to slip his name at least once into every subsequent phone conversation. Julia was trying to see why it was that both Lianne and her family considered Edward so terrific. Her mother had been so charmed by his old-fashioned good manners that she hadn't even blinked when she learned he was divorced.

Julia stepped back to let him into the flat. "Hello, Edward, you're right on time. You didn't have any problems with the traffic, obviously?"

"H-hello, Julia." Edward, usually a man of unflappable temperament, seemed stunned by her changed appearance. So stunned, in fact, that he stumbled over the doorsill and almost fell.

Cheeks splotched with angry red, he tugged at his starched shirt cuffs and smoothed his hair back into place, finding no humor in his near pratfall. Julia overcame an unworthy desire to giggle. "Guests are always tripping on that rug," she lied. "I'll have to move it."

Edward gave a final tug to his cuffs. "No harm done. Silly of me to trip, but I wasn't paying attention to where I was walking." He spoke calmly enough, but his gaze traveled rapidly down the length of her body and stopped at her thighs. His somewhat protuberant gray eyes showed signs of being about to pop out of his handsome head, but he was basically a courteous man and he hastily pulled his gaze back to her face.

He spoke jerkily. "The traffic's building up going toward the motorway. It'll take us a couple of hours to get to Lower Ashington, so we ought to be on our way. Are you ready to leave?" His Adam's apple bobbed as he swallowed. "That dress is rather, um...er... It doesn't look very warm. Do you need a jacket?"

With an inward sigh, Julia realized just how unsuited she was to the role of femme fatale. She'd bought this incredible bombshell of a dress and all she'd inspired Edward to say was that it didn't look very warm. His goggle-eyed amazement made her feel silly instead of feminine and sexy, but it was too late to wish that she'd bought a more demure dress, so she forced herself to continue smiling.

"I have a jacket in the bedroom, but I need your help first, Edward, if you don't mind. This is rather embarrassing, but the zipper is caught on the lining of my dress and I can't seem to disentangle it. If we stand directly under the light here, do you think you could loosen whatever's catching and zip me up properly?"

"Er...yes, of course." Edward waited while she positioned herself beneath the hall light fixture, then put his hands on her shoulders and turned her around. She jumped when his hands touched the bare skin of her back.

Edward cleared his throat. "I'm sorry if my hands are cold."

"It's quite all right," Julia said, although it wasn't. She hated the enforced intimacy, the fact that he now knew she was wearing no slip and a sun-yellow bra to match her dress, but she couldn't complain that he was taking advantage of the situation. Far from it. He scrupulously avoided touching her in any way that might be considered suggestive.

"There, that's got it," he said after a couple of minutes of careful tugging. "All done."

"Thank you very much." She swung around and realized that Edward hadn't moved away. Half a step forward and she would be in his arms. Julia felt momentarily paralyzed. She willed herself either to step briskly backward or to take that crucial step forward into his arms, but her feet remained glued to the area rug, her hands rigid at her sides, her insides churning.

In the end, Edward solved the dilemma for her. He murmured her name on a note of inquiry, and when she didn't protest, he clasped his arms around her waist and slowly bent his head toward her.

He'd kissed her before on a couple of occasions, presumably with modest satisfaction on his part. Julia hadn't felt anything, of course, but that wasn't surprising. She hadn't felt even a flicker of sexual desire for any man since the last time Gabe kissed her. She reminded herself that she was determined to cure herself of her stupid fixation on Gabe. If she concentrated, she was sure she'd finally be able to inject some pizzazz into her response to Edward. Eyes squeezed shut, she tilted her mouth up to his.

His lips closed eagerly over hers. His kiss felt like…nothing in particular. Determined to work up some enthusiasm, Julia imagined that he was Hugh Grant and she was Emma Thompson in *Sense and Sensibility*. She imagined they were succumbing to their love for each other after months of silent yearning. When Julia realized that her mind had drifted off into a mental review of the movie, she decided she'd picked the wrong fantasy. Jane Austen was obviously too chaste to inspire an appropriately passionate response. She needed a more contemporary scenario. How about Richard Gere and Julia Roberts in *Pretty Woman*? Their kisses had been hot enough to melt the celluloid they were filmed on.

Julia concentrated on visualizing Edward as Richard Gere, but her imagination failed her. Edward remained stubbornly Edward, and her blood refused to catch fire or even to send out a hopeful spark or two. His kiss tasted of peppermint toothpaste, which wasn't a bad thing for a kiss to taste of, she supposed, but she wished she could forget about the mechanics and just go with the flow. When she started to obsess about the fact that she couldn't

breathe and her nose was going to bump into his if she
came up for air too quickly, she decided it was time to do
them both a favor and break off the kiss. Belatedly it occurred to her that if she needed to pretend Edward was a
character in a movie before she could tolerate kissing him,
then their relationship didn't seem destined to scale the
heights of passion. At the moment, she reflected wryly,
they were doing a better imitation of Mickey and Minnie
Mouse than Richard Gere and Julia Roberts.

Edward, ever courteous, let go of her as soon as she
pulled back. Surprisingly, he seemed to have noticed nothing amiss with her tepid response. He was flushed and
breathing deeply when they drew apart, and Julia felt
guilty because she had been left so unmoved by an experience he seemed to have found arousing. What was the
matter with her? she wondered despairingly. Had she been
born with a defective sex gene that enabled her to feel
passion for Gabriel DeWilde and nobody else?

She was having a hard time finding something appropriate to say. Edward, fortunately, was not a man who
required his companions to provide their fair share of the
conversation. She'd learned on their earlier dates that he
could talk more than enough for two. He escorted her
down the street to the spot where he'd parked his BMW—
Edward could always find parking places—chatting enter-
tainingly about his work week. Julia listened, nodded in
all the right places, and wished he hadn't tucked his hand
beneath her elbow with such a proprietorial air.

It was after six when they approached the Winchester
exit from the motorway, but there was no risk of the light
fading before they reached Lower Ashington, since the sky
was cloudless and the sun was just beginning to bathe the
surrounding fields in mellow mauve light. They rounded
the bend in the road by the fifteenth-century village church
of St. Thomas and drove through the twilight to Briarwood
Cottage.

Lianne opened the door before they had a chance to ring the bell. "Jules!" She wrapped her friend in a warm hug. "You're so skinny and gorgeous, I can't stand it! Your hair looks terrific, your dress is to die for, and I think I hate you. I swear, if I get any bigger, we'll have to hire earth-moving equipment to haul me in and out of bed."

"You look wonderful," Julia assured her. "Glowing with health." She grinned. "Wait till next month and then you'll really find out what huge means. The day before she gave birth, my sister-in-law bore an uncanny resemblance to a beach ball with legs."

Lianne shot her a look of mock fury. "A fine friend you are. Rub it in that I have another four weeks of this torment to go. Just wait until you're pregnant."

"I feel quite safe from your revenge. My sister-in-law insists that giving birth causes instant amnesia."

"Don't count on it, Jules. I'm taking names and making written notes. I'm determined to remember every heartless comment from my so-called friends. What's more, I intend to pay them all back with interest."

Turning to Edward, Lianne held out her hand. "Nice to see you again, Edward. Come in, and Gabe can pour you a drink. Then, once you're fortified with alcohol, we'll expect you to be a dutiful guest and walk around the whole house, making admiring comments while we point out the magnificence of our new electrical wiring and what terrific ball bearings we have on our plumbing fixtures."

Edward smiled uncertainly. "I don't believe plumbing fixtures have ball bearings," he said.

There was a split-second pause before Lianne replied. "No, I don't suppose they do. Never mind, Edward. The idea I'm trying to convey is that you're supposed to be enraptured when we show you all the renovations. If you don't like what we've done, Gabe and I are hoping you'll lie."

"I'm sure we won't need to lie," Julia said diplomatically. "You've worked a minor miracle, Lianne, I can see that already. Did you keep the workmen chained to their hammers or something? Everything looks gorgeous."

"And so do you." Gabe came out of the drawing room and kissed the air to the right of Julia's cheek. "I like your new hairstyle. It's very dashing."

She willed herself to look straight at him and smile. "Thanks, Gabe. I decided it was time for a change."

"A very successful one." He returned her smile with one equally warm and just as impersonal. Julia's stomach performed its habitual somersault. Despairingly, she wondered if she'd still be fixated on Gabriel DeWilde when she was a doddery old woman, wandering from room to room in search of her false teeth. The image was absurd enough to make her laugh, and she murmured something appropriate to Gabe about being delighted to spend the weekend with him and Lianne, before escaping into the drawing room.

Two guests had already arrived. A man and a woman. The woman looked vaguely familiar, but Julia's smile froze as she recognized the man sitting in the window seat recessed into the deep bay window. Michael Forrest! What in the world was he doing here? Oh, Lord, of all the men to have underfoot for the next twenty-four hours, Michael Forrest was absolutely the last one on planet Earth that she'd have chosen. It was bad enough that she had to watch every move to make sure she didn't betray her feelings for Gabe. Now she'd have the added burden of being polite to a man who literally set her teeth on edge. Lianne and Gabe were normally sensitive to other people's feelings, but for some reason they didn't seem to have noticed that she and Michael practically came to blows every time they were in the same room for more than five minutes.

She'd met Michael for the first time a year ago this past spring, when she'd still been dating Gabe. She'd attended a gala benefit hosted by Grace and Jeffrey DeWilde, one of the last events she'd gone to with Gabe as her date. The evening had been ruined by her dawning awareness that Gabe wasn't in love with her—and the unfortunate circumstance that Michael Forrest had been seated next to her. Julia, who considered herself very easy to get along with, had felt her skin prickle with hostility from the first second her eyes met Michael's. He had clearly reciprocated her feelings. Their mutual antagonism had been instant, and noticeable enough to be embarrassing.

Michael had been the focus of attention all night long, telling a succession of scandalous stories about politicians and Hollywood celebrities that kept the entire table—except Julia—in gales of laughter. Even Jeffrey DeWilde had relaxed in a way she'd never seen before, engaging in a couple of exchanges with Michael that displayed not only Jeffrey's rapier-sharp wit and rather endearing sense of the ridiculous, but also a warmth Julia had never before associated with Gabe's somewhat intimidating father.

Even if there hadn't been that strange, inexplicable tension between the two of them, Julia wouldn't have enjoyed Michael Forrest's company. She wasn't normally judgmental about other people's life-styles, and she didn't care how many women he dated or even that he seemed to enjoy spending his time with people who were notorious chiefly for the reckless pace of their lives. What she couldn't forgive was the fact that Michael Forrest had a son he didn't seem to care about in the least.

As a teacher, she'd seen too many children who were emotionally neglected by their families, and she had no patience with irresponsible parents, especially when they were smart enough and educated enough to know better. Michael Forrest was a prime example of careless fatherhood.

Three years ago his affair with the movie superstar Cherie Lockwood had been the talk of the tabloids. For a few weeks their relationship blazed with a heat and passion that kept gossip columnists supplied with newsworthy items on a daily basis. Then Cherie Lockwood announced that she was pregnant and her affair with Michael heated rapidly to a boiling point. But by the time her son, Storm, was born, the relationship was over. Michael had the grace to acknowledge that Storm was his son, and for a month or two after the birth he spent the occasional weekend with Cherie and the baby. According to numerous media reports, his visits soon trickled away to nothing. At the celebration for Storm's first birthday, an astute reporter pressured him into admitting that the party was only the second time he'd seen his son in more than five months.

Fortunately, Storm's sad story had a more or less happy ending, although not one that shed a flattering light on Michael Forrest. Cherie had recently married Brad Stein, the Hollywood legend who'd directed her first movie. In a town famous for lack of integrity, Brad Stein was the well-known exception to the Hollywood rule. His devotion to his first wife, Terri, had achieved legendary status, and the entire movie industry grieved when Terri died after a brave, decade-long battle against muscular dystrophy.

Cherie and Brad were reported to have fallen deeply in love while she was trying to console him after the loss of his wife. They'd been married quickly and quietly, in a private ceremony notable for the absence of crass Hollywood trappings. Within weeks of their marriage, Brad had started legal proceedings to adopt Cherie's son, apparently without any opposition from Michael. Just a couple of weeks ago, *People* magazine had published a photograph of Storm feeding a bottle of milk to an orphan calf on Brad Stein's Texas cattle ranch. Julia wondered how Michael could bear to see such pictures and know that this wonderful little boy was being brought up by another man.

Despite her dislike of his casual approach to fatherhood, she hadn't been able to forget Michael after that first meeting. His face had lingered unaccountably in her mind's eye, a constant minor irritant that wouldn't go away, and she often found herself scanning the gossip magazines in search of an article about him. Presumably she did this out of a perverse desire to be annoyed, since that was always the state she found herself in after reading of his activities.

He was an American, a cousin of Grace DeWilde's who spent most of his time in Chicago and San Francisco, so she had no reason to expect to meet him ever again, especially after she broke up with Gabe. On a teacher's salary, she didn't frequent many of the dazzling galas, first nights and gallery openings that were Michael Forrest's habitual playground. Somehow, though, in the past three months, she and Michael had suffered the misfortune of ending up as dinner partners on at least half a dozen occasions, all of which had left Julia seething with fury for days afterward.

And now it was happening again. She stopped dead in the center of the drawing room. If she'd been a dog, she was quite sure her hair would have bristled. Michael sent her a look she couldn't interpret, then grinned and rose indolently from his seat. Why did he always look as if he owned the air around him, Julia thought angrily. He strolled across the room, hands stuffed in the pockets of his well-cut slacks, and stopped in front of her. He was at least two feet away, but her space felt crowded, and her nerve-endings jangled.

He bent his head in a mocking salute. "Hello, Julia, my sweet. I guess I'll have to come and do the honors, since you're obviously so delighted to see me that you can't move for sheer ecstasy."

She gritted her teeth—there, it had started already! Before she could come up with something halfway polite to reply, he took her hand and dropped a casual kiss on the tips of her fingers. Her skin prickled in instant outrage. Good heavens, didn't he realize how ridiculous it was for

a man to go around kissing a woman's hand in this day
and age?

She drew in a deep breath, determined to match his casually ironic manner. "Hello, Michael. What a surprise to
find you on this side of the Atlantic. I thought you were
still in the States, personally teaching the Dallas Cowboy
cheerleaders how to parachute."

He smiled, his green eyes lazily amused. "That was last
week," he said softly. "This week I'm planning to lead a
life of boring sobriety. Perhaps you'd like to keep me company?"

The implication that she was the ideal companion for
someone expecting to be bored wasn't lost on her. Julia
glared at him. "The paparazzi won't know what to do with
themselves if you're too discreet. They count on you for
at least one feature item per week."

"I guess next week they'll have to make do with Chuck
or Di." He brushed his thumb across her knuckles, and
she realized to her chagrin that he'd been holding her hand
all this time. She extracted her fingers from his clasp, her
breath coming too fast.

"You're looking great, Jules," Michael said carelessly.
"Yellow suits you."

"Thank you." She spoke stiffly, because she never
could relax around Michael, but his offhand compliment
was oddly reassuring. His womanizing was so notorious
that she could probably accept his judgment as that of an
expert witness. Since the Cherie Lockwood episode, Michael's name had been linked with half the movie stars in
Hollywood, and although Julia realized that every couple
featured in the tabloids hadn't necessarily met, much less
slept together, the gossip about Michael was so widespread
that she supposed there must be at least a grain of truth to
it.

"Julia, my dear, I brought you some champagne."

"What? Oh, thank you." Belatedly, Julia registered the

fact that Edward was standing right next to her elbow, and that she hadn't the faintest idea how long he'd been there. Being around Michael had all her senses alert to him, to the point that she forgot about other people. Glad of an excuse to break though the web of tension she and Michael always seemed to weave around themselves, she introduced the two men.

"Edward, do you know Michael Forrest? He's Gabe's cousin, and the president of the Carlisle Forrest hotel chain. Michael, this is Edward Hillyard. He went to school with Gabe, and now he's a barrister."

The men shook hands. "Good to meet you, Michael," Edward said jovially. "President of Carlisle Forrest, eh? That's an impressive job title for such a young man."

Michael's eyes narrowed, then he smiled. "I came by it the old-fashioned way. I inherited it."

Edward chuckled. "Well, being born to the right parents is always a good way to go straight to the top."

Michael's smile tightened only a fraction. "So everyone tells me."

"I feel as if I know you already," Edward said amiably. "The scandal sheets keep up with your exploits even on this side of the pond. I must say, Michael, I envy you your exciting life."

Michael bared his teeth. Julia supposed some people might have been misguided enough to think he was smiling. "You're a lawyer, Edward, so I'm sure you know you can't believe everything you read in the papers. The truth is, I routinely put in sixty- and seventy-hour work weeks and have virtually no time for socializing."

Edward chuckled. "I quite understand. And those lovely cheerleaders you were entertaining last week were strictly business, of course!" He grimaced in mock sympathy. "Bad luck, old chap, to have such a dreary job."

"Yes, some parts of my work do seem tedious on occasion."

Edward sensed nothing amiss, but Julia was acutely aware of the tension coiling inside Michael. She realized with a jolt that part of the reason being in Michael's company made her so uncomfortable was this sensation she always had that Michael was deliberately projecting an image that had little to do with the man underneath—and nobody seemed to notice anything wrong except her. The insight was disturbing, but her awareness of Michael's feelings remained acute. Superficially, he appeared relaxed, but she knew he was fighting for self-control as he turned and extended his hand to the woman who'd walked across the room to join them.

"Just in time, Tate darling," he murmured, tucking her hand beneath his arm and pulling her close.

The woman gave him a knowing glance, her eyes full of secret amusement. She leaned against him, her tall and shapely body folding into the curve of his arm with the ease of long-standing intimacy. Julia wondered if the two of them were lovers, then wondered how she could possibly doubt that they were.

"I'm Tate Herald," the woman said, holding out her hand, her smile warm and her voice friendly. "And you must be Julia. It's wonderful to meet you at last. Lianne's told me so much about you. Every time she shows me a piece of furniture or a color scheme in the house that I particularly like, she tells me it was your idea."

"Thanks for the compliment, but Lianne exaggerates the amount of help I've given her," Julia said. "I'm thrilled to meet you, Tate. You'll have to forgive me if I gush, but I'm a real fan of 'Grosvenor Square,' and I admire your acting talent enormously. You've built the role of Rowena Slade into something truly complex and intriguing."

Tate pulled a face, but her cheeks turned pink with pleasure. "Thanks for the kind words. I do try, although there are days when I get a little tired of scripts that seem to be devoted exclusively to finding more and more exotic excuses for me to take off my clothes in front of the camera."

"But, darling, you can't blame the producers," Michael murmured. "You look so exceptionally gorgeous lying on rumpled sheets, wearing nothing but a hungry smile."

Tate laughed. "Well, thank you, darling. It's always nice to get a compliment from a connoisseur. And the regular supply of money makes up for an awful lot of silly scripts." She grinned cheerfully at Julia. "I'm a weak woman, I admit it, but it's so nice to be rich after years of struggling to pay the rent."

"A television series is a good place to get your foot in the door," Edward interjected kindly. "Don't worry, Tate. Perhaps you'll have the opportunity to play some more worthwhile roles later on in your career."

There was an infinitesimal pause before Tate responded. "Yes," she said, her voice bland. "Perhaps I will."

Gabe joined them, carrying a bottle of champagne to fill any empty glasses and a Scotch and soda for Edward. "Sorry to keep you all waiting," he said. "Lianne and I have put away so many groceries over the past few days that I couldn't remember where we'd stashed the soda water."

Edward took the glass of Scotch and raised it in a toast. "Here's to you and Lianne," he said. "May this weekend mark the first of many happy occasions in your new home."

"I'll drink to that," Michael said, and they all raised their glasses.

"Speaking of Lianne," Tate said, "where is she?"

Gabe grinned. "When I last saw her, she was slandering the ancestry of the ducks she's cooking for dinner. I decided it would be smart to leave her alone until she and the birds come to terms."

"Oh, dear," Edward said. "Is there anything I can do to help? I enjoy cooking and I have quite a bit of experience with duck. Duckling à l'orange is a favorite with my mother.''

The man truly was a walking suitcase of admirable qualities, Julia thought. It was sweet that he liked to cook for his mother, and she was a perverse female not to be more appreciative of him.

"Thanks for the offer," Gabe said. "But as a man who has already survived an entire year of marriage, I can safely say that if Lianne wants help, she won't hesitate to let us know."

His words were punctuated by the sound of crashing crockery and a loud groan from the direction of the kitchen. Gabe rolled his eyes humorously. "Well, I guess we could interpret that as a request for immediate help."

The crash was followed by an ominous silence. "I'll go," Julia said, glad of an excuse to escape from three men who were all, for different reasons, rubbing her the wrong way.

She discovered Lianne leaning against the kitchen wall, eyes half-closed, a broken serving dish at her feet and steaming broad beans scattered over the newly resurfaced oak floor. Alarmed, Julia reached for her friend's hands. "What is it, Lianne? Did you burn yourself? You need to run your fingers under cold water quickly—''

"I didn't burn myself," Lianne said, her voice sounding simultaneously detached and overexcited.

Sensing something wrong, Gabe had followed Julia out of the drawing room. Squashing broad beans underfoot, he strode across the kitchen and put his arms around his wife. "Honey, what's up? Do you need to lie down?" He pressed his hand to her forehead. "Do you have a temperature? A headache? You don't look well, sweetheart."

"Don't I?" Lianne gave a crooked smile and drew in a deep breath. "I don't need to lie down, but I guess we do need to call Dr. Masham. Except he's away for the weekend, and even if he wasn't, he'd be in London, which isn't any use because I'm in Lower Ashington and I knew I should have lined up an obstetrician here, but I was going to do it next week—''

Gabe spoke with deliberate calm. ''Lianne, honey, you're not making much sense. You have to tell me what's wrong. Why do you need to call the obstetrician?''

''Well, I've had this nagging back pain all afternoon. I was busy, so I kept hoping it would go away. But it didn't, it got worse. And just now, I had a really strong contraction. It startled me so much I dropped the vegetable dish I was holding.''

''A contraction? You had a contraction?''

''Yes.'' Lianne shivered, although the kitchen was very warm. ''Gabe, I think I'm in labor.'' She looked at her husband with a mixture of panic and excitement. ''I guess this is the big moment, Gabe. We're going to have our baby.''

CHAPTER THREE

GABE'S EXPRESSION WENT completely blank. Julia was so accustomed to thinking of him as practical and efficient that it took her a few seconds to register that he wasn't staring at Lianne because his mind was weighing options and making crucial decisions, but because he was paralyzed by shock.

Edward had arrived at the kitchen door just in time to hear Lianne's announcement. He clucked in dismay, making vague flapping motions with his hands. "Oh, good heavens!" he exclaimed. "This is so unexpected! Whatever shall we do?"

"You and I are going to take a walk in the garden," Tate said, taking care of his flapping hands by putting another glass of whiskey into them. When he started to protest, she hooked her arm through his and led him firmly in the direction of the back door.

"I'll keep him out of the way," she murmured to Julia in passing. "That seems the most useful thing I can do for now. If you need me for anything else, just give a shout."

If Julia hadn't already been a devoted fan of Tate's, she would have become one in that moment. "Thank you," she said with heartfelt gratitude. "I owe you one."

"Darling, you most certainly do, and I'll be sure to remind you of that at some supremely inconvenient moment." Tate sailed out of the door, dragging a reluctant Edward behind her.

Gabe and Lianne continued to stare at each other like a

pair of puppets waiting to be animated. Julia spared a moment to reflect on how strange it was that prospective parents spent months planning for their baby's birth and then invariably seemed astonished when the big moment arrived. She waited for Gabe to take the elementary first step of calling the local doctor, but when she realized that he was showing no signs of doing that or anything else, she spoke up.

"Since Dr. Masham is away this weekend, you probably need to call your GP here in Lower Ashington," she said to Lianne, deftly removing a wooden spoon from her friend's clenched fingers and picking up the pieces of the shattered vegetable dish so that nobody would cut their feet. "You do have a doctor here, don't you?"

"Yes," Lianne replied, not moving.

"If you tell me where I can find his phone number, I'll give him a call and see whether he thinks you should drive back to London or have the baby at the local hospital," Julia prompted. "I don't suppose you've made arrangements to have the baby at home?"

Gabe finally snapped out of his stupor. "Lianne's mother made me promise we'd have the baby in a hospital," he said tightly. "She doesn't trust the idea of a midwife."

"Well, then, you just have to decide whether to go to Lower Ashington or make the drive back to London."

"The local hospital was closed three years ago," Lianne said, her voice high and breathless. "Nowadays, the nearest maternity unit is in Winchester. That's a forty-minute drive from here, and I'm not even sure exactly where in town the hospital is located."

"We can soon find out. Don't worry." Gabe looked so frantic that Julia gave his arm a few reassuring pats—the first time she'd voluntarily touched him since the night he told her he didn't love her. Surprisingly, all she felt was a sisterly sort of desire to calm him down so that he didn't upset Lianne with his panic.

"Gabe, you're worrying too much," she said, giving his hand a final consoling squeeze. "Babies come early all the time, and people who work on maternity cases expect the unexpected. At the moment, we need to focus on getting the best possible medical care for Lianne, whether that's in London or Winchester."

Lianne looked at Gabe, eyes brimming with guilty tears. "I should have made these arrangements weeks ago, instead of assuming we'd be back in London in time for the delivery. I can't believe I was so careless about something so important. I'm sorry, Gabe."

He put his arms around her. "It's my fault, sweetheart, not yours. I was the one who insisted on staying here until the renovations on the cottage were finished."

Lianne smiled mistily through her tears. "But I wanted to be here, Gabe. You know I love this cottage. It's my dream house come to life."

The parents-to-be seemed to have entirely forgotten the somewhat pressing problem of deciding on a hospital in which to have their baby, Julia thought. They stared tenderly at each other, lost in their own little world. She remembered her brother and sister-in-law saying that irrational behavior and the onset of labor went hand in hand, but she hadn't expected Gabe and Lianne, of all people, to demonstrate such classic symptoms of prenatal idiocy.

For some reason, Julia found her gaze drawn to Michael Forrest's. They exchanged amused, faintly exasperated glances.

Michael spoke softly. "It seems a shame to break up their lovefest, but I guess we should inject a note of reality into this discussion."

"I couldn't agree more. See if you have any better luck getting through to them than I did."

Michael tapped Gabe on the shoulder. "Guys, it's great

that you're so happy with your new home, but Julia and I would like to concentrate on a couple of more immediate issues right now. Like where Lianne is going to give birth. Which I guess could be right here in the kitchen if you don't talk to us real soon. Could one of you come down to earth for a couple of minutes and tell us the name and phone number of your local doctor?''

Gabe blinked, visibly forcing himself to concentrate. "Yes, you're right. We need to call the doctor right away. Her name's Emily Crane. That's right, isn't it, sweetheart?''

Lianne nodded. "Yes. And we have her phone number pinned up next to the fridge. At least, I think I put her business card there when the workmen left.''

Lianne barely finished speaking before she gave a smothered gasp of pain. Her hands fisted and she doubled over, cradling her hands around her swollen belly.

"Oh, my God!'' Gabe put his arm around her shoulders, his features twisted with worry. "Are you having another contraction, sweetheart?''

"Mmm.'' She clung to Gabe, squeezing his hand hard enough to turn her knuckles white. "Gabe, it hurts so much,'' she whispered.

When the contraction ended, Julia realized that she and Michael had both been holding their breath in sympathy. They let it out in unison as Lianne collapsed against the counter, panting. Gabe massaged her back and shoulders, but her face still appeared taut with strain. Julia felt a twinge of alarm. She was no expert on the course of normal childbirth, but she was fairly sure that the onset of labor was supposed to be more gradual than this.

Lianne slowly straightened, leaning heavily on her husband's arm as he helped her walk across the kitchen to a chair. "Jules, did you find the doctor's phone number?'' she asked.

"Yes, I have the card and I'm dialing the number now

this minute. Any special symptoms you want me to report to her?''

Lianne massaged her forehead, as if thinking was an effort. ''Just tell her that Gabe's driving me to the hospital in Winchester, and ask her what the admission procedure is, will you? To be honest, I don't think delivering this baby in London is a realistic option. I'm not sure we'd make it that far.''

Gabe's hair was already standing on end, he'd pushed his hand through it so many times. ''What the hell's going on here? Those last two contractions were only four minutes apart. I thought they taught us in our prenatal classes that labor starts out with contractions that are at least twenty minutes apart?''

''They taught us, Gabe. I guess they forgot to teach our baby.'' Lianne managed a small smile. ''He's obviously going to be a typical DeWilde and do things his own way and according to his own timetable.''

Gabe was too worried to rise to the offered bait. He gave his fingers another distracted push through his hair and winced when Lianne shifted uncomfortably in the chair. Sweat was beginning to break out on her forehead, and her face was pale except for two bright splotches of color on her cheeks.

Hanging on to the phone, waiting for the doctor's office to answer, Julia opened her mouth to suggest that Lianne might like a cool cloth to wipe her face, but Michael was ahead of her. He'd already found a clean tea cloth in one of the drawers and wrung it out in cold water. He handed it to Lianne without saying a word, and she pressed it gratefully to her forehead.

''The answering service is paging the doctor now,'' Julia said. ''Relax, Gabe. I'll have instructions on exactly how to get to the hospital and which entrance you should use in just a minute. I'll ask the doctor about any paperwork you might need, too.''

The seconds ticked by, freighted with tension. "Is the answering service having trouble finding the doctor?" Michael asked Julia, keeping his voice low.

"No, they know where she is and they asked me to wait on the line. They're paging her now. She's at the theater, but they've used a code to show it's an emergency, so she should respond soon."

"Let me handle the doctor while you pack an overnight bag for Lianne," Michael suggested.

"That's a great idea." Julia paused in the act of handing the phone to Michael. "Or perhaps Gabe should do the packing."

Michael shook his head. "Gabe's useless at this point. He'd probably pack jeans and a garter belt, and forget her robe and toothbrush."

"Lianne might not want me to go through her personal belongings—"

Michael reached out and took the phone. "You're being too considerate, Julia. Our about-to-be Mom and Dad are in shock and not functioning rationally. Any minute now, Lianne will have another contraction, and Gabe will go berserk. He'll start trying to take charge, but he won't be able to concentrate long enough to get anything done. He'll be running around, tripping over his own feet and bumping into the furniture. Strong, take-charge men who are crazily in love with their wives are always the worst at delivery time. Trust me on this, the only way we're going to get the pair of them out of here in the next half hour is if we make all the arrangements."

"You're right," Julia acknowledged. "I'll go and pack Lianne's bag. It shouldn't take me more than five minutes."

She located the master bedroom with no difficulty, but finding a suitcase proved impossible. In the end, not wanting to waste time, she took her own weekend bag, turned her clothes and toiletries out onto a bed in one of the spare bedrooms and hurriedly restocked the bag with the things she thought Lianne might need. She came downstairs again just in time to see Michael hanging up the phone.

He glanced at her inquiringly and she held up the bulging bag and the two pillows she'd brought down to put in the car for Lianne to rest against. He grinned and gave her a thumbs-up sign. "Great thinking. Lianne should bless you."

His smile banished his usual sardonic expression and gave his face an appealing warmth. Julia's stomach gave an odd little lurch, but there was no time to wonder why. Lianne gripped the arms of the chair as another contraction swept over her.

Gabe barely waited for the contraction to end before he shot into frenzied action. "That's it!" he exclaimed. "Only three minutes since the last one. We have to get to the hospital right away! This is an emergency!"

He put his arm around Lianne's waist and pulled her to her feet, then pushed her back into the chair. "No, you wait here. Don't move! I'll get the car."

He rushed blindly in the direction of the front door, knocking into a console table and almost sending a valuable Crown Derby jug flying.

Julia grabbed the jug while Michael grabbed Gabe's arm and hauled him back from the door. "Gabe, slow down. You need car keys before you can go anywhere."

"Right. Car keys." Gabe blundered toward the kitchen and Julia shot a warning glance toward Michael, shaking her head very slightly.

He nodded, picking up right away on her worry. "Yeah, well, on second thought, Gabe, why don't I drive you and Lianne to the hospital? That way, I can worry about the traffic, and you can sit in the back seat and hold your wife's hand. Remind her to relax and keep breathing, or whatever it is expectant fathers are supposed to do."

Gabe stared at Michael as if he no longer understood

simple English. Michael pulled a set of car keys from his pocket and jiggled them in front of Gabe's nose. "These are my car keys," he said. "We'll go in my car. Fortunately, it's parked right outside the front door so Lianne won't have far to walk."

Gabe nodded, his clumsiness vanishing as he turned to his wife. Tenderly, he helped her to her feet and took the pillows from Julia. "Are you ready to leave, sweetheart? Do you want an extra sweater?"

Lianne shook her head. "It'll be warm enough in the car."

At the front door, she and Julia exchanged hugs. "Good luck," Julia said softly. "I'm sure everything will be fine. And ask Gabe to phone us as soon as he can tear himself away from the new baby. I can't wait to hear if it's a boy or a girl."

"I'll make sure he calls," Lianne promised. She bit her lip. "I'm just a bit worried because the baby's coming so early. What if something's wrong, Jules? What if its lungs aren't properly developed?"

"These days, doctors are saving babies born eleven and twelve weeks before their due date. Four weeks barely counts as premature. Your baby's just impatient to get out and see the world. You said it yourself, a typical De-Wilde." Julia gave Lianne another encouraging hug. "You'd better hurry up and get into the car. Gabe's getting his wild and woolly look again."

Lianne's gaze softened as she glanced toward her husband. "He's excited, that's all. I've been feeling our baby grow inside me for eight months, but Gabe's had no role to play except to stand on the sidelines and watch my body go through changes he could do nothing about. That's hard for a man who likes to be in charge of everything."

"Yes, I'm sure it must be." Julia chuckled. "Tell him he can be in total charge of all nappy changes and any feedings between midnight and 6:00 a.m. for the next three months. That should help to make him feel truly involved in his baby's early development.''

Lianne smiled. "You always have the best suggestions, Jules. Oh, I just remembered! Call my mother for me, will you, please? She's had her plane ticket booked for the past six weeks. She's going to be really disappointed that she didn't get here in time for the birth.''

"I'll call her as soon as you and Gabe have left for the hospital,'' Julia promised.

"Call Gabe's father, too, would you?'' Lianne hesitated another moment before getting into the car. Then she turned her back on her husband and spoke quickly, almost as if she didn't want him to hear what she was saying.

"Grace is in London, Jules, but I don't know exactly where she's staying. Kate forgot to tell me. Will you find her and let her know that I've gone to the hospital? I really want her to come and see the baby as soon as she can.''

"I'll track her down,'' Julia promised. She knew Gabe had been estranged from his mother for over a year. Lianne had rarely talked about it, except to say a few weeks ago how relieved she was that things were finally improving between her husband and her mother-in-law. Though apparently not enough for Lianne to be sure that Gabe would invite Grace to come and meet her new grandchild.

Julia felt a spurt of unexpected anger toward Gabe. She understood why he'd been upset about the breakup of his parents' marriage. But Grace had left Jeffrey more than a year ago, and it was time for Gabe to get over it. If Megan and Kate could remain on good terms with both their parents, it shouldn't be too hard for him to do the same.

As soon as Lianne was settled against the pillows, Michael slipped into the driver's seat. "I'll leave everything here in your capable hands,'' he said to Julia, turning the key in the ignition. "And I'll call you as soon as there's any news about the baby.''

"Oh," Julia said. "I didn't realize you planned to wait at the hospital until the baby arrives."

Michael's dark eyes glinted with mischief. "Why, Julia, honey, if I didn't know better, I'd say you almost sound as if you're going to miss me."

"Ha!" Julia tossed her head, and her hair gave a satisfying swish as she flicked it over her shoulder. "Don't you wish."

Michael sent her a long, level gaze. "Yes," he said finally. "I do."

He drove off in a spray of gravel, leaving Julia to stare, speechless, at the retreating lights of his car.

CHAPTER FOUR

JEFFREY HAD ALWAYS considered that of all his children, Kate was the most similar to him in character. Sensitive, intense, driven and painfully intelligent, she'd inherited all his inhibitions about expressing her deepest emotions. The stormy course of her relationship with Nick Santos was exactly what Jeffrey would have predicted for his youngest daughter. What he wouldn't have predicted was the miraculous blossoming of her self-confidence since her marriage. With a mixture of pleasure and chagrin, Jeffrey was discovering that his daughter no longer hesitated to express her views about subjects she'd previously been careful to avoid.

When Grace had left him and moved to San Francisco, Kate had called to offer him polite sympathy, but she'd given no clue as to what she actually felt about the breakup. By contrast, during their most recent phone conversation, she'd informed him in no uncertain terms that his behavior over the past year had been idiotic.

"You want Mom to come back to you," Kate said. "And yet you can't bring yourself to tell her that simple truth. It's crazy, Dad. You're ruining your life because you're too proud to tell the woman you love that you behaved like a donkey's rear end."

"The situation's more complicated than that," Jeffrey protested. "Much more complicated."

Kate sighed audibly. "No, Dad, it's not complicated at all. You've spent almost a year and a half doing stupid things for no real reason except to make Mom's life miserable. And then, to crown it all, the pair of you spent a fortune on lawyers, arranging a divorce neither of you really wanted, chiefly because of that stiff-necked pride of yours—"

"You're confusing pride and dignity," Jeffrey said stiffly. "There were factors you aren't aware of that made our divorce inevitable." Pictures of Ian Stanley flashed into his mind: Ian dancing cheek to cheek with Grace, Ian kissing Grace, Ian making love to Grace. Jeffrey slammed the door on that last, excruciatingly painful image. Ian had been his friend for half a lifetime, but he and Ian hadn't spoken since the day Grace filed for divorce. Kate might be wrong about the details of his split from Grace, Jeffrey reflected, but she was dead right about the fundamentals. In the space of one short year, he'd lost his wife and his best friend. If he'd set out to make a major screwup of his life, he couldn't have done much better.

"I'm not confusing anything," Kate said. "We're two of a kind, Dad, and I know from experience that pride makes for empty days and lonely nights, and not much fun in between. The truth is, you rejected Mom's efforts at reconciliation one too many times, and she finally decided you meant what you were saying. Now you want her back, and you realize to your dismay that she isn't sitting around waiting for you to forgive her. That maybe she isn't going to come back unless you grovel. So I guess I'm wondering how long it will take you to come to your senses and start the groveling process."

"You seem to be forgetting that your mother left me," Jeffrey said tautly, the defense reflexive after months of using Grace's flight as an excuse for his own behavior. "I didn't leave her, it was the other way around."

"Dad, what happened to cause the breakup is almost irrelevant, can't you see that?" Kate sounded impatient. "The past is gone, and you can't change it. If I were you,

I'd start working on the future instead of obsessively reworking the past. Fortunately, Mom has a generous heart and a great sense of humor. I guess she's going to need both if you ever do the smart thing and beg her to take you back.''

Grace would need a sense of humor to take him back? It was one thing to think of the breakup of his marriage as a cosmic tragedy, quite another to think of it as a bad joke. Jeffrey scowled as he recalled the conversation with his daughter. Kate had been wrong in her assessment of his situation, he decided. For a start, his pride wasn't condemning him to empty days and lonely nights. On the contrary, his calendar was chock-a-block full, seven days a week, and not just with business appointments. If he wanted to, he could escort beautiful women to glamorous parties on a nightly basis. He stayed home so much because he preferred solitude, not because he had no alternative. Still, however hard he attempted to rationalize Kate's insights away, her words stung with the annoying prick of truth.

Determined to prove to himself that he was a man still in his powerful prime, rather than a lonely reject who was determined to behave like an idiot, Jeffrey managed to devise a Saturday schedule that promised to be a nonstop round of activity.

He breakfasted with a supplier from Taiwan, did a quick tour of a competitor's new store, had a late lunch with a vice president from the advertising agency to review next year's marketing plan for DeWilde's, and spent the latter part of the afternoon discussing a new look for his London flat with an interior decorator his secretary insisted was the best in London.

By the time the decorator left at five-thirty, Jeffrey was a hair's breadth away from committing murder. He wondered if he could have chosen a worse way to waste a sunny Saturday afternoon than thumbing through swatches of fabric with a woman who wielded her maroon nails like weapons and referred to half the wallpaper samples in any given book as "simply darling." But since the alternative was to continue living in a flat where every nook and cranny reminded him of Grace, Jeffrey suffered through the three hours of torment, and even acknowledged that the problem wasn't so much the decorator's grating personality as his own ambivalence about the fact that Grace was gone from his home, as well as from his life.

Which, he realized, brought him back full circle to the point he'd been at this morning when he set out on his round of frenzied make-work. The knowledge that his ex-wife was in town—that he knew the hotel where she was staying—was like a splinter under his thumbnail, constantly throbbing. To stop the ache, all he needed to do was pick up the phone and call her. But what would he say when she answered? Was he ready to grovel? Would it do any good if he did?

Jeffrey wanted to believe it was a good sign that Grace had personally brought him the long-lost DeWilde family jewels. What else could the gesture mean except that she was trying to bridge some of the emotional distance still yawning between the two of them? When he'd kissed her last night, she'd seemed perfectly willing to respond. But perhaps he'd been mistaken. God knows, he'd been seriously misreading Grace's signals for most of the past two years.

The harder Jeffrey tried to analyze everything that had happened in his office the evening before, the less he could remember exactly how his ex-wife had behaved. Was he imagining that she'd been deliberately sexy? Perhaps she merely wanted to get things back on a friendly footing with him for the sake of the children. Grace was too kind-hearted to want their strained relationship to mar the harmony of future family gatherings. But then again, she hadn't needed to kiss him with so much enthusiasm if all she wanted was to maintain a polite friendship. Jeffrey clenched his jaw in frustration. Lord, this was insane! He hadn't spent this much time worrying about a simple kiss since the cricket match when he missed his call to bat because he was behind the pavilion kissing the sister of the captain of the opposing team.

In the solitude of his kitchen, with his dinner of packaged soup heating in the microwave, Jeffrey finally acknowledged why he had never asked Grace to come back to him. It wasn't pride that held him back, it was fear. If he didn't ask Grace to come back, she couldn't refuse. And as long as Grace hadn't refused point blank to return, he could cherish the fantasy that one day they would be together again, the nightmare of the past two years wiped away.

Jeffrey watched the seconds count down on the microwave timer. He had every reason to avoid putting his fate to the test, he reflected gloomily. Grace was an attractive, intelligent woman, brimming with warmth and vivacity. He couldn't think of a single reason why she would want to come back to a dull stick like him. What in the world did he have to offer her?

The microwave beeped and he rotated his bowl of soup a precise quarter turn, then pressed the restart button. Once upon a time he'd have said that his marriage to Grace was a true partnership, and that his share of the bargain was to provide rock solid integrity and financial security, a counterbalance to Grace's contributions of beauty, warmth and sheer joy of living. He had destroyed the delicate balance of that bargain beyond repair. His affair with Allison Ames meant that he could no longer lay claim even to sexual faithfulness, let alone rock solid integrity. And Grace had proved with the success of her San Francisco store that she didn't need him for financial security or professional advice. As for the emotional balance he'd always believed he provided, Jeffrey had realized within days of Grace's departure that he needed her warmth a hell of a lot more than she needed his occasional calming influence and commonsense advice.

The microwave beeped again, and he stared at his bowl of bubbling minestrone with a grimace of distaste. The terrifying truth was that for all his wealth and for all his power in the world of business, he had no power at all over Grace. He could go to her and lay bare his soul, beg forgiveness for his adultery and tell her he loved her so much that he was going insane without her. And she would likely as not give him one of her sweet smiles and remind him that she'd already forgiven him for his affair with Allison, but that she hadn't the faintest desire to come and live with him ever again. Being a generous soul, she might even take pity on him and make love to him for old times' sake. Jeffrey couldn't make up his mind whether it would be more terrible to accept her offer or to refuse, knowing that she would never make the offer again.

The phone rang and he grabbed it fast, thankful for the interruption. At this point, anyone, even the maroon-nailed decorator, would be a welcome interruption to his own bleak thoughts.

"Mr. DeWilde?"

The caller was a woman, but she spoke with a soft, attractive voice that was vaguely familiar. Definitely not the decorator. "This is Jeffrey DeWilde," he acknowledged.

"Mr. DeWilde, this is Julia Dutton. You may remember that we've met a couple of times. Lianne used to share a flat with me before she married Gabe."

"Yes, Julia, of course I remember you. What a pleasant surprise to hear from you." She would never guess just how pleasant, Jeffrey thought ruefully. "You're a friend of Michael Forrest's, aren't you?"

There was an odd little pause before Julia spoke again. "Michael and I know each other," she said. "I'm calling from Briarwood Cottage, Mr. DeWilde, and I have some exciting news. Lianne's gone into labor and Gabe's taken her to the hospital in Winchester. He asked me to give you a ring to let you know that their baby will probably be born tonight or early tomorrow morning. He was hoping you might be able to come and meet your new grandchild sometime over the weekend.''

Gabe and Lianne's baby was about to make an appearance in the world! Jeffrey felt a rush of exhilaration so intense it caught him off guard. He'd been looking forward to the birth of his first grandchild, but until this moment, he'd had no idea how much. He laughed delightedly, remembering the excitement of the night Gabe and Megan were born, and experiencing some of the same deep-seated sense of wonder.

"Of course I'll come," he said. "What a splendid way to spend the weekend! I'll throw my shaving kit into an overnight bag and drive down right away. I should be there in a couple of hours, traffic permitting."

"I'm sure Gabe and Lianne will be thrilled to see you."

Julia had always struck him as a particularly nice young woman, but Jeffrey could detect a note of discomfort in her voice, as if she were hiding something from him. "Julia, is something bothering you?" His stomach lurched. "If there are problems with Lianne or the baby, I'd much rather hear about them now—"

"Oh, no, nothing like that," she said hastily. "I'm sure everything's going to be fine. I just have a slight problem that I'm not sure..." She paused for a moment. "Mr. DeWilde, this is rather awkward, and I apologize, but Lianne mentioned that her mother-in-law is in London. She wants me to let Mrs. DeWilde know...er...Grace..."

Julia stopped again. She drew in an audible breath and tried one more time. "Lianne wants me to let Grace know that she's in labor, and the baby should be here within a few hours. She would like her mother-in-law to come to the hospital as soon as possible. Unfortunately, I've called half a dozen London hotels already, and Mrs....um... Gabe's mother isn't staying at any of them. There's no reason why you should know her whereabouts, of course, but I wondered if you might happen to know which hotel she's staying in? Or if she's visiting with friends?''

Perhaps he was feeling so cheerful because of the imminent arrival of his first grandchild, but Jeffrey found the poor young woman's frantic efforts to avoid saying "your ex-wife" almost entertaining. "I'm glad you thought to ask me,'' he said, a note of amusement creeping into his voice. "Yes, by fortunate coincidence, I know exactly where Grace is staying.''

"Oh, super! Could you give me the name of her hotel, please?''

"I'm sure you must have a dozen other things to do besides call Grace,'' Jeffrey said, barely restraining himself from giving a whoop of glee when he realized that he'd been presented with the absolutely perfect excuse to contact his ex-wife. "Let me take one task off your plate, Julia. Why don't I call Grace and tell her the news?''

"Well, if you're sure you don't mind, that would be a big help—''

"It will be my pleasure,'' Jeffrey said, with absolute truth. "In fact, Julia, it's only sensible for me to drive Grace down to Winchester. I'm sure she'll want to rush down there the minute she hears the news, and there's no point in her hiring a car to go to exactly the same place as I'm going.''

"Wonderful. I'll try to get a message to Lianne and Gabe at the hospital in Winchester to let them know you'll both be on your way shortly.''

"Do you have directions to the hospital?'' Jeffrey asked.

"Yes, Michael wrote them down. I'll repeat them for you.'' She gave him clear and concise instructions on how to find the hospital. They exchanged goodbyes and Jeffrey hung up, humming the theme song from the most recent James Bond movie as he poured his unwanted soup down the garbage disposal. He looked up the number for the Goreham hotel and dialed quickly, heart thumping.

Yesterday the DeWilde jewels had come home, and now his first grandchild was about to be born. Plus, he was going to spend several hours in Grace's company! He smiled broadly as the hotel telephonist answered his call. One way or another, this was shaping up to be quite a weekend.

JEFFREY STRODE ACROSS the polished marble floor of the Goreham hotel lobby. Skirting a fountain that he barely noticed was there, he found the concierge desk with the unerring instinct of a man who had stayed in hotels the world over. "I'm Jeffrey DeWilde," he said crisply. "I've been trying to reach Mrs. DeWilde since half past eight. I rang earlier, and when she didn't answer the phone, someone on your staff was kind enough to check her room and confirm that she was out. I need to get in touch with her urgently, and it occurred to me that she might have asked you to help her with theater tickets, or some such thing."

The concierge checked in a small ledger, then shook his head regretfully. "I'm sorry, sir, I can't help you. Mrs. DeWilde didn't ask us to make any bookings on her behalf. But if you would care to leave another message, I'll make sure that she knows to get in touch with you the minute she returns."

Jeffrey glanced at his watch. Not quite nine o'clock. It would take less than two hours to drive to Winchester at this time of night, and the impatience he felt to get on the road was caused by eagerness rather than any sense of emergency. Since he very much wanted to be with Grace when they met their first grandchild, the most sensible thing for him to do was to control his impatience and remain at the hotel until she returned from her evening's engagement.

"I'll order a sandwich while I wait for her to come back," Jeffrey told the concierge. "Could you point me in the direction of the coffee shop, or wherever it is you serve light snacks at this time of night?"

"Of course, sir. Our coffee shop and tearoom are located to the rear of the atrium, on my right, behind our indoor garden." The concierge swiveled around to point toward a veritable forest of tropical greenery. He swung back as Jeffrey was on the point of walking away. "I just thought of something, sir. It's possible that Mrs. DeWilde is in our Oak Room restaurant. We've won several awards for our outstanding menu of all-British food, and many of our guests choose to eat there rather than going out to dinner. Since you're heading in that direction, you might want to take a quick look before you order your sandwich and see if Mrs. DeWilde is in the Oak Room."

"Good thought," Jeffrey said. "I'll certainly take a look. Thanks for your help."

Winding his way through a sea of Doric columns, he wondered why an architect would choose to design the lobby of an English hotel to look like a cross between a Roman emperor's palace and a Hollywood sound stage. There wasn't even any design consistency, he discovered on reaching the restaurant. In contrast to the chilly brightness of the atrium, the Oak Room was paneled in somber oak, carpeted in hunter green and furnished with overstuffed leather chairs to look like a nineteenth-century gentlemen's club. The heavy white damask cloths covering the tables glowed with ghostly luminescence against the surrounding gloom. The overhead lights were so dim that Jeffrey couldn't imagine how diners were supposed to connect their forks with their food, much less read their all-British menus.

The maître d' was busy settling a group of eight Japanese businessmen into their seats, and most of the other tables seemed to be filled exclusively with men, without even a token wife or female executive to leaven the masculine atmosphere. Although this seemed the last sort of place in which Grace would choose to eat, Jeffrey decided he might as well make a quick tour of the restaurant before escaping to the coffee shop and ordering a sandwich.

He heard the soft ripple of Grace's laughter before he saw her, and he strode forward, calling her name almost in the same instant that he recognized the man seated beside her in one of the booths along the far wall. Damn it to hell, his wife was eating dinner with Ian Stanley!

Jeffrey halted in midstride, consumed by a white-hot jealousy as irrational as it was fierce. Almost worse than the jealousy was the stark realization that he had no right to question Grace's choice of dinner companion. Perish the thought, but for all he knew, he might be interrupting their engagement dinner. Drawing in a couple of quick, deep breaths, he stepped forward with grim determination, trying to greet his ex-wife and his former best friend with the easygoing courtesy he knew was appropriate. But, as always happened when he was confronted by emotional situations he didn't know how to handle, he froze. The casual words he sought so desperately wouldn't come.

For a tense moment, nobody moved or spoke. Then Grace looked at Ian, her gaze quizzical, and Jeffrey could sense some unspoken question and answer pass back and forth between the two of them. He would have sworn nothing could have made him feel more jealous of Ian Stanley than he already did, but witnessing the silent intimacy of that exchange, he realized for the first time the full enormity of all that he'd lost when Grace left him. Anger and jealousy both disappeared in an overwhelming rush of sadness.

"Jeffrey, please join Ian and me for coffee. We'll ask the waiter to bring another cup." Grace turned to him and held out her hand, the gesture unconsciously appealing, as if she expected him to do or say something hurtful and wanted to prevent a scene. It was a depressing commentary on his recent behavior that she should so obviously feel nervous. "Were you looking for me, Jeffrey, or is this meeting just a coincidence?"

"I was looking for you," he managed to say. "The concierge suggested I might find you here." He fixed his gaze on a knot in the oak paneling and tried to sound polite, instead of sarcastic. "I trust I'm not intruding at an inconvenient moment."

"No, of course you're not. Sit down, Jeffrey. You're so tall looming over us that I'm getting a crick in my neck. Ian and I were just discussing his plans for the rest of the summer."

His plans? Did that mean Ian was expecting to spend the rest of the summer alone, without Grace? Jeffrey willed his legs to bend at the knee and slide into the booth opposite Grace and Ian. He wondered how in God's name he'd ever arrived at the point in his life where being asked to drink a cup of coffee at the same table as the woman he loved and the man who'd been his best friend should seem like a test of endurance equivalent to dipping his fingers into a tub of acid.

But, damn it, he wasn't going to ignore Ian's presence just because he was insanely jealous. Ian was in no way responsible for the breakup of his marriage, and it was past time to stop blaming everyone except himself for the fact that Grace had left him. Jeffrey cleared his throat. "How are you, Ian?" he asked coolly. "Keeping well, I trust?"

Grace and Ian exchanged another of those infuriating silent dialogues. "I'm doing—very well," Ian said. "And as I was just telling Grace, I have exciting plans for next month. I've made arrangements to visit China. I'm going to spend three weeks in a small town west of Beijing."

"How interesting," Jeffrey said woodenly. "Is it a business trip? Does the bank have plans for an investment there?"

"It's much more exciting than that," Grace said. "Ian has been supervising the fund-raising to rescue three hundred orphaned girls whose home burned down last winter. They've built a new home for the orphans, and now he's trying to get permission to build a high school for them. You know that girl babies in China are abandoned at ten times the rate of boys, and very often they receive almost no education, because in country districts the traditional beliefs about female inferiority still hold sway. Ian's been working like a fiend to cut through all the paperwork and government red tape to get this orphanage built, and the provincial authorities have invited him out for the grand opening. It's quite an honor, because the central government usually doesn't like to have foreigners spending too much time outside the official Foreign Enterprise Zones."

Jeffrey would have been only slightly less shocked if Grace had told him Ian planned to spend the next month learning to pilot an alien spaceship. "You're going to spend three weeks in a Chinese village, drawing up construction plans for a school?" he exclaimed, unable to conceal his surprise.

"You could try sounding slightly less amazed, old chap." Ian spoke with his usual self-mocking irony, but Jeffrey thought he could detect a faint note of hurt behind the seemingly flippant words. "Even frivolous people like me have their occasional bursts of nobility, you know."

"You don't have to convince me of your good qualities," Jeffrey said quietly. "You're the one who always seemed hell-bent on showing the world that you didn't give a damn. I'm surprised you're willing to destroy the image you've always worked so hard to project, that's all."

Ian didn't reply for a moment. "Sometimes life has a way of flicking its tail and catching you unawares," he said finally. "I've learned some valuable lessons about myself over the past year, and I've discovered that I don't want to look back on my life and realize that the most useful thing I've ever done is provide entertaining gossip for my ex-wives."

The past year had taught Jeffrey a lot, too. Not least of the skills he'd acquired in Grace's absence was the ability to hear what was being left unspoken, as well as what was being said out loud. He looked at Grace for guidance, but she seemed intent on rearranging packets of artificial sweetener in a pile around her plate, and she stubbornly refused to raise her eyes.

Jeffrey pushed the floral centerpiece to one side and looked across the table at the man who had been his friend for almost forty years. "What's going on here, Ian?" he asked. "Something's wrong, and not just with the treatment of girl babies in China. What is it?"

Ian smiled, but he didn't meet Jeffrey's eyes. "Nothing's wrong, old chap, quite the contrary. I'm going to China to make sure that the orphanage meets the specifications we agreed on and that corrupt officials haven't siphoned off any of the funds for their private profit. But the trip isn't going to be all work and no play. There will be plenty of free time in which I can indulge all my familiar bad habits. I understand that now the regime has relaxed its dress code, young women have gone back to wearing gorgeous silk cheongsams instead of those dreary Mao suits. I'm looking forward to meeting many beautiful women and making them very happy."

"Don't," Jeffrey snapped. "Ian, I'm your oldest friend. Don't pretend with me. What the bloody hell is going on here?"

For the first time, Ian allowed his gaze to drift upward until it locked with Jeffrey's. "Are you my oldest friend?" he asked. "Funny you should say that. I rather had the impression that we were no longer speaking, at least about anything meaningful. Which would make you my oldest former friend, wouldn't it?"

Ian's words hurt in ways Jeffrey would never have expected. "I've done a great many things over the past two years that were remarkable for their foolishness," he said. "Believing that I could deny our friendship was one of the most foolish. Of course we're still talking to each other about things that matter, Ian. Or at least my part of the *we* is still talking. And you may as well accept that I plan to keep on talking until you start answering. Really answering, as opposed to pushing me away from you by erecting a barrier of smart comebacks."

Ian smiled, this time with genuine warmth. "I'll be damned, Jeffrey, that was almost eloquent. Although, I suspect that it would take somebody who's known you since prep school to appreciate how out of character that speech was."

"Fortunately, you qualify," Jeffrey said.

"Yes." Ian was silent for a moment, then he looked up and grinned. "Since it seems a shame to throw away so many years of putting up with you, old chap, I suppose I'd better accept that we're destined to be best friends forever." He hesitated for another moment, then held out his hand across the table. "Here's to old and trusted friends, Jeffrey, and a lifetime of good memories. Let's shake on it."

Jeffrey grasped Ian's hand, swallowing over a sudden lump in his throat. "You should have given me a swift kick in the pants several months ago," he said gruffly.

"The temptation to do just that was frequently overwhelming," Ian said. "However, Grace persuaded me that you were being so rock-hard stubborn that I risked breaking my toe without bringing you to your senses. And I had no particular desire to sacrifice my toe in a lost cause."

Jeffrey shot a quick glance at Grace, but she still refused to meet his gaze. He sighed and turned back to his friend.

"I'll be honest with you, Ian. If you and Grace end up married to each other, I won't see as much of you in the future as we did in the past. I'm not a generous enough man to totally put aside my own feelings and enjoy watching your happiness. That doesn't mean I don't…that I won't always care about you. About both of you."

Grace finally stopped poking at the packets of sweetener and gave an impatient sigh. "I told you weeks ago that Ian and I have no intention of getting married," she said. "For a smart man, you can take an annoyingly long time to get a simple idea into your head, Jeffrey."

"Possibly," he said, thinking how incredibly beautiful she looked in the soft candlelight. "But for thirty-two years I relied on you to keep pounding away until I got the message, Gracie. It's a little difficult to develop alternative coping methods at this stage in my life."

The silence that fell over the table was broken by Ian. "Since the waiter seems to have decided that we're not worthy of a second cup of coffee, I think I may go up to my room and leave you and Grace to discuss whatever business it is that brings you here, Jeff." He rose to his feet. "Grace, darling, I'd love to clamber over those luscious legs of yours, but since your ex-husband is sending dagger looks in our direction, I think we'd better be discreet. Could you stand up and let me slide out?"

Grace stood up at once, but Jeffrey wasn't looking at her. He stared at Ian with new eyes, taking in the gauntness of his friend's cheeks and the way his expensive, perfectly tailored jacket hung from shoulders that no longer seemed broad and strong, but shrunken and horrifyingly frail. He slid out of the booth and stood himself. "Ian?" he said hoarsely, his stomach plummeting. "Ian, for God's sake, stop lying to me. Tell me what's wrong. Have you been ill?"

For a split second, Ian hesitated. Then he shrugged. "Do

I look that bad?'' He managed a rueful smile. "And to think my doctors are all rather pleased with me.''

"Your doctors?''

"God, yes. I've a positive retinue of the creatures. But at the moment, we're all on very good terms with one another. They've postponed my death sentence by several months because I'm responding to treatment so well. One of them confidently expects to win a prize for the paper he's writing about the beneficial effects of the drugs he's dosing me with.''

Jeffrey looked from Ian to Grace and back to Ian again. Grace's face confirmed the worst. He didn't insult his friend by pretending not to understand. "How long?'' he asked tersely.

"Possibly as much as another year,'' Ian said. "I told you, my doctors keep postponing the moment of execution, but a year seems to be about the outer limit.'' He put his hand on Jeffrey's shoulder. "Don't look so shattered, Jeff. I've learned there's a certain satisfaction to be derived from ensuring that you make each hour count. Life takes on a whole new perspective when you're forced to count exactly how many days of it you may have left.''

"And I've already squandered four months of the time we could have shared,'' Jeffrey said. "What idiots we both are, but especially me. For God's sake, Ian, why didn't you tell me when you first got the diagnosis?''

"I wasn't sure you'd be willing to take my phone call, and I wasn't quite feeling in the mood to have my oldest friend refuse to speak to me.''

Jeffrey wanted to protest that he would never have given Ian the brush-off if he'd had even a hint that something was seriously wrong, but remembering some examples of his own stupidity during the past year, he was appalled to realize that he might easily have refused to listen to Ian long enough to discover the extent of his friend's problem. Dismayed at how close he'd come to throwing away something of enormous value, he put his arm around Ian's wasted shoulders in a rare gesture of physical affection.

He swallowed over the lump in his throat two or three times before he could speak normally. "I'll phone you next week so that we can arrange to spend some time together before you take off for China. Perhaps you could come down to Kemberly for a couple of days, give Mrs. Milton a chance to show off her cooking, and let me boast about how I've learned to take care of Gracie's rose garden. I want to hear all about this high school you're building. It sounds like an intriguing project."

"I'll wait for your call. And if there's a chance of squeezing a donation out of you, I'll even bring pictures and architectural drawings of what we're doing in Beijing."

Ian smiled, but now that he was paying closer attention, Jeffrey could see that it was costing his friend real effort to conceal his pain.

"Bring the pictures, Ian. Knowing your silver tongue, I'm sure before the weekend's over you'll convince me that it's always been my lifelong ambition to support an orphanage in China. I might as well see the details of what I'm buying into."

Ian grinned. "I'll make a note to bring pictures." He took Grace's hand and carried it to his lips with typical flamboyance. "Good night, sweetheart. By the way, as one of your oldest and dearest friends, it's my duty to warn you that this Jeffrey DeWilde fellow has a shocking reputation with the ladies. Don't let him talk you into going anywhere with him unless you're willing to let him take you to bed."

Grace blushed. "I'll keep your advice in mind, Ian. Good night, sleep well. And thank you so much for a lovely dinner."

"As always, it was definitely my pleasure. Good night,

Jeff." Ian strode purposefully across the room, stopping at the maître d's station to pay the bill.

"How long have you known he was dying?" Jeffrey asked abruptly as he and Grace sat down again at the table.

"Since I was in Nevada, waiting for our divorce to come through."

"You should have told me, Grace."

"He asked me not to, and I respected his wishes. It was the least I could do."

"He's been in love with you for years. You know that, don't you?"

"Yes." Grace had returned to piling up her packets of sweetener. "But Ian is aware that although I love him dearly as a friend, I'm not in love with him."

"It would be a horrible mistake to marry him because you're sorry for him—"

"For heaven's sake, Jeffrey, how many different ways do I need to say it? I'm not planning to marry Ian. He knows it. I know it. Can we please drop the subject?"

"I'm sorry," he said stiffly. "But for once I wasn't thinking about you and me when I gave that advice. I was genuinely thinking about Ian. He would hate to be married out of pity."

"And I don't plan to marry him out of pity or for any other reason." Grace pushed her empty coffee cup to one side and looked up at him questioningly. "You said you were searching for me, Jeffrey. What did you want to see me about?"

Jeffrey felt a return of his former excitement, although it was tinged by sadness for Ian. He reached across the table for Grace's hand, smiling as happiness about the soon-to-arrive new baby overtook his other emotions. "I had a phone call this evening from Julia Dutton. Do you know her?"

"Mmm, yes. She dated Gabe for a while, didn't she?"

"Maybe, but it can't have been serious, because I've

seen her at a couple of dinners seated next to Michael Forrest. Even I noticed the sexual tension the two of them were generating—''

"Michael Forrest and Julia Dutton?" Grace's eyes lit up. "Now, that's a surprising combination, but oddly enough, it might be a good one. His parents' marriage was so horrible, he used to swear that he'd never marry, and given the way my cousin Maddy behaved toward Michael—"

Jeffrey almost laughed at how swiftly their conversation had wandered off track. It was so typical—so marvelously typical—of the conversations he used to have with Grace. "Gracie, dearest, if we could please stick to the subject—"

"But I thought Julia was the subject."

"No, she's not. Except that she phoned to say that Lianne went into labor earlier this evening, and Gabe wants us to go to the hospital right away so that we can meet our new grandchild."

"Oh, how wonderful! Our grandchild is here! Are Lianne and the baby all right? Is it a boy or a girl?"

"When Julia called, Lianne was still in labor. But by the time we arrive at the hospital, the baby could have put in an appearance."

Grace's entire body seemed to spark with delight. "Oh, Jeffrey, what great news! This is so exciting! My first grandbaby, can you imagine? It doesn't seem possible." She reached for her purse and stood up. "Shall we take a cab together? Then we can have a glass of champagne to celebrate, or even several glasses, without worrying about drinking and driving."

"A cab isn't an option, unfortunately," Jeffrey said. "Lianne and Gabe were spending the weekend at Briarwood Cottage, so Lianne isn't having the baby in London as she planned. Apparently there wasn't time to make the drive back into town, so she's having the baby in the local hospital, which is in Winchester."

Grace's forehead crinkled into a frown. "Everything's going to be all right, isn't it, Jeffrey? I know Lianne's taken wonderful care of herself during the pregnancy, but it's always worrying when a baby arrives too early."

"According to all the reports I've been given, everything's splendid," he said. "But we need to get a move on if we're going to see our new grandchild before he's a day old."

"He? You're such a chauvinist, Jeffrey. I've told you this baby is definitely a girl."

Jeffrey let his mouth curve into a predatory smile. "How much are you betting, Gracie?"

She looked at him thoughtfully. "Are we talking money?"

He shook his head. "Of course not. That's no fun at all. I had something more along the lines of our traditional bets in mind."

He couldn't tell whether she was shocked or not. Her gaze traveled slowly from his face to his chest and then back up again. "All right," she said at last. "We'll bet one hour."

"Two," he said instantly.

She hesitated for a moment. "All right," she agreed. "Two hours."

He couldn't believe it had been that simple. Jeffrey spelled out their bet, just to make sure. "If it's a boy, for two hours you do exactly what I order you to do. Agreed?"

"Yes." The flush in Grace's cheeks darkened. "And if the baby's a girl, for two hours, you'll do exactly what I order you to do."

"It's a deal," Jeffrey said softly. He touched her lightly on the cheek. "I'm sure you remember that I always collect on my bets, Gracie."

"Yes." She turned abruptly, so he couldn't see her face

and had no idea what she was thinking. "I need to change into something more comfortable for the drive," she said.

"Of course." Jeffrey overcame the impulse to dance a quick jig. "And it might be wise to pack an overnight bag, in case we decide to stay in Winchester tomorrow night."

Grace turned back to him at that, and her cheeks were flaming. "All right, I'll pack a bag. I shouldn't be more than fifteen minutes."

"Would you like me to help you pack?"

She gave him a flustered, half-amused glance that made Jeffrey's toes curl inside his polished loafers. "Thanks, but I think I'll probably be ready more quickly without your help."

Jeffrey tugged at his collar and discovered he wasn't even wearing a tie. He cleared his throat but his voice still sounded hoarse. "I'll wait for you by the concierge's desk."

Grace pressed the tips of her fingers against his mouth. "Fifteen minutes," she murmured. "I'll join you in the lobby."

CHAPTER FIVE

JULIA ABANDONED HER VIGIL by the phone and ran to meet Michael the instant she heard his car turn into the driveway. "What's the news?" she called, scarcely waiting for him to step out of the car. "How's Lianne? Has the baby arrived?"

"No baby as yet," Michael said, walking with her into the house. "The doctor's giving it another three hours, then if things aren't progressing the way he wants, he may decide to do a C section."

"A cesarean?" Julia pulled a face. "Oh, no, what's the problem?"

"Nothing drastic, according to Gabe." Michael sat down on the sofa and stretched wearily. "Where are Tate and Edward?"

"Gone back to London." Julia glanced at the clock. "They should have arrived a few minutes ago if they didn't run into traffic. Tate says she'll phone you on Monday night. Now, tell me what's happening with Lianne and the baby."

"Gabe wasn't too coherent, but as far as I could understand, Lianne's early contractions were so powerful that the baby moved too rapidly down the birth canal, and so far, the cervix hasn't effaced sufficiently for the baby to be born. The doctor scheduled the C section just to be on the safe side, so that the baby won't have to spend another five or six hours banging the top of its skull against Lianne's cervix."

Julia curled up on the sofa next to Michael, tucking her feet under her. "My sister-in-law had a cesarean, too. If the baby's not in the right position or the labor's not progressing as it should, it seems to be the safest choice."

"That's pretty much what Lianne's doctor said," Michael agreed. "And Gabe seems confident the doctor's making the right decision."

"What sort of shape was Gabe in when you left the hospital? Do you think there's any chance he'll remember to phone us when the baby does finally arrive?"

"I wouldn't count on it," Michael said wryly. "When we spoke, he seemed to be having a hard time remembering his own name. But with luck, his brain will start operating on full power again once the baby's born and Lianne's recovering."

"I still can't believe how he went to pieces!" Julia shook her head. "Men are so useless where babies are concerned."

Michael looked amused. "Actually, I'd heard rumors that we're somewhat essential to the process of baby-making. Are you about to disillusion me?"

"Heavens, no. I wouldn't dream of arguing with an expert."

Michael tensed for a moment, then yawned and flexed his shoulders. "Very wise of you, my sweet."

She turned her head when she realized she was staring at the muscles rippling beneath his shirt. "I wish you wouldn't call me that."

"Call you what?" His voice was lazy; his eyes were anything but.

"My sweet."

"Why not? Aren't you sweet?"

There was a knot twisting tight in the pit of her stomach. "Not particularly. And I'm certainly not yours. You sound so blasted patronizing when you call me that, and I hate it."

He said nothing for a moment, his eyes on hers. "I'm sorry. I never intended to sound patronizing."

The knot twisted tighter. "Then how did you intend to sound?" she demanded. "Sarcastic? Condescending? If so, it worked."

"I've apologized already. What more do you expect me to say?" Michael got up and strode into the kitchen.

Julia marched after him. "I expect an explanation. As far as I can tell, you've been deliberately setting out to needle me ever since I've known you. What's your problem, Michael? What in the world have I ever done to offend you?"

"Not a damn thing." He slammed the fridge door shut and swung around to face her. "Or maybe this," he said, and pulled her into his arms.

The instant Michael's lips touched hers, Julia knew that, at some deeply buried level of her consciousness, she'd been waiting for him to kiss her since the night they first met. He kissed her hard and long, his mouth open, his tongue thrusting aggressively against hers, his hands hot and urgent on her body. She kissed him back with equal hunger, drawing his tongue deeper into her mouth, her skin jumping with little shocks of pleasure everywhere he touched her.

He held her tight. Her arms wrapped around him and clung. She registered a fleeting sense of astonishment that being held by Michael Forrest should seem so incredibly right, but even that hazy awareness soon vanished, burned away by the heat and passion of their kiss. He unzipped her dress and tugged it from her shoulders. It didn't occur to her to protest. She moved restlessly against him, the blood roaring in her head so loud and fierce that it drowned out everything else, even her thoughts. She only knew that the longer they kissed, the more she wanted.

It was Michael who finally drew away, Michael who stepped back until a gap opened up between the two of them. He rubbed his hand briefly over his eyes, leaning against the door of the fridge, his chest rising and falling as if he'd just run a hard race.

Her body was throbbing with a need that reduced her normal inhibitions to rubble. She wasn't ready for their lovemaking to end, and for once, she was ready to take the initiative in carrying things further. She moved blindly toward him, but he grabbed her wrists and held her at arm's length, forcing her to keep her distance.

"Back off, Julia." His voice was rough. "You're tempting as hell, but I make it a rule never to go to bed with a woman who's in love with another man."

She flinched at his rejection. A dozen conflicting emotions rose inside her, but anger seemed the safest one to allow to the surface. He'd turned away, and she moved, positioning herself directly in his line of sight. "As far as I can recall, I didn't say anything about going to bed with you, Michael, not a single word."

"You didn't need to say the words. Your body was carrying on a very explicit conversation."

Julia shoved her arms into her dress and yanked it up onto her shoulders. Her pulse raced and her heart was pounding. Her breasts still tingled, and her nipples ached because Michael was no longer touching her. It was insane—absurd—that someone she didn't like could have this much of an effect on her. Edward had kissed her only a few hours ago, and she'd experienced nothing more than mild boredom. Michael kissed her and she erupted like Mount Vesuvius. Sometimes, Julia thought, life could be really infuriating.

She glared at Michael, because being cross with him was a lot more satisfying than being angry with herself. He returned her look with a cool, knowing stare, and her stomach gave a treacherous lurch of desire. Her stupid body apparently didn't have enough sense to accept that the man had just flat-out turned her down.

He finished buttoning his shirt, but didn't bother to tuck it back into his trousers. To Julia's supreme annoyance, his resulting appearance wasn't in the least disheveled. Instead, by some subtle alchemy, he managed to convey the impression that well-dressed men this season were wearing their hair rumpled and their shirts hanging over the belt of their trousers.

Meanwhile, she undoubtedly looked a wreck. No lipstick, hair tumbling every which-way, and her dress undone. Julia reached behind her back and yanked at the zip. It glided halfway up, then stuck. She muttered several creative curses about tight yellow dresses, bought for all the wrong reasons, then tugged again. To no avail. The wretched zip wouldn't budge.

Michael popped the top on a can of lager he'd taken from the fridge. "Would you like some help?" he asked.

His politeness scraped on her nerves like a drill on tooth enamel. With Michael, she always seemed to be waiting for the sharp edge of his mockery to poke through the velvet-smooth courtesy. "I can manage," she said curtly, her skin turning hot and then cold at the thought of him touching her again. Amazing how different this hot-and-cold sensation was from the feeling Edward had aroused when he rescued her from zip failure earlier that afternoon.

The thought of Edward reminded her of Michael's strange comment when he ended their kiss. "Whatever gave you the idea that I'm in love with Edward Hillyard?" she demanded, still tugging at her dress. "Edward and I are barely acquaintances, let alone lovers."

"Edward?" Michael was silent for a second or two, then his gaze locked with hers. "I wasn't talking about Edward Hillyard," he said. "I was talking about Gabriel DeWilde."

Julia's hands froze, then fell to her sides. Gabe. She was so shocked to have forgotten about Gabe that she wasn't even humiliated by the realization that Michael knew of her abortive love affair. When Michael implied that she was in love with another man, why in the world hadn't she realized he was talking about Gabe, she wondered. Why hadn't Gabe's name even crossed her mind?

The answer struck her with the illuminating force of a hammer smashing through a barred and shuttered window. "I'm not in love with Gabe," she said.

She listened to herself speak the incredible words, then repeated them, just to be sure she registered their truth. "I'm not even a tiny bit in love with Gabe. He's an interesting, successful man who happens to be married to my best friend. You're mistaken if you believe anything else."

Michael finished his lager and crushed the can. He gave her a long, assessing look. "You were in love with Gabe."

It was surprisingly easy to admit the truth. "Once. A long time ago. Not anymore."

He tossed his empty can into the trash. "I'm glad you corrected my mistake," he said. He leaned back against the counter and smiled, his manner newly relaxed. "Now, are you sure you wouldn't like to reconsider my offer of help?"

His smile really did have the most extraordinary effect on her. Not least, it seemed, on her ability to understand simple sentences. She blinked. "Your offer of help? What for?"

"With your zipper." He wiggled his fingers. "If you're interested, I have ten certified zipper masters at your service."

"I'll just bet they're certified," Julia muttered, but she clearly wasn't going to get her dress fastened by herself, so she turned around, holding up her hair to prevent it getting caught.

He fastened her dress within a few seconds, his fingers coming into contact with her skin only once, when he had to glide the zip over the hook of her bra. Her body, demonstrating a total lack of good sense, responded with an instant flood of renewed desire. Remembering her indifference to Edward, Julia wondered if there'd ever been a scientific study done that explained how and why a woman could react so differently to the touch of two men, neither of whom she could even see. She supposed there must be some obscure hormonal reason for her response to Michael Forrest, because nothing else explained the effect he had on her.

She moved away the moment he was finished. "Thanks."

"You're welcome."

She wasn't nearly comfortable enough in his company to allow silence to fall between them, so she searched for something to say. Something bland and uncontroversial. Since they were standing in the kitchen, she came up with food. "You probably haven't eaten dinner, Michael, and you must be hungry. Could I make you a sandwich or something?"

"A sandwich would be great, but I can make my own. What about you? Have you eaten?"

"Oh, yes, before Tate and Edward went back to town. It turns out Edward wasn't exaggerating when he claimed gourmet cooking was a hobby of his. He rescued Lianne's ducklings from certain incineration, kept the wild rice warm while he tossed up a fabulous salad, and even helped clear away the dirty dishes when we'd finished eating. Thanks to Edward, we ate a truly scrumptious meal."

"He sounds like a regular paragon of virtue," Michael muttered, pulling a loaf of bread and a hunk of cheddar cheese from the fridge.

"A man without vices," Julia agreed.

Michael put two slices of bread onto a plate and cut a wedge of cheese. "Have you ever noticed how tedious perfect people are?"

She chuckled. "Yes, especially since I met Edward."

Michael looked at her, his expression arrested. "You don't laugh much," he said quietly. "You should do it more often."

"I'll make it a midyear resolution," she said tartly. "Laugh often, even when I'm not amused."

"Keep up with that tightly pursed mouth and haughty squint, honey, and in another few years, you're going to be able to do a damn fine imitation of Queen Victoria."

She should have been offended, but she found herself laughing, instead. Michael was right, she reflected. She did have a tendency to clamber onto her high horse for no particular reason. And he was also right that she should laugh more often. She'd wasted too much of the past year making a catastrophe out of a minor problem. If she hadn't been determined to cast herself in the role of tragic heroine, she'd have recovered from her infatuation with Gabriel DeWilde months and months ago. It was a disquieting realization. One of several tonight, all of which she owed to Michael.

She watched him put together his sandwich. "That looks awfully dry," she said. "Why don't you add some cucumber or something?"

"You want me to mix cheese and cucumber?" Michael wrinkled his nose. "Sounds like a mighty odd combination to me."

"British people eat it all the time."

Michael's silence was eloquent enough to make her smile again. "You're in no position to make rude comments about British cooking," she said.

He put on an injured expression. "I didn't say a word! Did I say a word? No."

She gave him a repressive look. "Your silence spoke volumes, and you, Michael Forrest, come from a country where people pour syrup on pancakes and then put bacon and sausages on the *same* plate as the syrup. Not to mention serving fried chicken with honey. Honey and fried chicken! Don't you dare talk to me about gross combinations."

Michael grinned. "A golden brown chicken drumstick, fried in cornmeal and served with honey and biscuits, doesn't appeal to you, huh?"

Julia shuddered.

"Why don't we do a deal?" Michael suggested. "I'll put cucumber on my cheese sandwich, if you'll have breakfast with me one day and eat pancakes served with real maple syrup and bacon."

"It's a deal," she said, taking the cucumber out of the fridge and searching for a sharp knife to slice it.

He eyed her with justifiable suspicion. "You agreed to that much too easily."

"Not at all. I have no plans to weasel out of the deal." She gave a sly smile. "Although by great good fortune, I don't think there's anywhere in London that actually serves American breakfasts."

"How little you know your own hometown," he murmured.

"I'll take my chances." She quartered his cheese sandwich, now brimming with cucumber, and handed it to him with a smile. "Here you are, Michael. Eat up and admit you were wrong."

He took a small, dubious bite, chewed for a moment, then looked at her with wide-eyed astonishment. "It's not bad!" he exclaimed. He took another bite. "I must be hungrier than I thought. This actually tastes pretty damn good. The cucumber adds crunch."

Julia smiled graciously. She could afford to be generous since she knew Michael wouldn't bother to invite her to breakfast. That thought didn't make her quite as happy as it should have, and she sat down opposite him at the kitchen table, feeling a renewed attack of restlessness.

"Gabe should have called by now," she said. "It's past midnight."

"It seems a long time to us because we're just hanging around, but it's less than six hours since Lianne went into labor. That's nothing, especially for a first baby."

She drummed her fingers on the tabletop. "Yes, I know. The waiting's difficult, though."

He covered her hand with his. "Do you want to go to bed? I can wake you as soon as I hear something."

"Thanks, but I'm too keyed-up to sleep. This is my godchild that's about to make his or her debut in the world."

Michael finished his last bite of sandwich. "Mine, too." His gaze met hers across the table, eyes gleaming. "Does that make us related, do you think?"

"In medieval times, the church used to claim that it did." She made an apologetic gesture. "I'm sorry, ignore that. It's my teacher-reflex kicking in. I have this annoying habit of taking other people's throwaway remarks and responding with a minilecture."

"A sentence is hardly a minilecture," Michael said. "Besides, who told you it's an annoying habit?"

"My brothers," she said ruefully. "They're both engineers, and they tend to explain things much better with charts and diagrams than they do with words. They really dislike it when they make some casual comment or other, and I respond by branching off into a long and usually irrelevant byway that I find fascinating and they find boring in the extreme."

"I'd say that's their problem, not yours." Michael stood up and carried his plate over to the sink. "For two people who are about to become relatives, at least according to ancient church doctrine, we don't know much about each other, do we? Why don't we choose some comfortable chairs in the living room and tell each other our life histories while we're waiting to hear from the hospital?"

Having heard Michael tell plenty of amusing stories about himself, Julia was more than willing to have him entertain her until Gabe phoned. "You go first," she said, following him out of the kitchen.

Michael shook his head. "I'm a traditionalist at heart. Ladies should always go first in this sort of situation." He sat down in a Queen Anne-style wing chair that was conveniently close to the phone.

"Well, all right," Julia said, taking a seat on the sofa. "But this isn't going to take me long. Let's see. I was born in London and I've more or less lived there all my life. I'm thirty, and planning to stay that age for the next three or four birthdays. I have two older brothers, who are both married, and two nieces, who are seriously adorable. I teach French at a private girls' school in Kensington. Now it's your turn."

"In a minute. I think your biography could be expanded a bit. How old are your nieces? Do you spend a lot of time with your family?"

"My nieces are three and five, and we see quite a lot of one another since we all live in the London area."

"Your brothers are both older than you?"

She nodded. "They're thirty-six and thirty-seven. I was the proverbial unexpected afterthought, although my mother swears that she was thrilled to have a daughter after being surrounded by men for the first ten years of her marriage. Nowadays, it's my father who says he's surrounded, what with two granddaughters and two daughters-in-law."

"Do you like your sisters-in-law?" he asked, stretching out his legs in front of him.

Julia plumped up an oversized down cushion and tucked it behind her. "They're very good women, both of them."

"Ah." Michael smiled. "You can't stand 'em."

"I didn't say that," she protested.

"Yes, you did," he said cheerfully. "I know the feeling. I have a brother-in-law who drives me nuts. He's a surgeon, saves lives on a daily basis, but I think he had his sense of humor clinically excised when he was in medical school.''

"One of my sisters-in-law has plastic flowers planted in her front garden because real ones are too messy," Julia said. She caught Michael's eye and they both burst out laughing.

"We won't waste any more time discussing our boring in-laws," he said. "Tell me why you became a teacher. Was it something you always wanted to do?"

"In a way. When I was growing up, I was quite sure I wanted to be a teacher. I was accepted at King's to read French—"

"Whoa! Translation time," Michael said. "What does that mean exactly?"

"King's is one of the colleges that make up London University," Julia explained. "And for my degree, I read French—"

He looked puzzled. "Didn't you have to write it and speak it as well, to get a degree?"

She laughed. "Reading French means that the main subject I studied at university was French. It doesn't mean that all I had to do was read French to get a degree."

Michael's frown cleared. "I never heard that expression before. Okay, I understand now. In the States we'd say that when you were in college, you majored in French. Go on."

"I graduated when I was twenty. Then I took a year off, working at odd jobs all over France. I had a great time, especially when I got to the south. We Brits always go a bit crazy when we're exposed to bright sun." Julia smiled at a sudden rush of memories. "I fell madly in love with a handsome Frenchman called Jean-Paul Rossier and almost married him."

"What stopped you?"

"My guardian angel," she said. "Either that, or I got tired of competing with his mother for his attention."

He laughed. "Sounds as if you had a lucky escape."

"Definitely. Anyway, having run away from Jean-Paul and Madame Rossier in the nick of time, I came home to England and took a teacher's training course for a year. When I had my diploma, I applied to teach French at the middle-school level."

"At the school in Kensington where you are now?"

"No, at that point in my life I was full of high ideals about shaping young minds and transforming the world through the miracles of education. I took a job at a state school in one of London's poorest districts." Julia paused for a moment, remembering. "That was a pretty devastating experience. For the first two years I assumed I was a total failure as a teacher. By the end of the third year, I realized I wasn't all that terrible, I just wasn't good enough to compensate for parents who didn't care, and a school system that had provided my students with years of rotten education long before they reached my classroom."

"Did you quit?"

"Not for another year. But it was hard to make my French lessons anything but drudgery when half the students in my class couldn't distinguish between a noun and a verb in English, let alone in a foreign language."

"You can't blame yourself for the failure of an entire system," Michael said.

"Perhaps not. But you know, there were a couple of teachers at that school who managed to inspire their students class after class, week after week, year after year. One of them taught remedial reading, and the other taught history. I saw the miracles that a truly dedicated and talented teacher could work, even with children everyone else had rejected as hopeless. Watching those two old-timers, I realized that I was never going to measure up. With time and patience I could learn to be a competent teacher, but I didn't have the fire inside me that was going to transform me into an inspirational teacher. By the very best standards, I wasn't going to make the grade."

She paused again, wondering why she was telling Michael something about herself that she hadn't confided to anyone else, not even to Lianne. "It was a difficult thing to accept about myself—that I was a second-rater in my chosen career."

Michael didn't insult her with a facile reassurance that she was probably a better teacher than she realized. He steepled his fingers and looked at her over the top. "I guess the obvious question is why are you still teaching? It's not only your students who deserve something better, Julia. You deserve it, too. You have way too much intelligence and guts to waste your time doing something that doesn't command a hundred percent of your energy."

She grimaced. "Have you any idea what the jobless rate is in this country? I may not be a superb teacher, but I'm a good one, and I like the people I work with at Kensington Academy—"

"Those are all excuses for not making a change," Michael said. "They're not reasons."

"They're pretty good excuses," Julia said hotly. "I have to support myself, you know. My father was forced to take early retirement, so he and my mother have just enough income to scrape by. My brothers have young families to think about, and more children on the way. I have a huge mortgage on my flat, and the building society isn't going to be in the least bit interested if I tell them that I can't afford to make any more payments because I'm taking a few months off to beat bongo drums and try to find myself."

"I think it's men who are supposed to beat bongo drums," Michael said. "But I get your point. You can come out of your attack dog mode."

Julia grimaced. "I wouldn't have reacted so strongly, but the truth is, you touched one of my hot buttons." She drew in a deep breath. "I very badly want to make changes in my life, but it's a scary prospect."

"Change usually is."

"Mmm, especially for me." She leaned forward, hands clasped around her knees. "I was brought up to believe that taking risks was irresponsible, that sensible people found a solid career and plugged away at it, nine to five, week after week. But I watched Lianne when she came over here from the States, with nothing much behind her except talent and determination. The truth is that I not only admired her courage, I envied her willingness to stake everything on the slim chance of making a success as a designer. If I'd been in her shoes, I'd have weighed the odds, made a careful analysis of the marketplace and come to the logical conclusion that I had no chance at all of succeeding. Lianne simply had faith in herself and her talent. She knew she was an innovative and creative designer, so she hung on, through one setback after another, until she won the chance to show people how good she was. And look at how brilliantly she's succeeded."

"Lianne also had some help from her friends," Michael said. "She's told me that there were plenty of days when she wouldn't have been able to eat if you hadn't been subsidizing her talent with your hard-earned cash."

Julia flushed. "Lianne paid me back twice over the second she started work at DeWilde's."

"I wasn't criticizing Lianne's faith in herself, or the fact that she relied on you when times were tough. I'm pointing out that even talented people need a helping hand on occasion."

"That's true." Julia smiled. "Well, if I ever discover that I have a secret talent, I'll start looking round for some helping hands. And now you've pried all those confidences out of me, it's your turn."

"You already know everything there is to know about me," Michael said lightly. "You're the person who keeps reminding me that the tabloids carry a running account of my life.''

As so often happened, she felt that something in his body language didn't quite fit with the casualness of his voice. Julia examined him thoughtfully, weighing the implausible idea that Michael might actually have been hurt by some of her sarcastic comments about his life-style. ''There must be a few private moments for you to fill between flirting with cheerleaders and drinking champagne with movie stars,'' she said, matching his light tone, leaving him free to decide whether he wanted to talk honestly or hold her at arm's length, as she suspected he did with most people who tried to get close. ''What do you do when the paparazzi aren't on your heels? Do you go fishing? Deep-sea diving? Listen to jazz? Read Plato? Shakespeare?''

He raised an eyebrow. ''Read Plato and Shakespeare? You're joking, right?''

''No,'' she said quietly. ''I'm not joking. Far from it.''

''I work,'' he said abruptly. ''Eleven or twelve hours a day, six days a week. Two or three nights a week, I have some function to attend that's geared strictly toward generating maximum publicity for the hotels. Those are the events that usually make a splash in the gossip columns. Sundays, I take off.''

''And what do you do on Sundays?''

He looked away. ''I spend a lot of Sunday sleeping. Sometimes I try to spend a few hours with a friend, a real friend, not someone who has gossip value for the hotel's PR flacks.''

''And…'' she prompted.

''I also play the piano,'' he said, as if he were admitting to a guilty secret. ''Chiefly Bach and Mozart. I'm very bad, but nobody has to listen except me.''

It occurred to Julia that for a man constantly surrounded

by other rich men and beautiful women, Michael Forrest led a lonely life. "Why do you work so hard?" she asked.

He shrugged. "For the past year, mainly out of habit. Until then, I worked my tail off because the prestigious and famously gracious Carlisle Forrest hotel chain was about to slide into extremely ungracious bankruptcy."

She was startled. "I thought the Carlisle Forrest hotels in the States were like the Ritz in Paris, or Claridges in London—part of a tradition that had never lost its luster."

"I can't speak for the Ritz or for Claridges, but as far as our hotels are concerned, when I took control of the company, we were doing a fabulous job of providing all the comforts and services that you might have expected from a superb hotel prior to World War II. We polished shoes and had a maid on each floor ready to serve tea at four in the afternoon, because those were services my great-grandfather had instituted when he built our original hotel in Chicago. If you can believe it, we didn't have a computerized billing system, and most of our hotels only had one fax machine to serve the combined needs of the guests and the hotel staff. We were catering for a clientele that simply didn't exist anymore, and if we hadn't done something to spruce up our image and attract convention business, the entire chain would have gone under. We'd been operating at a loss for more than five years."

"You had to fight the existing management to get the changes you wanted implemented," Julia guessed.

"Yes." Michael got up from the wing chair and started pacing. "Unfortunately, existing management happened to be my father."

"I'm sorry," she said with real sympathy. "Was it very bad?"

"The pits." He shoved his hands into his pockets. "My father had a heart attack the week after I took over his job. He died a year later, and my mother hasn't spoken to me since."

"I'll bet she cashes her dividend check," Julia said tartly.

"You'd win your bet," Michael said. His smile didn't quite reach his eyes. "She's the only person I know who disapproves of my life-style more than you do."

"Until tonight, I had no idea what your life-style was."

"You knew about my relationship with Cherie Lockwood. And about Storm."

"Yes."

"You don't approve."

Julia chose her words carefully. "When you're a teacher, you see a lot of children whose parents neglect them. I don't care what sort of a relationship two consenting adults choose for themselves, but I don't think men or women should have children unless they're willing to be real parents."

Michael hesitated for a moment. "Cherie doesn't want me to spend time with Storm," he said finally. "I would see more of him if Brad Stein didn't strongly object."

She believed him, Julia realized. Astonishingly, she even found herself feeling sympathy for his plight. Her voice softened. "I'm not a complete idiot, Michael. I realized long before tonight that what the gossip magazines write about you probably bears only a glancing relationship to the truth. I'm sorry that my teaching experiences distorted my judgment when it came to your relationship with Storm and Cherie. I should have known there was more to it than the line being pursued by the tabloids. Lord knows, I shouldn't have been so credulous. These are the same journalists who keep reporting that the Loch Ness monster is eating the local milkmen."

"Is she?" Michael asked innocently.

Julia smiled. "With all that good salmon in the loch? I'm sure poor old Nessie's got better taste."

Michael came and stood in front of her. "Thank you for the vote of confidence." He grasped her hands and tugged her gently to her feet. He framed her face with his hands and looked down at her with a rueful gleam in his eyes that she couldn't quite interpret. "You're the most incredibly beautiful woman, Julia. You know that, don't you?"

No, of course she didn't know anything so ridiculous, but Michael sounded almost convincing enough to persuade her. "You make me believe it," she said huskily.

"Believe it all the time, because it's true." He ran his hands through her hair, and she closed her eyes, letting the magic of his touch shimmer through her veins. She wished this night would go on forever. She wished they could meet again, talk again, discover more about themselves and each other. She wished they could make love. Here. Now.

Her eyes flew open. Michael had stopped touching her, but he stood very close, his green eyes dark, almost brooding. She reached up and stroked his cheek before she had time to consider what that oddly tender gesture might signify. "I've enjoyed the time we spent together tonight," she said softly. "Thank you, Michael."

"I'm the one who should thank you. It was definitely my pleasure." He glanced away, then abruptly turned back and looked down at her. "You know, it's damned inconvenient, but I really want like hell to take you to bed."

His words were casual, but the heat in his voice made her cheeks burn. She swallowed, moistening her dry throat. "What's stopping you?"

"The remnants of my conscience." He traced the outline of her mouth with his thumb. "The certainty that we'd end up making each other very miserable."

The fact that she knew he was right didn't lessen the fierce regret that seized her. She realized suddenly that this overwhelming sensation of sharp, sexual hunger was what had been missing from her relationship with Gabriel DeWilde. Belatedly, she gave thanks that Gabe had had the sense to realize the lack before it was too late, even if she hadn't.

Julia tilted her head back so that she looked straight into Michael's eyes. What she saw there made her wonder if the pleasures of making love to him tonight might not outweigh the misery of the inevitable parting in the morning.

He leaned toward her. "Julia…" He murmured her name against her mouth. "God, don't look at me like that."

"All right," she whispered. She closed her eyes, but he kissed her, anyway. He kissed her with a passion that left her shaking, then held her tightly in his arms to still her trembling. No wonder she'd always been so tense and prickly around him, Julia thought. Her subconscious had been smart enough to sense the danger, even if the rest of her had been pathetically slow on the uptake.

Their kiss went on, and this time Michael didn't draw away. The longer they kissed, the faster Julia's inhibitions scattered, and the less she cared about the inevitable reckoning in the morning. Her head pounded with the roar of her blood, and it was a while before she realized that what she heard was a real noise, coming from outside the house.

"Michael…" She dragged herself back to awareness of their surroundings. "Michael, there's a car in the driveway. Someone's here."

He rested his forehead against hers. "Can't we tell them to go away again?"

"I don't think so. They must have seen all the lights are on."

"If it's your friend Edward, I'm not likely to be polite." Michael sighed. "Turn around. I'd better do up that damn zipper of yours again before we have to answer the doorbell."

But the doorbell didn't ring. Instead, an attractively

husky female voice called out from the entrance hall. "Hello! Is anyone there? This is Grace DeWilde."

Julia shot an appalled glance at Michael. There was only one reason she could think of for Gabe's mother to make such a noisy announcement. "She must have come in already and seen us," she hissed.

He gave a wry smile. "Yes, I guess she did." He raised his voice. "Grace, come on in. We're in the living room."

Since the floor failed to open and swallow her, Julia made a dash for a dark corner, but Michael clamped his arm around her waist and refused to let her go. "Julia, honey, I think Grace and Jeffrey have probably seen two people kissing before."

"There's kissing and then there's kissing," Julia muttered.

He grinned. "Yeah, and I guess we were definitely doing the latter."

Grace came into the room before Julia could say anything more. She'd changed her hairstyle since the last time Julia had seen her, and the shorter cut made her face look softer and younger. Or perhaps it was just her glowing happiness that made her look so youthful. Jeffrey DeWilde followed behind his ex-wife, his face wreathed in a smile as broad as hers.

Grace gave the pair of them a faintly amused glance, then she crossed the room and swept Michael into a warm embrace. "Michael, how nice to see you on this side of the Atlantic. And Julia, my dear, thank you. I understand from Jeffrey that you're the person who told him to track me down so that I could come and visit my new grandbaby."

"Yes, that was me. How are you, Mrs. DeWilde?"

"We're both wonderful." Jeffrey took his wife's hand and tucked it around his arm. "We've just come from the hospital," he announced proudly. "Lianne gave birth to a baby girl just after midnight. Grace and I are grandparents."

"Congratulations!" Michael and Julia spoke in unison.

"I'll get some champagne," Michael said. "This deserves a toast."

"Lianne must be thrilled," Julia said. "I know she and Gabe were both hoping for a daughter. Have they decided on a name for her yet?"

"Elizabeth Gabrielle," Jeffrey said. "It seems a good mix of plain and fancy, don't you think?"

"It's a lovely combination," Julia said. "Have you seen the baby yet?"

"Of course. But only a quick glimpse before the nurses shooed us out and told us to come back tomorrow," Grace told her. "She's six pounds, two ounces, and utterly beautiful."

"She's bald as a coot," Jeffrey said. "However, based on past experience with our three, I'm optimistic that the condition isn't permanent."

"Her skin is very fair, not red at all," Grace said. "I think she's going to look a lot like Gabe."

Jeffrey chuckled. "Trust me, that's a likeness only a new grandmother could spot. Personally, I think she bears a startling resemblance to Winston Churchill."

Michael came back carrying a tray with four brimming glasses of champagne. "How's Lianne doing?" he asked, handing the glasses around. "Is she exhausted? More to the point, maybe, how's Gabe holding up?"

"We left him incoherent but edging toward sanity," Jeffrey said dryly.

"Lianne's sleeping," Grace said. "She had a C section in the end, and she was pretty groggy when we saw her, but there were no complications and the doctor expects her to be out of the hospital in five or six days." Her face lit up. "Isn't it wonderful to think we have a new person to welcome home within the week? This is so exciting."

"It certainly is." Jeffrey raised his glass. "Here's to Elizabeth Gabrielle," he said. "The first of the new generation of DeWildes."

"May her life be long and full of love." Grace touched her glass to Jeffrey's, then looked quickly away.

"And here's to Lianne and Gabe," Michael added. "The proud parents."

Julia smiled and lifted her glass. "Not forgetting the new grandparents."

"I'll drink to all of the above," Grace said happily.

The four of them drank their champagne, and Grace sighed contentedly as she put down her glass. "This has been such a good night," she said. "But I suppose we should get to bed if we're going to drive back to the hospital tomorrow morning."

"Why don't you two take Gabe and Lianne's bedroom?" Michael suggested. "That room has its own bathroom and it's at the back of the house, where it's quieter. You'll rest better if your room faces away from the road. Not that this lane gets much traffic."

Jeffrey and Grace looked at each other, then both seemed suddenly fascinated by their shoes. Grace was blushing, and Jeffrey appeared as thoroughly embarrassed as a sophisticated, mature man can manage to appear.

Julia was horrified by Michael's gaffe. How could he have forgotten that Grace and Jeffrey were divorced? "Of course you don't have to share—"

Michael stepped firmly on her toes. "Why don't you two go on up?" he said, as if Julia hadn't spoken. "We'll take care of locking up and turning off all the lights down here."

"That's very good of you," Grace said faintly.

"Well, good night, then." Jeffrey cleared his throat. "I'll get your overnight bag from the hall, Grace."

"Thank you." Without looking at either Michael or Julia, Grace made her way to the staircase. She walked upstairs, gaze fixed rigidly ahead. Jeffrey followed, a bag in each hand. The sound of footsteps along the upper hallway was followed by that of a door closing.

Julia stared wide-eyed at Michael. "They were divorced three months ago!" she exclaimed. "Michael, what in the world is going on here?"

He gave a small smile. "A reconciliation?"

"But according to Lianne and Gabe they've spent the past year making each other's lives totally miserable!"

Michael's smile became rueful. "True love," he said wryly. "Ain't it grand?"

CHAPTER SIX

JEFFREY SUPPOSED that he had endured more embarrassing situations in his life than walking upstairs to bed with his ex-wife under the fascinated scrutiny of a man and a woman young enough to be his children. Right at the moment, however, he couldn't recall one. Intellectually, he realized there was something comic about feeling so wicked at the prospect of sharing a bedroom with Grace. Emotionally, he was incapable of appreciating the manifold ironies of the situation. The truth was, at this moment he could think of nothing beyond the fact that Grace had publicly agreed to spend the night sleeping in his bed. That simple fact left him torn between lust and panic. He'd blown every previous chance for reconciliation by his own stupid behavior. What if he blew it again? God knew, he had no clever or sophisticated plan for wooing her back. Telling her how much he loved her and begging for her forgiveness was the best he could come up with, and he had a dreadful fear it wouldn't be enough.

He cleared his throat. Damn! Grace was going to think he'd developed defective vocal chords if he did that one more time. "Gabe and Lianne have done a splendid job with the remodeling of this cottage, haven't they? This room looks very comfortable." Trying not to stare with too much interest at the rather small four-poster bed, he put their overnight bags on the window seat and looked around for a suitable place to hang his clothes.

Yawning, Grace kicked off her shoes and dropped her

linen jacket onto a chair. She turned around and gave him
a glance that appeared equal parts affection and amusement. Not quite what he yearned to see, but a lot better
than the hurt and angry glares of their recent past. "Briarwood Cottage is lovely, Jeffrey. In some ways it reminds
me of Kemberly, although a much smaller version, of
course." She opened her overnight bag. "The bed isn't
very big, is it? Still, it looks comfortable."

"Very comfortable," Jeffrey said stiffly. He hadn't realized men of his age could blush at the mere mention of
the word *bed*. In the nick of time, he remembered not to
clear his throat. "Would you like to use the bathroom first,
or shall I?"

Grace gave another yawn. "You go first. I'll finish un-
packing while you're in the bathroom."

She sounded so matter of fact. The appalling thought
struck Jeffrey that perhaps she intended to spend the entire
night sleeping.

She couldn't possibly be planning to lie next to him for
seven hours and just sleep. Or could she? Was that why
she was yawning? To warn him she was tired?

Grace shook out the folds of a silk robe before dropping
it onto the bed. "Would you like me to unpack for you,
too, Jeffrey?"

He winced. Thirty-plus years of marriage suggested he
should decline, but Jeffrey decided to be brave. How much
damage could she do to a pair of slacks and a blazer?
"Thank you, if it's not too much trouble. Perhaps you
could find a spare coat hanger or two in the wardrobe. I'll
take my shaving kit and dressing gown into the bathroom
and leave everything else to you."

They might have been two polite strangers, he thought
gloomily as he brushed his teeth. He combed his hair, relieved that although it was rapidly turning gray at the sides,
at least he hadn't gone bald since Grace left him. He
splashed on after-shave and peered in the mirror, hoping

Grace would think his new gray hairs looked distinguished. Thank goodness his three-times-weekly squash games kept him fighting fit and he still had a few muscles to be proud of.

When he realized that he was actually standing in front of the bathroom mirror flexing his biceps, Jeffrey recovered his sense of humor. He reached for his dressing gown, smiling ruefully. Love, it seemed, could always find new ways to make sensible men behave like fools.

He walked back into the bedroom and paused in midstride, his breath catching in his throat when he saw Grace. In his absence, she had kicked off her shoes and climbed onto the bed, where she sat cross-legged in the middle of a heap of pillows, reading a magazine. She glanced up at the sound of the bathroom door opening and smiled at Jeffrey as she took off her glasses and put them on the bedside table.

For a few seconds, he would have sworn his heart literally stopped beating. He wondered what Grace would say if he told her that of all the things in their marriage that he missed, the familiar sight of her perched in the middle of his rumpled bed, reading, was the one he missed most.

Her smile was replaced by a look of concern. "Jeffrey? Is something wrong?"

"Nothing," he said hoarsely. "The bathroom's all yours."

"Thank you. I'll shower later, I think."

Later? But it was already past one o'clock in the morning. Jeffrey wondered what the hell he was supposed to do next. Climb into bed still wearing his robe? Discard it casually somewhere in the ten feet separating him from the bed? The etiquette of sharing sleeping quarters with an ex-wife entirely defeated him.

Grace twisted around so that they were facing each other. "Actually, Jeffrey, I was sitting here wondering if you'd remembered about the bet we made earlier this evening.''

He'd been thinking of little else ever since they left the hospital. "I remember. I believe you said our new grandchild would be a girl. I predicted the baby would be a boy."

"Which means I won the bet." Grace looked contemplative. "As I recall, that means you owe me two hours of...service. That is what we agreed, isn't it?"

The way she said "service" was so heavy with innuendo that Jeffrey managed, just barely, to refrain from choking. "Er...yes, I believe two hours is what we wagered."

Before the divorce, their finances had been so intermingled that betting for money had seemed pointless. Over the years, they'd developed a system where they staked time instead of cash, with the loser having to do whatever the winner specified for the stipulated number of hours. Sometimes that had meant Grace agreeing to watch one of Jeffrey's beat-'em-up movies, or Grace dragging Jeffrey to one of the avant-garde art shows she loved and he hated. Once Jeffrey had been condemned to prune the roses at Kemberly, and in retribution the next time he won a bet, he'd forced Grace to balance their quarterly household accounts. Quite often, though, the bet had turned into a sexual game, with the loser required to make love in whatever way the winner commanded. On those occasions, by the time the bet had been paid, it was difficult to remember who had been the winner and who the supposed loser. Jeffrey hardly dared to hope that Grace was going to claim payment of their recent bet by demanding sexual favors from him. That seemed like rewarding him for losing with every fantasy of the past year rolled into one giant gift package.

Grace examined him thoughtfully. "Since we're here

together, this seems like a good time to claim my payment."

"Er...yes. I suppose now is as good as any other time."

She smiled, a slow, sexy smile that had his stomach doing handsprings. "It's one-thirty," she said. "You realize that under the terms of the bet, you have to do exactly what I say until three-thirty?"

He shoved his hands into the pockets of his dressing gown to prevent himself running to the bed and grabbing her. "Yes. Until three-thirty." He rocked back on his heels, pretending reluctance. "Not a minute longer, mind."

"Of course not." She slid off the bed. "Come here, Jeffrey."

Somehow, he managed to control his eagerness and walk toward her without stumbling over his own feet. "Gracie," he murmured, reaching out his arms. "Gracie, I've missed you so much."

She quickly stepped backward, eluding him. "The first rule is that you're not allowed to talk."

He drew in an uneven breath. "All right."

She shot him a disapproving look. "No talking means no talking, Jeffrey."

He nodded.

She smiled. "And the second rule is that you're allowed to move only if I give you permission."

He stared straight ahead.

"Very good," she murmured. "Make sure you remember those two simple rules."

Jeffrey wanted to ask what would happen if he broke the rules, but Grace reached up and drew her hand across his cheek in a slow, intimate caress, so he decided to postpone his question. When she reached his mouth, she hesitated, then stroked across his lips, parting them so that she could slip her finger into his mouth. By the exercise of supreme self-control, Jeffrey obeyed orders and refrained from responding with his tongue to the erotic thrusting of her forefinger.

When he was almost at the point of moaning in frustration, Grace changed her form of torment, trailing her hands down his chest until she reached the belt of his dressing gown. "Is there anything you'd like me to do right now, Jeffrey?" she murmured.

He closed his eyes and clenched his fists.

She frowned. "Hmm. I'll consider that an attempt on your part to obey my rules." She didn't untie the belt of his robe, but she did at least part the lapels and rest her head against his chest. Before he even realized what he was doing, he'd fastened his arms around her, one hand on her hips, the other tangled in her hair.

For about twenty tantalizing seconds she allowed herself to be crushed against him. Then she twisted out of his embrace. "Four minutes," she said in mock reproach. "Goodness, Jeffrey, you're even worse at honoring your bets than you used to be."

He bit back his protest that he was a man, not a block of stone, and that he wanted her so desperately tonight that he was amazed he'd lasted four minutes without tumbling her onto the bed. She smiled, as if she knew how badly he wanted to speak, and dropped a quick kiss in the center of his chest before moving away and positioning herself on the other side of the room.

Pretending not to have noticed that he was staring at her with almost hypnotic fascination, Grace began to unfasten the leather belt at her waist. She slid the belt from the loops of her slacks with a seductive skill that would have done a professional stripper proud, playing with it for a couple of seconds before tossing it in the direction of the old-fashioned wardrobe. Sweat broke out on Jeffrey's forehead. If this was her way of punishing him for breaking the rules, he wasn't sure that it was succeeding. She was tormenting him, all right, but some torments were fiendishly enjoyable.

Her gaze locked with his, and her eyes gleamed with the satisfied knowledge of precisely what she was doing to him. She unfastened the button at the waistband of her slacks, lowered the zipper and shimmied out of them with a sinuous sway of her hips.

Jeffrey drew in a gasping breath and realized two things simultaneously. First, that he didn't have a hope in hell of surviving two more minutes of this crazy bet, let alone two more hours. And second, that for a woman who'd recently divorced him, Grace seemed delightfully willing to seduce him.

To hell with caution and restraint, he decided. This was the woman he loved, and he was starving for her. In a few quick strides, he covered the distance between them, sweeping Grace into his arms, tilting her head back and kissing her with blind, hungry passion. Oh, God, she felt so wonderful in his arms after months of harrowing abstinence.

She returned his kiss with all the fire he'd dreamed of, rubbing against him, her body lithe and still marvelously supple. Her arms came around him, stroking his shoulders, linking her hands with his, urging him backward onto the bed.

Jeffrey couldn't have been more willing to follow her lead. He tumbled onto the mattress, pulling Grace on top of him. He started to roll over, to reverse their positions so that he would be on top, when he realized that he couldn't move his right arm. Grace scrambled off him, and he sat up, staring in disbelief at his wrist.

"You've handcuffed me to the bedpost!" he said, gazing incredulously at the velvet-lined, stainless steel manacle that he'd seen once before, when Grace delivered the DeWilde jewels to his office.

She grinned mischievously. "Honestly, Jeffrey, you

promised not to speak for two hours, and now you're not only speaking, you're shouting."

"I didn't expect to be chained to the bedpost!" he yelled.

"It's punishment for breaking the terms of our bet. You know I always take our bets very seriously."

"For God's sake, Gracie, how could you expect me to stand there like a statue? You were deliberately driving me crazy!"

Grace appeared unrepentant. "I hope this bedroom has thick walls," she said. "Otherwise Michael and Julia are going to think we have a very kinky relationship."

"They'd be dead right! We do have a kinky relationship, or at least a totally ridiculous one!" Jeffrey drew in a deep breath, wriggling his wrist to no avail. "Come on, Grace, be reasonable. Undo the handcuff."

She eyed him coolly. "No."

He lunged for her ankle, but she moved, swift as quicksilver, tucking her feet under her.

"This is insane," he said, struggling to control his frustration. "Grace, if you don't want me to make love to you, you don't have to lock me up. You just have to tell me. I'll be disappointed, of course, but I'm not about to force you against your will. For God's sake, what do you think I've turned into? Some kind of monster?"

"I don't think you've turned into anything, Jeffrey. I think you're just what you've always been, a proud and stubborn man."

"I'm not in the least stubborn, and pride isn't necessarily a flaw!" Jeffrey said hotly. He moved instinctively toward her, but was brought up short by the handcuff. "All right, Grace, I'll beg if you want me to. Please, let me out of this damned thing."

"If I do, are you going to try to make love to me?"

It took him a while, but finally he managed to say it.

"No, I already told you that. Not if you don't want me to."

"I don't know if I want you to. It depends." She dangled the silver key chain from her index finger, waving it gently back and forth.

"On what?"

"On you, as it happens. Have you any idea how much heartache you've put me through over the past nineteen months, Jeffrey? Do you even begin to fathom how badly you hurt me?"

He didn't have to stop and think about his answer, even for a moment. "Yes," he said, his voice hoarse with regret. "I know how much I hurt you, Gracie, because I hurt myself every bit as much. If there were some way to unravel time and go back to before this whole mess started, I'd do everything differently, I swear. But there isn't a way, and all I can do now is tell you how sorry I am and ask you to forgive me for destroying our marriage."

She continued to wave the key. "I left you. I was the one who flew off to San Francisco."

"To outsiders it may have seemed that way. We both know the truth. You didn't leave me, Grace, I drove you away."

"Nineteen months ago—six months ago—I'd have given my right arm to hear you admit that. But now apologies for the past aren't enough, Jeffrey."

He felt sick, and the pain was even worse because he knew he had no right to expect a different answer. "Enough for what?" he asked harshly.

"For us to build a future on." Her voice shook slightly, and Jeffrey realized her composure was nowhere near as complete as it seemed. "I guess this is the big moment, the point where we both have to make a decision about our respective futures. Tonight is the last time I'm ever going to ask you this question, Jeffrey. Are we going to spend the rest of our lives together or apart?"

"I want us to be together," Jeffrey said, clinging to the frail hope that she would show him a way to redeem himself, a way out of the quagmire he'd created. "God, Gracie, you can't even begin to imagine how much I want that."

"You want us to be married again. Is that what you're saying?"

Married again to Gracie. Jeffrey shut his eyes. He wanted that with such fierce intensity that he could barely respond. "Yes."

"Why?" she asked. "You have to tell me why you want us to be married, Jeffrey. I need you to give me the words."

Grace knew him too well, he thought. She knew how hard it had always been for him to express his feelings, to lay his vulnerability on the line, to run the risk of being rejected by the person he cared about most in the entire world. She knew how much easier it would be for him to make passionate love to her, then glide back into their relationship without ever verbalizing how much he loved and needed her, how much he regretted his past failures. But she didn't recognize yet how much he'd changed during the months of their separation. Losing Grace, suffering through their divorce, had taught him many things. Not least the lesson that love, freely given, was never wasted, and that whether Grace accepted or rejected his feelings for her, he would be richer for having expressed them.

He looked at her, the words flowing easily from his tongue, because they came straight from his heart. "I want us to be together again because I love you," he said. "You're my delight, my joy, my friend, and the best part of everything that I am. I don't deserve your forgiveness, but if you'll agree to marry me again, Gracie, I shall be the happiest man on God's earth."

To his absolute horror, Grace began to cry.

"Gracie! Don't! Please, don't cry! I didn't mean to upset you. If you don't want to marry me, you don't have to.'' He scrambled onto his knees and discovered that by stretching out his left hand, he could just manage to touch her cheeks. He tried to stem the flow of tears. "Gracie, please don't be sad. I can't bear it if I've hurt you again.''

She took his hand and held it against his cheek. "You haven't hurt me.'' She sniffed. "Goodness, Jeffrey, have you forgotten so much about me already? I always cry when I'm happy.''

She was happy! Relief left him limp. "You cry when you're sad, too. How is a mere man supposed to tell the difference?''

She reached for a tissue from the box standing on the bedside table. "I don't know. A woman would never be in the least bit confused, but men are so hopelessly inadequate—'' She broke off. "Jeffrey what are you doing?''

"Unlocking this damned handcuff,'' he said, freeing himself. He held up the key he'd stolen, dangling it just out of her reach.

She lunged for him. "Jeffrey DeWilde, stealing that key while pretending to console me was not the behavior of a gentleman.''

He let her momentum topple him backward, so that she lay straddled along the entire length of his body. "Gracie, darling, chaining me to the bedpost was not exactly the behavior of a perfect lady.''

She wriggled, pretending she wanted to get away and actually making not the slightest effort to escape his grasp. He put his arms around her and rolled sideways, capturing her firmly beneath him. "Are you going to ravish me?'' she asked.

He looked down at her, smiling. "Yes, I believe I am.''

"Thank God.'' She linked her hands behind his head and pulled his mouth down to hers. "It's about time.''

CHAPTER SEVEN

JULIA SLEPT UNTIL AFTER nine the next morning, and woke to the sound of the village church bells ringing outside her open window. When she came downstairs, Michael was in the kitchen with charts and flow sheets spread over the table, the *Sunday Times* unopened at his elbow and the smell of brewing coffee permeating the air.

"Good morning." She headed for the coffeepot. "You look as if you've been up for a while. And working, too."

"Yeah." He rubbed his hand over his unshaven chin. "I woke at five and couldn't get back to sleep. Jet lag catching up on me, I guess."

He looked exhausted, Julia thought, and she'd bet good money that his insomnia had been caused by more than jet lag. Having spent the past year tied in knots over Gabriel DeWilde, she recognized the symptoms of someone wrestling with problems that refused to go away. "It's really annoying when you can't sleep," she said, keeping her voice casual. "You lie there wondering how you can feel so tired, and yet not be able to doze off."

He shrugged. "Insomnia's inevitable when you fly across the Atlantic as often as I do. Eventually your body goes on strike and decides it's sticking to San Francisco time regardless of where it happens to be."

"At least you don't have to work today." She gestured to the charts and flow sheets arrayed in daunting piles in front of him. "That's the great thing about papers filled with columns of figures. You know they'll still be there tomorrow.''

Michael's answer was a noncommittal grunt while he swiftly collated the papers and stashed them into his briefcase. Julia sighed and poured herself a cup of coffee. She'd woken up feeling totally confused about what had happened between her and Michael, and his attitude was doing nothing to clarify things. She'd enjoyed his company last night more than she would have believed possible. She'd sensed a camaraderie between the two of them, almost as if they understood each other without needing to find the words to verbalize their feelings. This unexpected sense of intimacy would have been mystifying enough, even if he hadn't kissed her. But he had kissed her, twice. And on both occasions his kisses had aroused instant desire. Julia was still trying to come to terms with that startling fact. She couldn't understand why she'd responded so strongly to a man she wasn't sure she approved of. How could she fantasize about making love to a man who'd abandoned his own child? Wasn't she the woman who'd always considered a man's attitude to fatherhood as the litmus test of his true character?

Julia stirred milk into her coffee and delivered herself a quick lecture. Having fallen out of love with Gabriel DeWilde, she had no desire to tumble into a doomed relationship with Michael Forrest. Quite apart from her own ambivalence about what was going on between them, the kisses that left her in turmoil had probably created no more than a minor blip on Michael's emotional radar. At this point, the smart course of action would be to stop trying to strengthen a bond that existed only in her imagination.

Fortunately, in the aftermath of her affair with Gabe, she'd become highly skilled at chattering brightly about nothing in particular. "Have Grace and Jeffrey gone to the hospital already?" she asked, carrying her cup of coffee to the kitchen table.

"No, there hasn't been a sound out of them." Michael's eyes gleamed. "I'm guessing they had a long and active night. I think they may sleep for quite a while yet."

"An active night? Do you mean they...? Surely they can't have..." Julia realized Michael was laughing at her and she grinned reluctantly. "All right, so I'm being ridiculous. Of course they did. But, Michael, they're divorced."

He leaned across the table, lowering his voice to a conspiratorial whisper. "If you don't tell anyone, I won't, either."

She laughed, although she was bothered by the fact that she'd been so caught up in her own feelings last night that she'd been oblivious to Grace and Jeffrey's. "I was horrified when I heard you suggest that they should share Lianne and Gabe's bedroom. How in the world did you know they wanted to sleep together?"

"It wasn't exactly an inspired guess, Julia. The pair of them might as well have carried a twenty-foot banner."

"But they barely glanced at each other!"

"That was my first clue," he said dryly.

Julia shook her head. "All right, I admit I don't understand what's going on. The DeWildes were married for half a lifetime, and then they spent a year hurling legal hand grenades at each other. Finally, less than four months ago, they got a divorce. And now you're telling me they arrived here last night dying to sleep together. Michael, that makes no sense at all. None."

"Why would you assume that sexual relationships have to make sense?"

In view of the way she'd responded to Michael last night, Julia realized she had no valid answer to that. "If we were talking about my students, I wouldn't be so surprised. I don't expect people falling in love for the first time to behave rationally, not in the beginning when there's so much to discover—about yourself as much as about the other person. But since Grace and Jeffrey DeWilde managed to stay married for more than thirty years, you'd think they'd have worked out whether or not they actually love each other *before* they filed for divorce."

Michael got up and poured them both more coffee. "Sometimes people get carried away in a situation, and they have to reach some kind of closure before they understand that they've galloped off at full speed in the wrong direction."

Julia stirred her coffee without drinking it. "It's really hard to imagine Grace and Jeffrey DeWilde having such a...such a torrid relationship. They always seemed settled, as if they had every detail of their lives under control. Especially Jeffrey. I can't imagine him galloping off anywhere, let alone in the wrong direction. He's so calm and sophisticated, and he has that wonderful ironic wit, as if nothing anybody did would ever surprise him."

"A dangerous man to get close to," Michael said softly. He shoved the newspaper to one side with unexpected force. "Here's some advice for you, Julia. Beware of men who hide their feelings behind a facade of indifference. Too much cool and witty sophistication usually means there are hot and powerful emotions churning behind the mask."

Michael should know, because he and Jeffrey DeWilde were two of a kind. Julia felt a moment of astonishment that she'd taken so long to recognize something so obvious. Michael was less urbane and more cynical than Jeffrey DeWilde, more provocative and less dignified, but he played the same game. He'd learned how to protect his privacy not by hiding, but by stepping forward and deliberately thrusting a false image into the glare of the media spotlight. For whatever reason, this weekend Michael had allowed her to catch a few glimpses of the real man behind the public image, and Julia realized that she was hungry for more.

She looked up at him. "Are you warning me that you're a dangerous man to know, Michael?"

He hesitated a fraction too long, and she realized he wasn't going to let her step any further behind the mask, at least for a while. "I thought we were talking about Jeffrey," he said. With a skill she'd come to recognize, he segued into one of his ever-ready anecdotes. "I guess I was one of the few people who wasn't surprised when Grace and Jeffrey broke up. The hotel business teaches you that people are endlessly amazing, in good ways and bad. Our flagship hotel in Chicago just hosted a wedding reception for a seventy-five-year-old groom and his seventy-eight-year-old bride. Their most recent divorce had lasted for six years and this was their third wedding."

She knew he was deliberately distracting her, but he made it so entertaining to be diverted. "It was their third wedding to each other?" Julia said.

"Yep, it sure was. They had both their other wedding receptions at our hotel, too, the first one in 1947 and the second one in 1965." He grinned. "Maybe next time I should give them a discount for being such loyal repeat customers."

"Michael, don't say that, even in fun! Heavens, I hope it's third-time lucky for them."

"The groom is very optimistic. I stopped and chatted with him for a few minutes while he was paying his bill. He informed me that the difference in their ages had always been a problem, but that he believed this time they had it licked." Michael managed to look solemn. "He felt he finally had a more mature attitude, and he planned to ignore snide comments about the age gap from his pals."

"How old did you say they were? Seventy-eight and seventy-five?" Julia shook her head.

"Yep. One of my grandmothers was an immigrant from

Poland and she was full of wise peasant sayings. Her favorite was that we grow too soon old, and too late smart. I guess she had a point."

She laughed. "All right, Michael, you win. Obviously it's completely unreasonable of me to expect the DeWildes to have their act together just because they were married so long. By this reckoning, they've got at least another quarter century to go before wisdom strikes."

Michael leaned back in his chair, twisting a gold pen between his fingers. "While we're on the subject of Grace and Jeffrey, we should make plans for the day. They might be pleased to have the house to themselves this morning, don't you think? Why don't we clear up here as quickly as we can, then drive into Winchester and see Lianne and Gabe and the new baby?"

"I'd like that. We can leave a note for Grace and Jeffrey to let them know what we're doing." Julia smiled at Michael, realizing that despite her confusion, she felt lighthearted, anticipating the day ahead in a way that had been foreign to her for much too long.

Michael stared at her for a long, silent moment. Then he pushed back his chair, the movement abrupt. "I'll see to things upstairs. Why don't you take care of cleaning the kitchen?"

"All right. I've packed my case, so I can be ready inside thirty minutes. How about you?"

"Sounds good to me," he said. "Meet you in the front hallway."

HIS PARENTS' MARRIAGE had not inspired Michael with any fondness for the institution, or any respect for the idea, fashionable in some quarters, that staying in a failed marriage was a more responsible choice than getting out. As for love and passion, his experience with Cherie Lockwood had convinced him that human beings would be far happier if they could take a lesson from amoebas and learn how to clone themselves without benefit of a partner.

Storm's birth had confirmed his opinion that long-term relationships carried penalties that far outweighed the dubious benefits, and he'd been careful in the past three years never to get seriously involved. He didn't lead the wild sexual life that the tabloids suggested, but he never dated a woman who might want more from him than the little he was prepared to give. Where relationships between the sexes were concerned, Michael was very much in favor of keeping things shallow—and therefore painless.

Julia Dutton tempted him to break all his own rules. He wasn't quite sure why her naive sexuality should be such a turn-on. He hoped like hell that he hadn't reached the point where he was so jaded that he needed innocence to spark a response in his cynical soul. If ever he'd heard a game plan for disaster, that was it. He couldn't risk getting sexually involved with a woman too unsophisticated to understand what sort of person she was dealing with.

Frowning, Michael unlocked the car. He'd been in a strange mood ever since Julia's arrival at Briarwood Cottage yesterday evening, and he'd found this morning's visit to Lianne and Gabe unsettling, to say the least. His brief encounter with their new daughter had brought back memories of Storm's birth that he would have preferred to keep safely buried. Damn! He thought it was women who were supposed to get sentimental over helpless infants, not men who had no intention of adding any offspring to the already overburdened planet.

"Wasn't Elizabeth Gabrielle beautiful?" Julia slid into the passenger seat and gave him a smile that made his heart race. Her cheeks glowed, her eyes sparkled, and the sun struck flashes of fire from her hair. Looking at her made his throat ache.

The fact that she seemed oblivious to the effect she was having on him only made her appeal more powerful. He watched, torn between self-mockery and fascination, as Julia shook her hair out of her eyes and adjusted the shoulder strap so that it lay more comfortably between her breasts. He'd noticed from the first that she was a restful person to be with, not someone who needed to fidget. As soon as the seat belt was in place, she clasped her hands lightly in her lap and turned to him with another smile.

"I agree with Grace, don't you? Elizabeth definitely looks like Gabe. And did you see her hands? They were so crumpled and perfect. I love looking at a newborn baby's hands."

She sounded wistful and he wanted like hell to kiss her. Right before taking her to a room with a large bed and twenty-four-hour room service. He was aware of an odd tenderness winding its way through his other feelings, hooking itself onto what had started out as a perfectly straightforward case of sexual desire. The sensation was alien enough to make him edgy, unwelcome enough to annoy him, and he leaned forward, turning on the ignition as an excuse to avoid responding to her smile.

Best to get the conversation onto neutral territory as quickly as possible, he decided, backing out of their parking space. "Lianne looked well, didn't you think?"

"Yes, she did, considering how exhausted she must be. And Gabe was back to normal, thank goodness."

Michael raised an eyebrow. "I guess you could call it normal. Providing you overlook the fact that he spent ten minutes debating whether Elizabeth should enroll at Oxford or Harvard. Personally, I think it would be great if the kid got to open her eyes and look around the room before her parents started obsessing about her college applications."

She laughed. "You're forgetting how precocious our godchild is. According to Lianne, she's not only opened her eyes, she's already smiled. Remember?"

"No, I forgot. That improbable gem must have been

dropped right around the same time Gabe told me that he was sure Elizabeth recognizes the sound of his voice."

"Perhaps she does." Julia patted him on the knee. "You're just a cynical old grouch, Michael."

He wanted to take her hand and guide it straight to the zipper of his slacks. He gripped the steering wheel and took a deep breath. "You're right," he said. "I'm a grouch. I guess hunger's making me bad-tempered."

"No wonder. You only had a sandwich for dinner and neither of us ate breakfast. We should find somewhere to have lunch. There's a restaurant not far from the motorway that isn't too bad."

He had enough phone calls and faxes waiting to occupy every minute of the afternoon and most of the night, not to mention the fact that he had arranged to spend at least three hours with Clive Browne to discuss hotel business. Michael hesitated for a second, then realized he had better things to do than waste time pretending to debate something that was already decided. The truth was, he'd been planning ever since last night to take Julia with him to Ashby Hall.

"There's somewhere I'd like to take you for lunch," he said. "Somewhere special, but it's out of our way. Are you in a hurry to get back to London?"

She shook her head. "I have no plans for tonight, and my first class isn't until ten tomorrow. It's the last week of school, so I'm basically wrapping up the year's work and suggesting some summer reading assignments, so I don't have any real preparation to do."

Michael doubled back the way he'd come, negotiated a busy traffic roundabout with the flair of a native Brit, and took the road that was signposted for Weyhill.

"Where are we going?" Julia asked. "Although, it's such gorgeous weather that almost anywhere with trees and a view of the sky would be great."

"I'm taking you to a place called Ashby Hall. It's about fifteen miles from here."

"Is it a restaurant?"

"A hotel, converted from an eighteenth-century country mansion."

"Oh, lovely! My favorite sort of place to eat. How did you hear about it? This road's pretty, but it's definitely off the beaten track."

"Grace brought me here a couple of years ago. The gardens at Ashby are famous among rose enthusiasts, and she wanted to see a particular variety of antique rose growing here that has been lost almost everywhere else. I believe it was called Autumn Damask. She was hoping the owners might agree to give her a cutting for the garden at Kemberly."

"And did they?"

"The head gardener decided she was worthy enough to be put on the waiting list. Grace said that was the gardening equivalent of winning an Olympic medal. After her split from Jeffrey and their divorce, I don't know whether she actually got the rose in the end."

"Isn't it unusual for a hotel to be cultivating rare and antique roses?"

"They don't just cultivate roses. Wait until you see the place. The gardens are amazing. The house has an interesting history, too. It was originally built for the local lord of the manor, who had no children, so it was inherited by a cousin, who also had no children, and that continued for another two generations, until the place began to acquire the reputation of being cursed. In 1860, when it came on the market, nobody would buy it until a man came along called Blodget, who'd made a fortune manufacturing decorative tins and canisters, and he snapped at the bargain. He already had ten children, so I guess he decided a sudden attack of sterility might not be all that bad."

She chuckled. "Blodget—what a great name! It sounds

like something out of Dickens. Did the family move in and live happily ever after? Please don't tell me all the Blodget children died, or something horrid like that.''

''As far as I know, the ten little Blodgets lived long and happy lives, but their parents didn't have any more children, which means either Mr. Blodget failed to break the curse, or Mrs. Blodget got smart and locked him out of her bedroom.''

''Or they discovered the miracle of family planning,'' Julia suggested.

''In the 1860s? I doubt it. Anyway, the moment Mr. Blodget's name was on the Ashby Hall deeds, he started to go through the house 'improving' it with artistic additions.''

Julia pulled a face. ''Let me guess. He added mock turrets to all the chimneys—''

''Sure.'' Michael grinned. ''Not to mention a central Gothic tower with a striking clock, fake vaulted ceilings in the drawing room, and enough stained glass windows to decorate a small cathedral.''

''Oh, Lord.''

''You haven't heard the best. For his final flourish, Mr. Blodget brought an artist over from Italy to paint cherubs on every available ceiling and Chinese landscapes on all the door panels.''

''He had an Italian artist painting the Chinese scenes?'' Julia asked.

''I guess so. Mr. Blodget probably had the typical Victorian attitude and considered one foreign country interchangeable with another. Italian, Chinese, what's the difference?''

''None, obviously. They both eat noodles, don't they?''

Michael laughed, and realized he'd laughed more with Julia over the past twenty-four hours than with anyone else in the preceding six months. ''Let's not be too hard on poor Mr. Blodget. To give credit where credit's due, the guy also overhauled the drains and modernized the plumbing. He even installed a bathroom in the attic for the servants, which was quite an innovation for his time."

"The bathroom was a nice touch, but isn't it strange how entire generations can suddenly lose their collective taste? It's horrifying to see what happened at the end of the last century. Aristocrats were tearing down magnificent old buildings and spending millions of pounds to build houses we can hardly look at today without flinching."

"Some of what they did was close to vandalism," Michael agreed. "But fortunately for posterity, Mr. Blodget ran out of money before he could totally wreck Ashby Hall, and his descendants were too strapped for cash to do any more damage. They continued to live in the house until the end of World War II, at which point they were done in by inheritance taxes, so the land was sold off to various enterprises and the house was turned into a hotel. And that's what it's been ever since."

"An interesting history. Is the hotel owned by one of the mega-corporations?"

"Until five months ago, it was run by the same family partnership that bought it right after the war. They never made much money, but they didn't seem to care. They were fanatically keen gardeners, so they chugged along, enjoying the gardens and not trying to do much more than keep their heads above water as far as the hotel proper was concerned. Then last year, the three original partners died in quick succession and the rest of the family decided they'd lost the heart to continue running the place. When I heard it had come on the market, I decided to buy it."

"You mean you bought the property on behalf of the Carlisle Forrest Corporation?"

He shook his head. "No, it wasn't a Carlisle Forrest deal. I've gone out on a limb and bought the place personally." He smiled wryly. "And in fifteen years or so, if all goes well, I shouldn't owe the bank a penny more than a million bucks."

Michael had expected her to be interested in his plans for Ashby Hall, but he hadn't anticipated the expression of intense longing that flickered across her face. "I envy you," she said huskily. "If your renovation project is successful, it'll be a wonderful way of giving new life to a house that's steeped in local history. What a terrific project! You must be so excited."

Excited? It was a word he would never have used to describe his own feelings, but Michael realized she was right. He did feel excited, although his enthusiasm was tempered by frustration. His obligations as president of the Carlisle Forrest chain consumed a minimum of fifty hours a week, which didn't leave him much time for moving ahead with his plans for Ashby Hall. He'd reached the point where he needed to block out a month where he could stay in England and get the project off the ground, instead of nibbling at the problems piecemeal during harried three-day trips, punctuated by jet lag. At the moment, however, finding such a month seemed about as likely as finding an honest man among his mother's coterie of lovers.

"I'm excited," he said finally. "But mostly I'm scared as hell." Which was a truth he wouldn't have admitted to another living soul.

"You? Scared?" Julia's expression changed from interest to astonishment. "But you've been so successful with your hotels, and this project seems more of the same. Right up your alley, in fact."

"I'd say it's more like taking a flying leap across the alley with a strong chance that I'll land flat on my backside in a heap of garbage."

She grinned. "You need to borrow a parachute from one of your Dallas cheerleader pals. You wouldn't look good sitting in garbage, Michael. Slapstick's not your style."

She surprised another laugh out of him. Then he sobered. "I can't afford to fail, Julia, and the truth is, this project's a huge gamble."

"You've developed a winning strategy before. You can do it again."

His mouth turned down. "I was a lot younger when I seized control of Carlisle Forrest, and too ignorant to know what enormous risks I was taking. Now, unfortunately, I'm a lot smarter. Smart enough to be worried. In some ways, the hotel industry is an incestuous community. If I screw up with my plans for Ashby Hall, it won't be long before there are rumors all over the place about my failure. And the rumors won't just affect me personally, they'll have an impact on my position as CEO of Carlisle Forrest, too. Nothing succeeds like success, and nothing drags you down quicker than failure. Before you know it, our stockholders will be invading the annual general meeting to ask questions about my competence—"

"What would they find to complain about? Everyone agrees you've done a brilliant job."

Her confidence was touching—and totally unrealistic. "You don't run a major corporation without making enemies, Julia, so everyone doesn't agree that I've done a brilliant job. Besides, you can be sure that stockholders who are looking for trouble will find something legitimate to complain about, because every president of every corporation screws up occasionally. If you make a hundred decisions a week and get ninety-nine of them right, I believe that's better than making fifty correct decisions and letting the other fifty issues slide into oblivion because you're afraid of being wrong. But every incorrect decision leaves you exposed when someone wants to cause trouble. If Ashby Hall goes into bankruptcy, there are enough hostile board members remaining from my father's day that you can bet one of them will want to know why I'm the president and CEO of ten giant Carlisle Forrest hotels when I can't even run a rinky-dink little English inn like Ashby Hall at a profit.''

"So this really is a high-risk venture for you." Julia stared straight ahead. "Now I envy you even more."

"Why?"

"For the same reason I admire Lianne. For having the courage to chase your dream even though you know in advance that you may be a spectacular failure."

"I'm not sure I'd call that courageous. Try stubborn."

Julia smiled. "All right, then. Stubborn and courageous, how's that?"

"Flattering." Until Julia's queries, Michael hadn't realized how much he'd begun to question the wisdom of his decision to buy Ashby Hall. And in responding to her comments, he was reminded of all the reasons why he wanted to tackle the challenge of developing a hotel from scratch, and strictly to his own specifications. "Now, to return to really important subjects, if you're as hungry as I am, you'll be delighted to know that once we turn the next corner, we're on Ashby property."

He heard the faint rasp of her indrawn breath as Ashby Hall came into sight, but she said nothing. She simply looked around her in wide-eyed silence until he'd parked the car in the new, tree-scaped lot he'd had built at the side of the hotel. Without waiting for him, she got out of the car and walked to the canopied front entrance, standing with her back to the hotel so that she could look out over the stretch of private road they'd just driven along.

He joined her, not breaking the silence.

"It's literally breathtaking," she said at last. "Those horse chestnut trees lining the driveway are spectacular. They must be eighty feet tall."

"Or more. They're old, too. So are the oaks around the eastern perimeter. Some of them are approaching their hundredth birthday. The copper beeches are newer. They were mostly planted in the fifties and sixties."

"You said the gardens were famous among rose lovers, but I didn't imagine anything this...grand. I don't think I've ever seen such perfect landscaping anywhere. And the flower beds! The colors in those terraced beds are almost unimaginable."

"Wait until you see the lily pond in the back, and the gazebo across the stream from the weeping willow tree. Not to mention our famous rose garden, of course. The grounds were laid out by Capability Brown for the original owner, and even Mr. Blodget had enough sense not to mess with the fundamental design."

"How in the world are you going to maintain the gardens without bankrupting the hotel?"

"An excellent question."

Julia looked at him in alarm. "You are planning to keep them up, aren't you? It would be almost criminal to let a garden like this get overgrown and neglected. Although, I'm afraid to ask how many full-time gardeners you need to maintain the place to such a high standard."

"Less than you'd think. The landscaped area looks bigger than it is because the hotel is set on a hillock, creating the illusion that acres of gardens slope away and melt into the horizon. So far, we're managing with just two full-time gardeners, with a lot of the heavy-duty work contracted out to specialists. The gardeners don't waste time cutting the grass or lopping tree branches or applying weed-killer. They concentrate on caring for the decorative shrubs and the flower beds."

"Still, those are costs that most hotels don't have to carry. I'm beginning to understand why taking this place on is such a challenge."

"On the plus side, the gardens are a strong selling point as well as an expense. And I hope I've come up with a concept for marketing the hotel that will justify the high costs."

"What's that?"

"We'll talk over lunch." Michael put his hands on her shoulders and turned her toward the hotel entrance. "I'm going to start eating the delphiniums if I don't get some food soon. Let's go inside."

Julia's comments about the decor and layout of the entrance lobby showed Michael that Lianne hadn't been exaggerating when she claimed that Julia knew more about interior design than many professionals. He watched as she bent down and inhaled the scent from a bowl of cream-colored roses set on a console table near the window. She straightened, smiling when she realized he was looking at her, then stood admiring the view of the garden in contented silence. Michael felt a sudden surge of intense pleasure that Julia was with him, allowing him to see Ashby Hall through her eyes. His overall tension decreased a couple of notches. He still had a briefcase stuffed full of urgent company business to deal with, but so what? If he could make a success of Ashby Hall, a few more eighty-hour work weeks wouldn't seem so bad.

He recognized the woman at the reception desk, and remembered that her name was Jean and that she coached the local girls' swimming team. Her last name escaped him. He made a mental note to have all employees wear name badges, a standard practice in the States.

The receptionist greeted him with a crisp, professional smile. Clive Browne had his staff well trained. "Welcome back to Ashby Hall, Mr. Forrest."

"Thanks, it's good to be here," he said. "How have you been keeping, Jean? Won any good races recently?"

Her smile became warmer, less professional. "The county championship," she said proudly. "Last year the team came in fourth, so the girls are thrilled to have moved up so fast."

"Congratulations. You must have worked hard, all of you."

"We did." The receptionist picked up the phone, dialing as she spoke. "I'll page Mr. Browne to let him know you're here. He's been expecting you."

Clive Browne didn't keep them waiting long. A short, stout man with thinning hair and ruddy cheeks, he'd been hired as a stopgap manager a few weeks before the previous owners decided to sell out. Clive was in his early fifties, and Michael had originally kept him on simply because he'd been too busy to hire a replacement. In this case, dumb luck seemed to have worked better than brilliant planning. Clive had no college degree, and he'd never run a big hotel, but Michael was fast reaching the conclusion that the guy was the most astute general manager he'd ever dealt with.

"Michael, good to see you." Clive shook hands, his manner friendly but not effusive. "How was the drive down from London? Heavy traffic, I expect. The sunshine always brings out the weekend drivers."

"We didn't come from London," Michael said. "Julia and I spent the night in Winchester." He knew exactly what impression he'd create by saying that, and yet he said it, anyway. And then was annoyed when Clive directed a swift, speculative glance toward Julia.

Clive was much too savvy to let his curiosity become blatant, even though Michael had never before brought a friend—male or female—to Ashby Hall. Turning his assessing glance into a polite nod, Clive gestured toward the dining room. "I have a table saved for you in the Terrace Room, if you'd like to have lunch before we start work."

"We'd definitely like to eat right away. We're both starving." Michael put his arm around Julia's waist and drew her forward. The proprietary gesture felt good, too good considering he'd just decided that he didn't want Clive speculating about their relationship.

"I should introduce you two," he said abruptly. "Julia, this is Clive Browne, the general manager of Ashby Hall. Clive, this is Julia Dutton." He added no explanatory tag to her name, chiefly because he had no idea how to describe her. As an acquaintance? A friend? The woman he lusted after but didn't dare sleep with?

Clive extended his hand. "Nice to have you with us, Miss Dutton."

She shook hands, wrinkling her nose. "Please call me Julia. Otherwise I'll feel as if I'm back at school with my students."

"You're a teacher?" Clive asked, leading the way to the Terrace Room.

"Yes. I teach French at Kensington Academy in London."

"French was one of the many subjects I failed at school," Clive said. "Funny that, because when I went to work in France for a couple of years, I picked up more than enough of the language to get by. I still remember a lot of it, too."

Julia rolled her eyes. "Don't get me started on the subject of how foreign languages are taught in our schools. I promise you, Clive, that's a two-hour lecture you don't need to hear."

"If someone as attractive as you had been my French teacher, I might have paid a bit more attention." Clive honored her with one of his rare smiles. "Then again, I might not. I was a bit of a lout as a teenager. Now, if you'll follow me through this crowd, I'll show you the table we saved for you. I hope you'll be pleased with the way the decorating turned out, Michael."

"Were you satisfied?" Michael asked.

"More than satisfied. And the restaurant's already stirring up attention in local circles. Mostly word of mouth from customers, which is the best advertising you can get, of course."

When Michael last visited the hotel in June, the Terrace Room had been shrouded in drop cloths. Now the shabby wallpaper left over from the fifties had been replaced by an elegant Regency stripe in burgundy, gold and ivory. The marble cherubs had been removed from the fireplace, revealing the clean lines of the original structure and the superb craftsmanship of the carved wooden panels directly above the mantel. A thick, close-pile burgundy carpet deadened the inevitable noise of the busy dining room, and rose pink table linen added a frivolous touch to a room that might otherwise have seemed too formal.

Michael had found the heavy velour draperies that originally covered the triple French doors especially ugly, but these had been replaced with lighter ones made of chintz, in a pattern of summer wildflowers against an ivory background. Right now, the drapes stood open to take advantage of the sunny view across the lawn, but at night, or in winter, they could be drawn tight to block out the damp and chilly darkness.

The decorative changes were successful beyond his hopes, but as far as Michael was concerned, the best change of all was the crowd of customers who filled the room. At least thirty men and women of varying ages, in couples and larger groups, all seemed to be enjoying their meals. He let out a sigh of profound relief. His first gamble, hiring a talented younger chef full of enthusiasm and innovative ideas, seemed to be paying off.

"This is great, Clive. You told me the restaurant renovations had gone well, but the photos you sent didn't do the room justice."

"I'm glad you approve."

"And the chef's working out? From your point of view, as well as the customers?"

"He has to be the least talkative person I've ever met, but his cooking speaks for itself, and he's excellent at the administrative side of things. Not so good at explaining what he wants done to the line cooks. But, yes, he's working out very well. That was a good hire, Michael."

Clive directed them to a table near the French doors and

handed them menus. "I'll send a waiter to take your orders. Have someone page me when you're ready to start work, Michael. I'll be waiting."

CHAPTER EIGHT

CLIVE PUSHED HIS CHAIR back from the computer. "Good Lord, Michael, look at the time! Julia will be furious that I kept you so long."

"What?" Michael tore his gaze away from the spread sheet on the computer screen and struggled up from the subterranean dungeon in which he'd been wrestling with the problem of expanding the client base for Ashby Hall. He stared bleary-eyed at the clock on the wall of Clive's office. Seven-thirty. Almost dinnertime.

"Seven-thirty!" He shot out of the chair. "My God, why didn't you say something? We've been working for five and a half hours straight."

"I didn't say anything because I didn't notice." Clive pulled a contrite face. "Sorry, Michael. It's no use setting one workaholic to keep track of another. That's worse than expecting the cat to guard the bird sanctuary."

Michael shut off his computer program and closed his laptop, wondering how in hell he was supposed to explain to Julia that he'd started outlining a promotional strategy for Ashby Hall and had totally forgotten the time. Julia was going to be madder than hell, and she had every right to be. It was one thing for him to spend an hour catching up on urgent business while she took a leisurely stroll through the gardens with one of the staff. It was quite another to have ignored her for the best part of six hours.

"We'll get back to this first thing tomorrow morning," he told Clive. "The restaurant is a bright spot in the financial gloom, but the room occupancy rate is still way too low. We need to come up with a marketing concept that boosts reservations on a year-round basis, and that's a tough sell. Ashby Hall has no golf course, no tennis courts, and not enough space for conference rooms, which means we're not going to make up our occupancy shortfall with business meetings.''

Clive rubbed his forehead. ''I'm brain-dead at the moment. We'll come back to it on Monday. Maybe a good night's sleep will bring some inspiration.'' He hesitated for a moment. ''Are you and Julia going to spend the night here? If you are, you can take your pick of rooms. Unfortunately, we have at least fifteen vacancies.''

''No, Julia and I will be going back to town.'' Michael slipped his computer disks into a carrying case. ''I'll be ready to start work at seven tomorrow morning, if that's okay with you.''

''Certainly.'' Clive didn't probe Michael's plans. He picked up his briefcase, which bulged at the seams with papers. ''If you don't need me anymore, Michael, I'll call it a day. I should go home and try to make peace with my wife. I've just remembered we were supposed to be playing bridge with the neighbors.''

''Good luck,'' Michael said. ''Explaining how you forgot that could be quite a job.'' He sorted rapidly through faxes and printouts, deciding what to take with him to deal with tonight after he drove Julia home. ''Tell me something, Clive, how do you keep the hours you do and stay married?''

''I've no idea.'' The manager's smile contained little humor. ''Christine's my fourth wife,'' he explained.

''Oh.''

Clive's smile tightened. ''Yeah, there's not much else to say, is there. The only thing I did right was I never had kids.''

Clive's laconic words just about summed up the situation, Michael reflected, heading toward the lobby in search of Julia. When you worked sixty hours a week and spent most of your remaining waking hours obsessing about the work you'd supposedly left behind, something had to give. And usually what gave was the person's marriage. He'd seen the pattern with his grandparents, who hadn't divorced but had led separate lives while supposedly sharing the same household. To this day, Michael had only to visualize his grandparents' living room in order to feel a tangible chill. He could never remember an occasion when he'd seen his grandparents actually touch each other, except by accident. And the pattern of isolation-without-divorce had been repeated in a much more destructive form in his parents' marriage, where his father had alternated between excessively hard work and equally excessive contrition, while his mother filled her empty hours with affairs, punctuated by hysterical reconciliations with his father.

As a teenager, Michael had found his father's guilty attempts to patch up his marriage and relate to his wife and children almost more unbearable than the lengthy periods of neglect. He'd been even more alienated from his mother, whose clandestine affairs had never been clandestine enough to remain undiscovered, but had still left her far too busy covering her tracks to have time for him and his sister.

For a while, Michael had hoped to break the patterns of the past in his own relationships, but ever since his affair with Cherie Lockwood, he'd decided that the Forrest men weren't cut out for marriage, and he'd come to consider loneliness a small price to pay in order to avoid creating his own sick variation on his parents' destructive marital theme. Like his father and grandfather before him, Michael had a flair for choosing precisely the wrong woman when it came to serious relationships.

He passed the bar and library, poking his head into both. No Julia. It was possible she was in such a snit that she'd

called a cab, gone to the station and caught a train back
to London. He stopped at the reception desk and forced
himself not to snarl. God knows, it wouldn't be the clerk's
fault if Julia had left. "I'm Michael Forrest," he said to
the young man on duty. "I'm looking for a friend of mine,
Julia Dutton. Do you have any idea where she is?"

"Yes, sir." The clerk referred to his notepad. "She left
word at four-fifteen that when you were ready to go back
to London, she would be waiting for you in the Salisbury
suite."

Four-fifteen. Three and a half hours ago. He hoped to
God someone had pointed out the library and that she'd
helped herself to a book. He had no one to blame but
himself if a member of staff had simply dumped her in the
Salisbury suite and left her to twiddle her thumbs. In retrospect, he couldn't understand how he'd become so
wrapped up in his work that he'd made zero effort to see
that she was entertained. Feeling uncomfortably guilty, Michael took the key offered by the clerk and headed for the
guest rooms.

The Salisbury suite had been made over from Mr. and
Mrs. Blodget's bedrooms, and it was the largest in the
hotel. At least Julia hadn't been stuck in one of the small
back rooms on the third floor that hadn't yet been refurbished. Ignoring the elevator, he raced up the curved staircase two steps at a time, inserting the key in the lock at
the same time as he called out to let Julia know he was
coming in. Prepared to grit his teeth and apologize even if
she threw a mega-fit, he walked into the room.

She was sitting in a chair with her back to the window,
a giant pad propped on her knees. About twenty balls of
scrunched-up paper lay scattered around her feet. She had
one pencil in her mouth, another behind her ear and a third
in her hand. Whatever she was doing had her sufficiently
absorbed that she didn't seem to register his presence.

He spoke softly. "I'm sorry to have kept you waiting,

Julia, honey.'' The endearment sneaked out inadvertently, and he clamped his mouth shut, irritated by the slip.

He needn't have worried that she'd misinterpret the sappy way he'd said her name. She spoke around the pencil, her voice vague to the point of abstraction. ''Hello, Michael.''

Another few seconds passed before she truly absorbed the fact that he'd come into the room. ''Michael!'' she repeated, taking the pencil from her mouth and smiling in the way that always made his stomach somersault. ''You're back!''

''Yes,'' he said, his voice sounding tight and strange even to his own ears. ''I'm back. I thought you'd be waiting impatiently for me. It's almost eight o'clock.''

''Heavens, I had no idea it was so late.'' She sprang to her feet, hurriedly gathering the crumpled balls of paper and stuffing them into the wastebasket. ''Sorry, Michael, I didn't mean to keep you waiting. I got carried away—''

Julia was apologizing to him. If her reaction hadn't been so unexpected, Michael might have found it comic. At best, he'd expected to be met with icy politeness, at worst, a full-scale tantrum. It had never occurred to him that she wouldn't even have noticed how long he'd been gone. He supposed there was an ego-crushing lesson somewhere in all this.

''Don't apologize,'' he said. ''I'm the one who should be doing that. I'm glad you kept busy, Julia, but I should never have left you alone for the whole afternoon and half the night. I'm sorry, really sorry. Clive and I started brainstorming, and time just ran away from us.''

''But you explained at lunch that you had a lot of work to get through, and I'd already told you that I was in no rush to get back to town, so I'm not sure what you're apologizing for.'' She found a second wastebasket and tossed in a few more paper balls. ''If I hadn't been willing to wait for you and Clive to finish your work, I'd have asked you at lunchtime to arrange for someone to drive me to the station so that I could catch the train back to London. I stayed because I wanted to.''

She sounded genuinely puzzled, as if she couldn't imagine anyone reacting differently to his hours of unexplained absence. If only she knew how unique her behavior actually was, Michael thought wryly.

"How did you entertain yourself for the whole afternoon?" he asked. "Did Brenda give you a tour of the gardens?"

"Yes, and the house, too. I saw everything, even the kitchens. Ashby Hall is wonderful, Michael. I've fallen in love. Quite desperately, I'm afraid."

He shot her a quizzical glance.

"With the house," she explained.

"Lucky house." There was no reason for him to have said something so suggestive. Why was it that with Julia his tongue always seemed to be racing two beats ahead of his common sense?

"Or lucky me." She gave him a rueful smile. "I've a suspicion that love affairs with houses tend to work out a lot better than love affairs with people."

"I'm sure you're right," he agreed, straight-faced. "Of course, the sexual aspect of the relationship can be a bit challenging."

She flashed a grin. "But enduring once you work out the kinks. Houses respond so well to a bit of loving care and attention."

If ever he'd heard an opening for a witty comeback, that was it. But when he looked at her, every wisecrack he'd ever known vanished from his head. He touched a curl that lay against her cheek, then brushed his thumb along her cheekbone. "You have a black smudge on your face. Hold still." He licked his finger and rubbed gently at the mark. "There, now it's gone."

"Thank you." She turned her head away. "I can never draw anything without getting pencil all over my face."

She'd just provided him with an easy out. He could ask what she'd been drawing when he came into the room and effectively break the tension building between them. Better yet, he could suggest going downstairs for dinner, where they could talk in the well-lit public safety of the Terrace Room. Hanging around with Julia in a room equipped with a large four-poster bed was a seriously dumb idea, leading to other, even more foolish ideas. Like canceling the trip back to town and spending the entire night making love under the stern gaze of Mrs. Blodget's portrait.

That would be seriously dumb, all right. Off the top of his head, he could come up with approximately thirty-seven reasons why he would regret having sex with Julia the minute the deed was done. And that was before he started counting the reasons why it would be a terrible idea from her point of view. All things considered, it was definitely time to get the hell out of Mrs. Blodget's bedroom.

He slid his hand from her hair to cup her chin and tilt her face to his. What he saw in her eyes set his heart pounding. The logic circuits of his brain sent out one final warning, then went into total shutdown. "Are you hungry?" he heard himself ask.

"Yes," she said, and her voice sounded as husky as his.

His thumbs shaped her lips, emphasizing the ambivalence of what they were talking about. "I'm hungry, too. Very hungry."

"We could order something from room service." Her cheeks flushed and her breath came quicker.

Odd, how something as ordinary as the heat of her breath against his fingers could be such a turn-on. "Yeah, I guess we could," he said, and closed his mouth over hers.

This was the third time he'd kissed her in the space of two days, and he should have been ready for the kick. He wasn't. Each time they kissed, he felt a jolt that squeezed his lungs, seared his gut and scrambled any small part of his brain that was still functioning. His mental guard down, Michael acknowledged that he hadn't forgotten about Julia this afternoon; he'd deliberately shut her out of his mind. He'd worked late because he'd wanted to offend her. He'd wanted to flaunt his bad habits in her face, to make her angry, to make her see how unsuited they were.

But his ploy hadn't worked. Inexplicably, she wasn't mad at him. She was yielding and passionate, and she felt so damn good in his arms that it was scary. Michael pushed his tongue against her teeth, finding his way into her mouth, drawing the taste of her deep inside him. She kissed him back, eyes closed, hips thrust hard against his body. Her kisses weren't sweet and demure; they were hot, and dark, and sent visions of fierce, stormy sex ripping through his head.

He couldn't stop thinking about the damned bed. It was right there next to them, a four-poster, piled with down pillows. He twisted his fingers in her hair, closing his eyes, shutting out his view of the bed. His mental image of the two of them lying together, naked and entwined, immediately became twice as vivid.

Michael gave up lying to himself. What was happening between them wasn't going to stop at a few hot kisses. He dragged her head back, kissing her throat, his knee thrust between her legs. Julia shuddered as his body slammed against hers. Her shudder was all pleasure and zero resistance.

Michael groaned. Julia was everything he wanted, and everything he knew he would later regret. Her kisses forced a response from him that was something more than passion, something more intense than desire. They were close, but he wanted to be closer yet, inside her, part of her. Her heart was pounding, her skin dewed with sweat, and he could smell the faint perfume of crushed rose petals on her skin. He imagined her walking through the gardens, the sun hot on her skin, and a rose tucked into her blouse. He breathed in the heady scent, too impatient to wait while she fumbled with the buttons of his shirt. Unable to bear the suspense, he ripped off his shirt, then tore apart her blouse, yanking it from her shoulders and tossing it onto the floor.

Her breasts were perfect, full and firm, filling his hands. He bent low and suckled. Julia made a small, incoherent sound and reached for the zipper of his slacks. Her hand slid inside. Sweat beaded on Michael's forehead. This must be what purgatory was like. The promise of heaven, not quite fulfilled. The threat of hell if she stopped touching him.

The posts of the bed loomed like giant sentinels at the corner of his vision. He imagined breaching their stern guard and sinking onto the bed with Julia in his arms. Sinking into those soft down pillows. Sinking deep inside Julia.

He reminded himself that there were thirty-seven good reasons not to have sex with her, but right now, he'd be damned if he could remember what a single one of those reasons might be. Her nails dug into his shoulders, and her body rocked in rhythm with his.

"I want you," he said.

"I want you, too. Make love to me, Michael," she murmured.

Her husky request snapped the last thread of his control. He reached for her, carrying her to the bed, tumbling onto the mattress, the primitive drumbeat of desire pounding in his ears and pulsing beneath his skin.

Together they scrambled out of their remaining clothes. He'd always assumed that making love to Julia would be sweet and tender. Until this moment, he hadn't understood that it was possible for sweetness and savagery to be wound so tightly together that the strands couldn't be pulled apart. There was a wildness in her that fed his hunger and increased his need, an urgency that swept away softer emotions. And yet, through it all, there was an aching tenderness, a yearning to feel the sort of closeness that he had never felt with another woman.

He trailed his mouth over the skin of her belly, and her shivers of pleasure quivered against his tongue. It was Julia's pleasure that had him gasping for air. Her pleasure that was sending him over the edge. Her face was turned sideways, half buried in the pillow, and he pulled her around so that he could see her expression.

"Look at me," he said harshly, although he had no idea why it was so important that she should. "I want you to look at me."

She opened her eyes. They were hazy with arousal, blurred with need. And full of trust, Michael realized. Damn it, she didn't even have the smarts to know that he would inevitably betray her.

It hurt to look at her, so he brought his head down and kissed her instead. His kisses were savage, ravenous, devouring. She gave him back all that he was demanding, and added a passion entirely her own. He plunged into her. Arching up, she welcomed him into her body, opening herself so that she could take more of him, wrapping herself around him, holding him tightly as her body convulsed, propeling him to his own climax. He collapsed on top of her, gasping, spent and—for a few seconds—ridiculously happy.

Julia stirred lazily, her body relaxed and boneless beneath him. Her face was flushed, her hair tangled, her gaze indolent and sated. Michael found her so beautiful that it made his throat ache.

And that was the thirty-eighth reason why he should never have made love to her.

Michael was still lying next to her, but Julia could feel the emotional distance he was putting between **them** as clearly as if he'd stood up and walked away. It was strange that she could divine Michael's feelings with relative ease when she wasn't at all sure what she herself was feeling. But then, nothing about her relationship with Michael was easy to understand. How long had she secretly been wanting to go to bed with him? For months, probably, given the way her body had reacted the moment he started to make love to her.

Julia sat up in the bed and wrapped her arms around her knees. The silence around them thickened, squeezing the air out of her lungs. She drew in a deep breath and spoke into the silence. "One of us probably needs to say something."

"Yeah." He gave her a brooding look. "We need a volunteer to go first and I pick you."

She was too shaken by the intensity of what had happened to be able to invent a face-saving lie. "I'm not sure what you want to hear, Michael. What should I say? That everything between us felt…right? That making love has never been like that for me before?"

He took her hands and turned them palms up, rubbing his fingers over the pulse in her wrist in a restless circle. "Julia, I'm the wrong man for you. You're warm, and generous, and easy to get along with. I'm egotistical, compulsive, driven, and where relationships are concerned, I'm unreliable and a hundred percent selfish. I should never have made love to you tonight, and I'm sorry."

Anger deadened some of the hurt his words might otherwise have caused. It was painful to hear him apologize for something she'd found so wonderful. "You're right about being egotistical," she snapped. "Why are you acting as though what happened here was entirely your choice? I'm not some inflatable sex doll, you know, programmed only to say yes. We both chose to make love, Michael, not just you."

"Then we both made a mistake," he said quietly.

"For a mistake, it felt pretty damn good."

At least that provoked a reluctant grin. "Mistakes often do."

Julia wanted to protest that what they'd experienced was an intimacy and a passion too special to be labeled a mistake. And yet part of her acknowledged that he was right. There was no future for the two of them, so what they'd started tonight had nowhere positive to go. Which was just another way of saying it had been a mistake. She was a teacher, living in a London suburb and dreaming of a husband and children of her own. How could she possibly fit into Michael Forrest's jet-setting life-style? Their sexual encounter had been spectacular, beyond anything she could have imagined. But sizzling sex was hardly a sensible basis on which to build her life's dreams. Right now, she was still floating in the afterglow of their lovemaking. When that glow faded, she'd be left to confront the fact that hot sex didn't take the place of shared values and a genuine liking for each other.

Now that she knew Michael better, she didn't believe that he'd casually abandoned his son. But she could easily imagine Cherie and Michael deciding that since their relationship was over, Storm would be better off growing up with his step-father, without confusing visits from his birth father. Storm was just one small example of the chasm between how she wanted to lead her life and how Michael had chosen to lead his.

What she'd tried to do tonight was to use sex to bridge the chasm, a doomed move from the start. More than doomed, it had been arrogant. She'd accused Michael of being egotistical, but she was guilty of the same fault. She'd been unforgivably conceited to assume that she could make love to Michael and he would instantly realize that he needed to reconsider the whole way he ran his life.

She should stick to falling in love with houses, Julia thought, then went cold. She hadn't fallen in love with

Michael. God, no. She refused to condemn herself to another year of pining for the unattainable. She swung her feet off the bed, her legs not quite steady. She found her blouse lying on the floor and shoved her arms into the sleeves, pulling the two sides over her breasts, keeping her back toward Michael. When they'd made love, she'd felt no inhibitions. Now it was uncomfortable to be naked in front of him.

"Julia, I'm sorry." He spoke from behind her, close enough for her to feel the touch of his breath on her neck.

She took a jerky step forward, afraid that she might cry, even more afraid that she might lean back and fall into his arms. "For heaven's sake, stop apologizing, Michael. If you recall, I didn't ask you for any promises or any commitments. We had sex. You seem to wish we hadn't. Personally, I enjoyed it. And before you say another word, you might like to know that at the moment I'm not feeling in the least sweet or easy to get along with, so you'd be wise to shut up."

She picked up her trail of discarded clothes and marched into the bathroom. "I'm going to take a shower. While I'm gone, maybe you can decide how I'm going to get back to town tonight. I assume you don't want to drive me."

When she came out of the bathroom, Michael didn't appear to have followed her instructions. He was sitting on the side of the bed, half dressed, the sketches she'd drawn that afternoon spread out over the rumpled surface of the bedspread.

"You can throw those away. I was just amusing myself by playing with some ideas." Julia crossed to the bed and started to bundle the drawings together. Her emotional state was too raw to sit and listen to Michael explaining how impractical and cost-inefficient her designs were.

He gripped her wrist. "No, leave them. They're very interesting. Where did you learn to draw?"

She shrugged. "Different places. I've taken a few adult education courses, quite a lot actually, but it's just a hobby, nothing serious." She sat down on the bed, absently re-examining the window treatments she'd drawn. "That's how I met Lianne. We were both at the London School of Design. Of course, she was enrolled full-time."

"But you were in the same drawing class?"

"From the school's point of view, drawing is drawing. They divide you according to ability, not according to your specific area of study."

"And the instructors considered you and Lianne to have equal ability?" Michael held a sketch in each hand. "What course were you taking?"

"Interior design." Julia frowned, not at all satisfied with her window treatments now that she looked at them again. Something was wrong, although she'd be damned if she could see what.

"How many courses did you take? Were you thinking of making a career change?"

Julia was only listening to Michael with half an ear. "I studied for quite a few years, although just at night and on the weekends. I got my diploma as a certified interior designer about a year and a bit ago, a few months before Gabe and Lianne were married."

She propped the drawing against the headboard and squinted at it to get perspective. The filmy curtains and draped satin side panels that she'd envisioned were a vast improvement over the heavy cretonne monstrosities currently hanging at the windows, but something was lacking. Gold! That was it. No Regency interior was complete without livening touches of gilt paint or gold tassels to break up the potentially lifeless elegance. She reached for the pencil by the phone.

Her reach was blocked by the sudden intrusion of Michael's torso between her and the bedside table. "You'd forgotten I was here, hadn't you?" His voice sounded amused.

She blinked and sat back. "Well, not exactly forgotten. I just realized that I'd made a mistake with the design for the window treatments in this room and I wanted to correct it before you saw—"

She shot him an embarrassed grin when she heard what she was saying. "All right, Michael, you can stop smirking. Yes, I'd forgotten you were here. I admit that when I get started on redecorating a room, I can get a mite obsessive."

"What's wrong with the decor of this room?" he asked, sitting next to her and propping a selection of drawings across her knees and his. "And before you waste time being polite, I'll tell you that I already knew something was wrong with the furnishings in here, so wrong, in fact, that I fired the decorator before she could move on to any other bedrooms. Unfortunately, I don't know exactly what's wrong, and neither does Clive."

"The design concept's fundamentally flawed," she said flatly. "I'm guessing the designer got cold feet and mixed two radically different styles in an effort to make the room look more welcoming. Is this the same person who worked on the Terrace Room?"

"No. The man who worked on the Terrace Room died in a boating accident before he'd given us more than a couple of preliminary sketches for the bedrooms."

"That explains the difference. The designer working on the Terrace Room had the courage of his convictions, and the result is something striking and wonderful. This bedroom is just a mishmash."

"Does mixing styles matter so much?"

"Not always. But the basic elements in this room have been refurbished in classic Regency style. You have rectangular plaster panels on the walls, a vine-and-leaf medallion on the ceiling, and off-white woodwork."

"I asked for that. We've tried to return the house to its original eighteenth-century form."

"Well, you made a wise choice. The simple Regency style is perfect for the proportions of the room."

"So what went wrong?"

"It isn't the furniture. Most of that is modified eighteenth-century reproductions. So far so good. But then the designer's added a floral carpet in a William Morris design, a heavy Victorian counterpane for the bed and draperies that match the carpet."

"Okay, enlighten me. What's wrong with William Morris?"

"Nothing at all. He's the artist who invented the whole concept of arts and crafts in the latter part of the nineteenth century. You know, the idea that you can have something that isn't a piece of great art like Michelangelo's *Pieta*, but is still something much more than a mass-produced plastic margarine tub. The problem is that the carpet and draperies in this room are potentially magnificent, but they don't belong here. They're almost a hundred years out of date for the rest of the room."

"So you think they're wrong because they're from the wrong period?" Michael asked. "I doubt if many of our guests would know that."

"No, I don't care that the date on the carpet's wrong, that's not the point. We're talking hotel decor, not an exhibit in a museum. Besides, you can easily mix antique and contemporary styles if you do it right. What's wrong with this room is that the exuberance and flamboyance of William Morris is clashing with the Regency desire for subdued, classical elegance. The end result is that everything in here ends up looking...diminished. Even Mrs. Blodget's portrait."

Michael glanced up at the oil painting on the wall opposite the bed. "I thought poor old Mrs. Blodget looked so stern because of all the goings-on in her bedroom. Are you telling me it's something more?"

Julia smiled. "Well, the goings-on in her bedroom may be part of the problem. But her portrait should be a focal point for the room. Instead, she looks out of place, don't you think? Like an aquarium in a dentist's office. You know it's meant to be soothing and take your mind off what's ahead. Instead, you keep looking at all those tropical fish and wondering what the dentist is going to do that's so bad he needs to divert you with swordtails and gourami. Mrs. Blodget looks as if she's been stuck on the wall to divert your attention from the curtains."

"A humiliating fate for a mother of ten and pillar of the British Empire." Laughing, Michael turned toward her, but his laughter died abruptly when their eyes met.

No, Julia thought frantically. No, she wouldn't let this happen. She edged backward on the bed. One mistake she could chalk up to experience. The second mistake she wouldn't be able to dismiss so easily.

"Julia…" Michael murmured her name and she stopped moving off the bed. And when he kissed her, she clung to him instead of pushing him away. His hands cupped her breasts and she felt the same helpless arousal as before. Her body burned with heat, consuming her from the inside out, making her writhe and twist at his lightest touch. How could she want him again with this fierce, aching intensity, when they'd only just finished making love?

"Julia." He said her name again, holding her chin so that she was forced to look at him.

"What?" she whispered.

"Spend the night with me."

She closed her eyes, fortifying herself against temptation. "I can't. I have a French class to teach at ten."

"I'll hire a limo to take you straight there."

The problem wasn't really her French class in the morning, and they both knew it. When she hesitated, Michael kissed her again, with passion and the merest hint of tenderness.

It was the tenderness that was Julia's undoing. "Yes," she said, cursing herself for a fool. "I'll stay with you tonight, Michael."

CHAPTER NINE

AFTER FOUR DAYS of glorious weather, heavy clouds had rolled in from the Atlantic. Jeffrey looked out of his window at the slate rooftops awash in rain, remembering another rainy morning, when his spirits had been grayer than the skies. Propping his feet on the sill, he watched the raindrops stream down the window in silver ribbons, washing away the summer dust.

A lot had happened in the fifteen months since that terrible Monday when he'd had to tell the world that Grace had left him, and although he would always regret the way he'd torn apart his marriage, this morning he felt the sort of joy that could only be experienced after living through months of real sorrow. Happy and a little scared, he felt like a young man standing on the brink of an exciting journey into new and unexplored terrain. He and Grace would soon be together again, but—for good or ill—Jeffrey doubted if he would ever again be able to take the comfortable routines of his marriage for granted.

A knock sounded at the door of his office, and he put his feet on the floor, swinging his chair around. "Come in."

Gabe walked into the room, his arms full of computer printouts. "Monica said that you needed to see me urgently."

"Yes, I do." Jeffrey smiled and gestured to a chair. "Sit down for a minute, Gabe. This isn't something we can discuss on the run."

"What's up?" Gabe put the printouts on the floor and settled into the chair. "I hope this is only a minor crisis. I promised Lianne I'd be back in Winchester by midafternoon."

"It's not even a minor crisis. In fact, I was surprised when Monica told me you were in the office. There's no reason why you shouldn't take the rest of the week off, Gabe. This is a time for you to be with Lianne and the baby, not worrying about next year's merchandising budget."

"Yeah, thanks, that's what I plan to do. I only came in today because I need to check on a few major projects before Lianne and the baby come home from the hospital."

"When is that going to be?" Jeffrey asked. "You must be looking forward to having the whole family at home."

Gabe smiled broadly. "Lianne should be able to leave the hospital by tomorrow, certainly by Thursday. I can't wait to see Elizabeth sleeping in her own crib, and I know Lianne's longing to be home."

Jeffrey raised an eyebrow. "That's rather early to leave hospital, isn't it, since Lianne had a cesarean? It's only three days since Elizabeth was born."

"Yes, but she's fine, not losing weight, and Lianne's recovering really well." Gabe grinned. "Besides, I think the doctor will be glad to get rid of her. My wife is a wonderful woman, but she isn't exactly what you'd call a docile patient."

Jeffrey chuckled. "Ah, yes, I've had experience with that sort of wife myself. When you and Megan were born, hospitals scarcely let mothers hold their own babies, much less change them or play with them. Grace lasted four days, and then she insisted on checking herself out, which was unheard of in those days, especially for a woman who'd just had twins."

"Did you and Mom ever wonder if you were doing the

right thing? Lianne's impatient to be home, and yet we're both a bit afraid that we're jumping the gun. We've read dozens of child-care manuals, and I can tell you all the stages of development for the baby's first year, but it's one thing to read about newborns in a book, and it's a completely different thing when it's your very own baby, and her head flops and her arms flail, and she's so scrunched up, you wonder if her legs will snap if you try to straighten them." Gabe's forehead creased in worry. "Elizabeth looks so fragile, I have to remind myself that she won't break if I don't hold her in exactly the correct position."

"Welcome to fatherhood," Jeffrey said dryly. "Of course your mother and I wondered if we were doing the right thing—parents spend a lot of nights lying awake second-guessing themselves. It's only adolescents who know they're right. Parents are generally a bit more humble."

"You mean I'm always going to feel this uncertain?" Gabe sounded appalled.

"It gets marginally easier as time goes on. At least until your angelic child turns into a teenager, and then you're back to square one." Jeffrey got up and gave his son a reassuring clap on the shoulder. "You're going to make mistakes because every parent does, but Elizabeth will thrive, anyway. Don't try so hard to be a perfect father that you forget to have fun."

Gabe grimaced. "I'm not shooting for perfect. Competent would suit me fine."

"You'll be much better than competent, Gabe, I'm sure. You love her, that's the most important thing by far." Jeffrey sat down again at his desk. "Keep in mind that children grow up much too fast, which everybody told us when you and Megan were born, and which we thought was nonsensical at the time, of course. And then one morning your mother and I woke up, looked around the house and realized it was just the two of us. Alone. Not a noisy, annoying teenager in sight. Somehow, while we weren't paying attention, you'd all three grown up and left us."

"Touching sob story, Dad." Gabe grinned. "But it would work better if I didn't know for a fact that you and my mother went out and celebrated your freedom with a luxury vacation in the Bahamas the week after Kate left for college."

"That was a case of drowning our sorrows."

"Sure, Dad."

"It's the inevitable fate of parents to have their sincerity questioned," Jeffrey said with mock solemnity. Although Gabe was right, of course, at least to a certain extent. He and Grace had relished the return of freedom and privacy to their marriage. Seeing three kids through the perils of adolescence was exhausting, physically and emotionally. Still, their vacation in the Bahamas had been only eighty percent celebration of the fact that they now had all their children successfully launched into adulthood. The remaining twenty percent had been consolation for their loss, and nostalgia for the years of parenthood that—in retrospect—had flashed by much too fast.

And now, with Elizabeth's birth, the generational cycle was starting over again, and Jeffrey was finding the experience far more satisfying than he would have anticipated. No wonder everyone said that being a grandparent was one of life's sweeter rewards. He stretched out his legs beneath the desk and smiled at his son, thinking how good life sometimes felt.

"When I pointed out that children grow up too fast, I wasn't asking for sympathy, Gabe, just advising you not to sweat the little things. Enjoy Elizabeth's company on a day-to-day basis, and try not to spend each stage of her babyhood wishing she'd move on to the next. When she's crawling, don't wonder how soon she'll start walking, and when she's playing peekaboo, don't wish it was chess." He shook his head, smiling ruefully. "And I swore I wasn't going to start passing on sage snippets of grand-fatherly wisdom at least until Elizabeth's first birthday.''

Gabe laughed. ''Well, we both know that was a lost cause, Dad. You've been sitting us down on the other side of your desk and dishing out homilies ever since we were old enough to listen. We three kids have actually grown rather fond of them in a perverse kind of way. Now, if I'm going to get out of here today, we need to get back to business. What was it you wanted to see me about?''

''It's about your mother.'' Jeffrey steepled his fingers and tried to look casual. ''Actually, about me and your mother.'' He could feel his smile grow stiff as he considered his son's probable reaction. Gabe had found the separation and divorce more troubling than either Kate or Megan, perhaps because he and his mother had once been especially close. ''We're…um…getting married again, Gabe. Some time quite soon, I hope. We're both…delighted…to be together again.''

''Are you serious?'' Gabe's head snapped up. Then he shook his head, looking bemused. ''Lianne warned me this was going to happen.''

''A woman of perspicacity,'' Jeffrey murmured.

Realizing something more positive than shock and disbelief was called for, Gabe got to his feet and crossed the room to pump his father's hand. ''Congratulations, Dad. I hope you and my mother will be very happy.''

In the old days, before his split from Grace, Jeffrey would have taken Gabe's words at face value and ignored the stiffness with which they were delivered. Not anymore. He leaned back so that his son was forced to meet his eyes. ''You don't sound very enthusiastic, Gabe, given that you've spent the past year complaining about our separation. What's your problem?''

''Nothing, Dad.'' Gabe's body was rigid. ''I'm very happy for you both. I guess.''

''Never try to make your living as an actor, Gabe. You'd

starve." Jeffrey turned around to stare out of the window, fighting the temptation to let the conversation slide into a comfortable pretense that everything was fine. The rain provided a sharp reminder of the dreary Monday morning when he'd been forced to tell Gabe that Grace had left for San Francisco and wasn't coming back. Gabe had been furious and Jeffrey had been mute with pain. He'd always understood that his son's angry bluster that day had been caused by hurt and feelings of abandonment at least as much as by genuine resentment, but he'd been too distraught to offer Gabe any help. This time, Jeffrey knew he owed his son something more.

He turned around to face the man who was his son. Strong, smart, and too handsome for his own good, Gabe would never find it easy to admit to the vulnerability of the child that still lurked within his aggressively masculine outer shell. But Jeffrey knew from personal experience how long it could take for that bewildered inner child to grow up. In his own case, it had taken fifty-odd years and the destruction of his marriage before he finally came to his senses and accepted that his own father, Charles DeWilde, had left him to fight a terrible war, not because he found his son unworthy. Now it was time to help Gabe accept at the deepest level that his mother had run away from the anguish of an intolerable marriage, not from her children.

Hard as it was for Jeffrey to give voice to his feelings, even to his son—or, perhaps, especially to his son—he forced himself to explain. "Fifteen months ago you stormed into this office and told me that Grace couldn't possibly have left me. You said that you knew we loved each other, that we'd been happily married for more than thirty years, and it was crazy for the two of us to split up."

"That was a long time ago," Gabe muttered. "A lot's happened since then."

"Yes, it has, but you were right about us, Gabe. Grace

and I do love each other, we always have, and we always will. It was crazy for us to split up, and, thank God, we've finally worked everything through to the point where we can put our lives together again.''

"Have you?" Gabe asked with barely concealed sarcasm. "And exactly how are you proposing to put everything together again, Dad? The two of you didn't just move into adjoining flats, you know. In case you've forgotten, my mother relocated five thousand miles to the other side of the Atlantic.''

"That's a logistical problem, Gabe, nothing more." Jeffrey hoped like hell that was going to prove true. "Since Grace and I are confident we can make our marriage work again, frankly I'm not sure why you need to worry.''

"I'm not talking about your personal life, although that's going to be hard enough to reconstruct. I'm talking about putting things together professionally, which for sure isn't something you can resolve just between the two of you.''

"Why not?"

"My mother used to work for DeWilde's. She doesn't anymore. She hasn't worked at DeWilde's for more than a year—and if either of you thinks she can come back and pick up where she left off, then you're badly mistaken. People have been promoted to take care of the projects she abandoned. We have a totally new reporting structure. Ask Megan and Ryder how happy they'll be to start filtering their decisions through Grace again. Ask Sloan DeWilde if he's anxious to have Grace second-guessing his activities in New York now that he's finally taking a real interest in the store and showing a profit—''

"And how about you, Gabe?" Jeffrey leaned across his desk. "Let's not leave you out of the discussion, because that's what this is really all about. Do you want to step down from your position as vice president and have Grace supervising your decisions again?''

"No, of course I don't," Gabe said curtly. "I understand that the breakup of your marriage had many complex causes, and just because my mother left you, doesn't mean she's the person who was at fault—"

"*Do* you understand that?" Jeffrey asked. "Or are you simply mouthing the words?"

Gabe drew in a deep breath. "I'm not just mouthing the words. Mother and I had a long phone conversation when she was in Nevada waiting for the divorce to come through. She helped me to realize that the breakup wasn't simply a case of her waking one morning and deciding she was bored and wanted out of the marriage. But your marriage and my mother's relationship with this company are two different things. Whatever problems the two of you were having, in my book that doesn't excuse her attitude toward this store. Damn it, she left this company in the lurch and she doesn't *deserve* to be taken back."

Jeffrey barely hung on to his temper. "It's bloody fortunate for you that I'm in such a cheerful mood, Gabe. That means there's a fifty-fifty chance we'll get through this discussion without me throwing a punch straight at your nose. In the first place, your mother didn't leave DeWilde's in the lurch. My behavior forced her away from this company every bit as much as from our marriage. In the second place, you obviously don't know your mother very well if you think she has the remotest intention of swanning back into DeWilde's and taking up where she left off, totally ignoring the feelings of her colleagues in the process. Even if I were stupid enough to propose such a thing, Grace is intelligent enough to refuse."

"I'm sorry." Gabe strode up and down the room, breathing hard, visibly struggling for control. "Okay, Dad, I'm sorry. My comments were out of line."

"Yes, they were. Grace would be the first person to acknowledge that she can't step back into DeWilde's as if she'd never been away."

Gabe said nothing and his mouth was set in a stubborn line. With a pang of regret, Jeffrey realized that despite his son's protestations, he still hadn't forgiven his mother. On a rational level, Gabe understood that Grace hadn't deserted her children and left DeWilde's in the lurch. On a deeper emotional level, he hadn't been able to reconcile his intellectual knowledge with his gut feeling.

Jeffrey sighed. He'd spent a lot of time over the past year wondering if he should tell his son the truth about what had precipitated Grace's flight to San Francisco. Until today, he'd always decided against revealing the sordid facts—and not just because it showed him in such a bad light. Jeffrey had felt that it somehow dishonored Grace to discuss his adultery with their children. Now he reached the reluctant conclusion that confessing the truth to Gabe was one more price he would have to pay if he wanted to heal the wounds he'd inflicted on his family.

He spoke quickly, before his courage could fail him. "Gabe, for reasons that will be self-evident, this is a conversation I never wanted to have with you, but I can see it's time for me to tell you the truth."

Gabe's head jerked up. "About what?"

"About the reason Grace left me and flew to San Francisco so suddenly." Jeffrey tried to meet his son's gaze and found that he couldn't. What if he redeemed Gabe's relationship with Grace only at the cost of destroying his own relationship with his son? He was making the unpleasant discovery that his sins seemed twice as black and three times as foolish when they had to be explained to one of his children.

He forced himself to speak the ugly truth. "Your mother left me because after several months of appalling behavior on my part, she discovered that I was sleeping with…that I was having an affair with…a woman young enough to be one of your sisters."

Gabe said nothing. The silence grew and deepened, until

Jeffrey finally found the courage to turn around and look at his son. Gabe was white-cheeked. "Do I know the woman?" he asked.

"No."

"I can't believe you did something so...tawdry. After all those years together."

"You can't begin to guess how much I wish it hadn't happened," Jeffrey said, reflecting that words had rarely been so inadequate for expressing what he felt. He had never wished more fervently that he could go back in time and eliminate those disastrous weeks of adultery. Even on the terrible night when Grace had caught him in his own tangle of lies, he hadn't felt much more ashamed of his behavior.

"There's nothing I can say, Gabe, that makes what I did seem less dishonorable. All I can offer you by way of justification is the feeble excuse that marriage is a complicated relationship, and it sure as hell doesn't get any easier as time goes by."

Gabe's voice shook. "I've spent fifteen months condemning the wrong person for the breakup of your marriage."

"Yes, I believe you have." Jeffrey spread his hands in a gesture of appeal. "I didn't keep silent in order to pass the blame onto your mother, Gabe. I kept silent because it seemed to me that this was a confession that would hurt the people who heard it more than it would hurt me to make it."

"Why did you change your mind?" Gabe asked harshly. "I'm not sure this is something I wanted to know."

"Because I couldn't think of any other way to make you understand—really understand—how badly you've misjudged your mother."

"I've misjudged you, too."

Gabe's unspoken accusation was more painful than a

blow. "Perhaps," Jeffrey said. "Or perhaps you're finally accepting the fact that your parents are human, both of us. I don't know if I'll ever be able to climb back onto the pedestal where you had me, Gabe, but that may not be such a bad thing. In the long run, I believe I'd prefer you to see me as I really am, warts and all."

Gabe spoke slowly. "If my mother's able to forgive you for what happened, then I guess it's not my place to pass judgment." He shook his head. "No wonder Mom left so abruptly."

"Yes." Jeffrey wasn't sure whether he felt relief that Gabe's opinion of his mother was clearly changing, or chagrin that he'd now effectively cast himself in the role of bad guy. For the moment, at least, he missed the familiar comforts of his pedestal.

Gabe stood up and paced across the room. "I guess this proves that nobody can tell what's going on inside a marriage except the two people involved." He clenched his fists. "My God, when I remember all the accusations I hurled at Mom! I don't know how she tolerated me."

"She loves you, and she's a very generous woman—as I know from firsthand experience."

Gabe swung around. "You're damn lucky she's taking you back."

"Yes, I am. Incredibly lucky." Jeffrey held his son's gaze. "But I hope I'm not going to lose you, Gabe, in the process of regaining Grace."

Gabe expelled a quick breath. "No, of course you're not going to lose me, Dad. Your halo may have been knocked out of alignment, but you're still the man I admire most in the world. Not least because I know you'd never have told me about your…affair…if you hadn't been so determined to make things right between Mom and me."

Jeffrey felt a hot spurt of relief race through his veins. Gabe looked and sounded almost like his old self. It would take a while for all the tangled strands of the relationship

between him and Gabe and Grace to be worked out, but
at least they were now heading down the right track.
"Thank you for trying to understand," he said. "Your
good opinion is very important to me, Gabe."

"You have it," Gabe said quietly. He ran his hand
through his hair, visibly gathering his thoughts and trying
to lighten the mood. "Well, Dad, if you're through with
the day's quota of startling announcements, could we get
back to the issue that prompted all these revelations?"

"I think I may have forgotten what that was," Jeffrey
said wryly. "Do you mean your mother's future role at
DeWilde's?"

"Yes. If Mom isn't going to rejoin the London store
when you two get married again, what is she going to do
with her free time? Somehow I can't imagine her retiring
to a life spent planning charity balls and heading up volunteer committees."

"The choice isn't just between taking up her old job at
DeWilde's and embarking on a life of leisure. You seem
to have forgotten that your mother has a heavy financial
and emotional investment in a store of her own."

"You mean Grace?"

"Yes. After we're married, she's planning to continue
running Grace, more or less as she's doing now."

Gabe stopped pacing and stared at Jeffrey. "But how
can she run a store that's in San Francisco when your home
is here in England? I assumed she'd sell Grace now that
the two of you are getting married again. "

He'd made the same rash assumption, Jeffrey thought
with a touch of chagrin. Grace had swiftly corrected his
error, with several pithy side comments on the arrogance
of men who, thirty years after the start of the feminist
revolution, still seemed to think that women only played
at their careers while marking time between husbands.
Still, his rashness hadn't been without its rewards. Grace's
demand for an abject apology had led to one of the more

amazingly wonderful half hours they'd spent in a night filled with stupendous memories.

Afraid that he might actually be blushing, Jeffrey walked over to the bar and poured himself a glass of mineral water. "Your mother is proposing that Grace should become the sixth DeWilde store," he said, dropping a few ice cubes into his glass and stirring. "She's suggesting that in exchange for surrendering her personal holding of DeWilde stock, the DeWilde Corporation should take over the start-up debt of her San Francisco store. Fortunately, the store is privately owned by Grace and her backers, so we can make the acquisition without going through a complicated public bid for shares. Financially, it seems a good deal for DeWilde's, so I shall probably recommend that the board accept her proposal."

Gabe rocked back on his heels, hands shoved deep in his pockets. "It's an interesting solution," he said. "What would you call the store? DeWilde's San Francisco?"

"No, we've already decided to keep the name Grace. It's too soon after the opening of the store to risk confusing the customers with a name change. After we complete the acquisition, the only immediate change we'll make is to ensure that the DeWilde signature product line is added to the merchandise the store already carries."

"But how is Mom going to continue personally running Grace after the two of you get married again? You need to be here in London, and she would need to be in San Francisco. In practical terms, I don't see how that's going to work out."

"Let's just say that this is an area of intense prenuptial negotiation," Jeffrey said dryly. He shrugged. "Grace's answer is that we'll spend a lot of time flying between San Francisco and London. My answer is that we'll appoint a general manager to cope with the day-to-day running of the store and Grace can act as a consultant. Fly out to San

Francisco for a week or ten days every couple of months, that sort of thing."

"Have you suggested that compromise to Mom yet?"

This time, Jeffrey was quite sure he was blushing. "Er...yes. Suffice to say, negotiations continue."

Gabe grinned. "Somehow I think I know how this one's going to work out. My guess is that you and Mom are going to be racking up a lot of frequent-flier miles."

"Well, San Francisco has always been one of my favorite American cities."

Gabe actually chuckled. "I have a suspicion that watching you two get together again is going to provide some memorable moments of family entertainment."

"You could be right. Just don't place any bets with Lianne on the details of the outcome. Take it from me, Gabe, she'll win every time."

"Good Lord, Dad, it didn't take me a year of marriage to work that one out." Gabe put his arm around his father's shoulders, and Jeffrey sighed with relief. He didn't think their discussion would have passed muster with some psychologists, but at least it was several steps higher up the evolutionary scale than his earlier attempts to communicate with Gabe about the subject of his marriage. And although there were a lot of regrets to go along with his confession about his affair with Allison Ames, he was confident that he'd done the right thing in telling Gabe. His mother's seemingly inexplicable flight had created a canker of resentment in Gabe's heart that could only be cured by drastic measures.

Gabe gave Jeffrey's hand a final squeeze. "I'd better get out of here or Lianne will have left the hospital in search of me." He paused in the doorway and tipped his hand in salute. "See you next Monday, Dad. Unless you and Mom can make it for dinner over the weekend?"

"I wish we could, but I think we'll be in San Francisco," Jeffrey said. "I need to see the store before I recommend buying it, and we also have to decide what to do about your mother's apartment. She thinks we may want to keep it so that we have a permanent pied-à-terre in the States. I'll call you before we leave, of course, and Monica will fax you a copy of my schedule."

"Speaking of which, where is Mom right now?"

"In Paris, with Megan and Phillip. She'll be back tomorrow night."

"I'll call her at the flat." Gabe drew in a visible breath. "I'd like to tell her how happy I am you two are getting together again."

"Actually, Grace isn't going to be staying with me. She's going to be staying at the Goreham."

"The new hotel in Knightsbridge? Why in the world is she staying there? Why not in your flat?"

Precisely because over the past fifteen months it had become *Jeffrey's* flat, not *their* flat anymore, although Gabe hadn't even noticed how he'd referred to it. "We have a few issues to iron out before Grace moves back in with me." The ice rattled as Jeffrey put down his glass of mineral water. He smiled bleakly. "In case you and Lianne ever decide to get divorced, Gabe, I advise against it. You were right in one thing you said earlier. Putting all the pieces of our marriage together again is proving complicated."

THAT WAS AN understatement of epic proportions, Jeffrey thought later that evening. He took off his jacket and hung it neatly on the valet stand in his dressing-room, then wandered into the bedroom and checked the messages on his answering machine. Grace had called to confirm that she would be catching an afternoon flight home from Paris tomorrow, and that she'd be waiting for him at the Goreham. She would arrange for dinner to be served in her suite at eight-thirty. "I love you," she'd said before hanging up. "I can't wait to see you again, Jeffrey."

He played that message three times before reluctantly moving on. The next message was from the interior designer, who wanted to know if he'd made any decisions about the swatches of curtain material she'd left behind. Jeffrey made a note to call her to apologize and say he was no longer planning to redecorate. The final message was from his mother, announcing that she assumed he was dead and the *Times* had forgotten to print an obituary. She could think of no other reason why she hadn't heard a word from him for the best part of three weeks.

The message was vintage Mary. Jeffrey would have felt considerably more guilty if he hadn't spent much of the past two weeks attempting to discover where his mother was. When last they'd spoken, she'd been in Boston, staying with friends. Where she'd gone next had been anyone's guess. He still wasn't quite sure where she was, since she hadn't done anything as helpful as leaving a phone number. However, since she talked about the *Times*, Jeffrey decided to try the phone number for her London flat.

Mary answered on the third ring. "Hello."

"Hello, Mother. This is Jeffrey. How nice to have you back in England again."

"And how nice to know that you aren't dead," she retorted. "Not that I expect you to telephone me with any degree of regularity, of course, even though I'm your mother—your frail, seventy-nine-year-old mother, I might add—"

"We both know you're eighty-one, and strong as a horse," Jeffrey said. His voice softened. "How have you been, Mother? More to the point, where have you been?"

"I went to Alaska," Mary said. "On a cruise, which was definitely a mistake. I've decided that people who go on cruises are either senile or prepubescent. Both of which are equally tedious when one is neither."

"I hope the scenery made up for the boring company."

"Oh, yes, it was very splendid, but I believe I shall

spend the rest of the summer in London. I woke up one morning on the cruise ship and realized that I was yearning quite horribly for a brisk walk along an English country lane. I took two aspirin and reminded myself that I loathe walking anywhere that I might see cows, but the yearning didn't pass, so here I am. It's a melancholy thought, Jeffrey, but I believe that as I grow older, I'm becoming incurably sentimental. The other day I found myself reminiscing at tedious length about the man who used to deliver milk to the house when I was a child. He brought the milk in big metal cans, with no refrigeration, on the back of a horse-drawn cart, and we used to dip a ladle into the cans to pour the milk into our own milk jugs. As far as I can recall, in the entire time I was growing up, the same man delivered the milk every day. I've no idea if he ever took a holiday. And I've absolutely no idea why I started talking about all this.''

"Because you're glad to be home,'' Jeffrey said. "And I'm delighted to hear you're going to stay for the summer.'' He realized that his mother didn't know yet that Lianne had given birth to Elizabeth Gabrielle and that she was now a great-grandmother. She would be thrilled to hear that the first member of a new generation of DeWildes had been born, even though she would pretend otherwise.

On the point of telling her about the baby's arrival, Jeffrey decided this was something too special to recount over the phone. Besides, if he had dinner with his mother, it would be easy to find the right moment to mention that he and Grace had decided to get married again. Mary was likely to have some trenchant opinions to express about that—Lord knew, she had trenchant opinions about everything—and the advantage of combining the news of his remarriage with news of Elizabeth's birth was that he could always redirect the conversation to the new baby if the going got too rough on the subject of his marriage.

"Mother, if you don't have any special plans for this

evening, I'd like to have dinner with you. You haven't eaten already, have you?"

"What a splendid suggestion! Are you planning to take me out on the town and wine and dine me? You know, I adore that new French place in Knightsbridge—"

"I was thinking of something a little more intimate and low-key," Jeffrey said. "Let me pick up some Chinese food and bring it over to your flat. I have some important news for you, Mother. Good news that I know you'll be happy to hear."

"Which we're going to celebrate by eating unidentifiable objects, coated in batter, out of paper cartons." Mary sighed, and for once her voice sounded thin and a little old. "Sometimes, Jeffrey, I really do miss your father almost unbearably. Now, there was a man who knew how to enjoy life in style."

"I miss him, too," Jeffrey said gently. "But I want us to be able to talk without running into half a dozen acquaintances or having the head waiter hovering at our shoulders all night long. And since neither of us can cook, we'll have to put up with Chinese take-away. The alternatives are fish and chips or Indian curry. Take your pick, Mother."

"Chinese," she said, and he could visualize her delicate shudder as clearly as if they'd been together. She sighed. "You know, Jeffrey, at moments like this, I almost wish I knew how to cook."

"No, you don't," he said cheerfully. "I'll see you in about forty minutes, Mother."

"I LAID THE TABLE in the dining room," Mary said, tilting her head to the side so that Jeffrey could kiss her cheek. "I though we might as well eat from real plates, even if we're not eating real food."

"Good idea." Jeffrey walked into the dining room and set boxes of rice, steamed vegetables and spicy, Szechwan-style seafood on the platters his mother had arranged on the table. He removed the bottle of chilled champagne from its insulated bag and put it on a place mat. Then he took Mary's hands and drew her into his arms for a quick hug.

"You're looking wonderful, Mother. The Alaskan cruise seems to have agreed with you."

"It probably did. One doesn't need to live for seventy-nine years to reach the conclusion that things that are boring and disagreeable are almost invariably good for one."

Jeffrey laughed. "I'm going to cheer you up despite your determination to spend the evening sounding like a curmudgeon." He popped the cork on the champagne and poured each of them a glass. "Here you are, Mother. I propose a toast to the newest member of the DeWilde family. Elizabeth Gabrielle DeWilde, born early Sunday morning, weighing in at six pounds, two ounces, and sporting a fuzz of decidedly red hair."

Mary turned swiftly, her face wreathed in smiles. "Lianne and Gabriel had their baby? Oh, Jeffrey, how exciting! Everything's all right, I'm assuming?"

"Everything's wonderful. Lianne had a cesarean, but she's recuperating well. And, in the way of newborn babies, Elizabeth has everyone convinced that she's totally adorable."

"I can't wait to see her." Mary put down her glass. "Heavens, Jeffrey, I'm a great-grandmother. That sounds such a dignified thing to be. I'm not sure I'm up to the task."

"I have every confidence that you'll rise to the occasion in your own inimitable fashion."

Jeffrey drew out a chair for his mother, and she sat down, her cheeks flushed with pleasure and excitement. "When did you say Lianne and the baby are coming home? I must send them a hamper of goodies from Fortnum and Mason's so that they can indulge themselves for a few days. And then I shall go to Harrods and buy an exquisitely impractical dress. Something in organdy with silk ribbons, don't you think?'' She was so busy making plans to go and see the baby that she helped herself to rice and seafood without a murmur of complaint.

The trouble with his ploy was that it had been too successful, Jeffrey thought half an hour later. Talk about Lianne and Gabe had led almost inevitably to talk about Kate and Megan and their recent marriages, and Mary's desire for more great-grandchildren before she was too old and dotty to appreciate them.

Finally, his mother leaned back in her chair, lighting up her cigarette in its long jeweled holder. She inhaled luxuriously, closing her eyes. ''You've no idea how good that tastes now that I only smoke five a day,'' she said.

''Yes, I'm sure it does,'' Jeffrey said absently.

Mary shot him a glance laden with suspicion. ''Are you quite well, Jeffrey? I can't remember any meal I've eaten with you for the last ten years when you haven't lectured me about how I need to stop smoking.''

''Since ten years of lecturing has produced no results, I've obviously decided to save my advice for more receptive listeners.''

''From anyone else, that explanation might be credible. From you, knowing how stubborn you are, it seems entirely unbelievable.''

Jeffrey pushed his empty plate to the side. ''All right. The truth is, Mother, that I have something else to tell you. It's wonderful news, and I'm very happy—''

''You're making me exceedingly nervous, Jeffrey. Please dispense with any further preamble.''

He drew in a deep breath. ''Grace and I are getting married again,'' he said baldly.

His mother didn't move or speak for a full five seconds. Then her face broke into a huge smile. ''Thank God,'' she said. "Oh, thank God! I was so afraid you wouldn't come to your senses in time to keep her."

"Mother, are you crying?"

"Of course not." Mary dabbed the corners of her eyes with her linen table napkin. "Oh, Jeffrey, you truly couldn't have brought any news that would have made me happier." She frowned. "But where is Grace? Why isn't she with you?"

"She's in Paris. She went to see Megan and Phillip, but she's coming back to London tomorrow."

"Wonderful. And when are you going to get married again? Quite soon, I suppose."

"That hasn't been decided yet." Jeffrey repositioned the half-empty champagne bottle between the steamed vegetables and the leftover seafood. "A lot of things have happened in the past year and a half," he said. "In many ways, my life stood still while I came to terms with the havoc I'd wreaked. But Grace's life moved on. She made new commitments, carved out a different role for herself." Jeffrey looked up. "For one thing, she discovered that she likes living in San Francisco. That much as she's grown to love England over the years, there's a part of her that misses the town where she was born and raised."

"I can certainly understand that," Mary said, stubbing out her cigarette. "Of course, if the divorce hadn't happened, she probably would never have acknowledged her homesickness, even to herself."

"But it did happen," Jeffrey said quietly. "And now we have to accept that although we want to be married again, Grace and I aren't quite the same people who were married to each other before. A lot of the issues we have to resolve appear purely practical, but when we start to scratch a little bit deeper, beneath the surface, we realize that the practical problems all have emotional issues underpinning them. Grace wants to be sure—we both want to be sure—that we don't solve the issue of what to do with her San Francisco apartment without solving the emotional problem it represents. And so on, down the line."

"Of all the astonishing things you've said to me tonight, Jeffrey, I believe that is the most astonishing. It inspires me to hope that you and Grace will eventually be even happier in your second marriage than you were in your first. I never expected to live long enough to hear you acknowledge that emotional issues can defy the logic of a situation."

Jeffrey gave his head a rueful shake. "I'm getting quite good at mouthing the right words, Mother. I'm not so good at feeling as generous and understanding as I sound." He stood up and walked over to the window, looking out into the rain-soaked darkness. "I want Grace back, Mother, and to hell with her need for terms and conditions. I want her to move back into our flat first, and then we can iron out the details of how we're going to rebuild our marriage later."

"And Grace doesn't agree with that timetable?"

"She says she's from the wrong generation to live in sin, even with an ex-husband." Jeffrey leaned his forehead against the cool pane of the window. "I think the truth is, she's afraid that if she moves in with me, I'll sweep away all her objections and force her back into the lives we were leading before the divorce."

"You're a very powerful man, Jeffrey, and not easy to resist. I can see why she might be worried."

Jeffrey's features tensed. "She has no cause to be. I just want her back, that's all. I'm not in the least interested in bargaining to make sure I come out as the partner with more power in the relationship."

"It seems to me that the answer to your problem is quite simple, Jeffrey. By implication, you've told me that Grace is the most important person in the world to you, and that you want whatever will make her happy. Tell her that, and

I have a strong suspicion that she'll be more than willing to start making plans for your wedding."

"Do you think so?" Jeffrey felt a surge of hope. "We're flying to San Francisco this weekend so that I can meet the executives running Grace's store. Perhaps before we leave, I could persuade her to slip out to Kemberly with me." He gave a small smile. "If the rose garden at Kemberly can't melt her heart, then I don't think anything will."

"Have you asked her to marry you?" Mary asked.

Jeffrey frowned. "Well, of course… I just told you that we've agreed to get married again."

"I wasn't talking about that. I was asking if you'd proposed. You know, gone down on one knee, put your hand on your heart, offered her your undying love and devotion, that sort of thing."

Did Grace expect a formal proposal from him? Surely she must realize that extravagant gestures like that weren't his style. Jeffrey shuffled from one foot to the other. "In the circumstances, Mother, don't you think that might be a little…excessive?"

She sent him a pitying glance. "Obviously, Jeffrey, your transformation into a man of sensitivity is not yet total. No, I wouldn't consider a formal proposal excessive. And in the circumstances, I think you'd be wise to make it as sincere and passionate and romantic as you possibly can."

"You haven't thought through what you're suggesting," Jeffrey protested. "Men traditionally hand over shiny new engagement rings when they propose to a woman, but what am I supposed to do? Grace still has the ring I gave her the first time I proposed, and it symbolizes everything that was good about what we shared for thirty-two years. I don't think either of us wants to put that aside and start our second marriage with new rings. So how do I set about making this romantic proposal you're advocating? Ask Grace to lend me her engagement ring for the night, so that I can put it in a box and give it back to her?''

"I will concede that you might have a small problem." Mary tapped her cigarette holder against the ashtray. "Wait here for a moment. I believe I may have the perfect answer to your problem sitting in my bedroom safe."

She returned carrying a worn leather jewelry box. "You've probably never seen this piece of jewelry before, and I don't believe Grace has, either. It might be the perfect gift for you to offer when you ask Grace to marry you again."

Jeffrey opened the lid and saw a gold, heart-shaped brooch, Victorian in style, open in the center, with diamonds at the point and two cherubs perched on either side of the elaborately decorated heart. The design was executed with exquisite craftsmanship, but the piece wasn't especially valuable, and the style struck Jeffrey as rather sentimental, not at all what he would have expected to appeal to Grace.

"Is this a piece of your own jewelry?" he asked, careful not to indicate by his tone of voice that he couldn't imagine why his mother counted on this pin to melt Grace's lingering resistance.

"I inherited it," Mary said. "This used to belong to Anne Marie DeWilde, your great-grandmother. As you know, most of her jewelry was lost or destroyed during the Second World War, so this has a unique value."

Jeffrey looked at the piece with increased interest. "Mother, thank you for the thought, but if I'm remembering family legend correctly, Anne Marie and Maximilien hardly had a happy marriage, so I'm not sure if this is quite the right piece to offer Grace when I'm trying to persuade her to marry me as quickly as possible."

"Like many family legends, the one about Anne Marie and Maximilien being miserably unsuited is only half true. In some ways, they had a very great love for each other."

Jeffrey had forgotten that his mother had actually known Anne Marie, although only briefly, since his great-grandmother had been killed by a bomb in the early years of the war. "Mother, I've just had a wonderful idea. Wouldn't this brooch be the perfect christening gift for Elizabeth Gabrielle? After all, Anne Marie was her great-great-great grandmother, and no doubt Elizabeth would treasure it as she gets older."

"I believe Grace would appreciate it more," Mary said. She looked at her son intently. "I'm gathering from what you're saying that Grace hasn't yet mentioned that while she was in Nevada, waiting for the divorce, she spent some time reading the personal diaries of Anne Marie De-Wilde."

"No, Mother." Jeffrey had a sudden vivid image of how he and Grace had spent most of their time together since their reconciliation—and it was a far cry from talking about the personal diaries of a DeWilde ancestor. He turned a gasp into a discreet cough. "I'm sure you understand that Grace and I have had a great deal to discuss."

"Yes, indeed. No doubt most of it prone and in a state of undress." Mary ignored her son's strangled murmur of protest. "I'll leave Grace to tell you more about what Anne Marie wrote in her diaries. Or if you should happen to find your curiosity piqued, I'd be happy to loan you the translation. Grace returned the diaries and translation to me with some nonsensical message to the effect that I was the family matriarch and the appropriate guardian of DeWilde history. I believe you'll find some of the information about your DeWilde ancestors quite—startling."

"If you say so, Mother. But what has any of this got to do with proposing to Grace and giving her that brooch?"

"Apart from the intriguing light they shed on the family history, the diaries also contain a moving story of Anne Marie's enduring love for Maximilien. I know Grace was profoundly affected by what she saw as parallels between her own situation and Anne Marie's. I'm confident that if you told her this was the brooch Maximilien gave to Anne Marie on their first wedding anniversary, at a time when their love was almost perfect, she would be deeply touched.''

Jeffrey closed the box with a snap and put it into his pocket. "Then, thank you, Mother. I'll trust your judgment on this one and give this to Grace when I ask her to marry me.''

"A wise decision." Mary touched his cheek in a quick, gentle caress that belied the briskness of her manner. "And your idea of giving Elizabeth Gabrielle a piece of family jewelry was an excellent one, which I shall take care of at once. Come and help me choose a christening gift for my new great-granddaughter. My goodness, hasn't this been a splendid evening?" She linked her arm through Jeffrey's. "We wouldn't have had nearly as much fun if we'd gone to a restaurant. I'm so glad I insisted that we should eat dinner at home.''

CHAPTER TEN

SHE DIDN'T WANT TO GET UP, even though her alarm was ringing. Eyes closed, Julia groped for the snooze button. The buzz stopped for a few seconds, then started again. Resisting the urge to pull a pillow over her head, she cracked open an eye. The neon red digits on her clock informed her that it was 5:47 a.m.

She sat up in bed and tried to remember why in the world she needed to get up at such an ungodly hour when it was the last week of the school year and her Wednesday classes didn't start until the afternoon. Absolutely no reason came to mind. In fact, it was frightening to contemplate how empty the days ahead seemed when she contrasted them with the color and excitement of the weekend she'd just spent with Michael Forrest. Closing her eyes, she slid back beneath the covers, unwilling to face reality this early in the morning.

The buzz started again and Julia finally realized the sound was coming from her front doorbell, not from her alarm clock. Stomach churning, she grabbed her dressing gown and hurried to the door. She could imagine few reasons for anyone to pay a surprise visit at the crack of dawn, and the ones that came to mind were all bad. On the verge of drawing back the safety bolts, she remembered to check the peephole.

Michael Forrest stood outside, leaning on her doorbell. Wearing running shorts, a T-shirt and a heavy layer of sweat, he managed to look sexy even through the distorting lens of the peephole.

Julia rested her forehead against the door, trying to summon the willpower to turn around and go back to bed. Ten seconds was all it took to convince her that she was coming up seriously short in the willpower department. Her stomach was churning again, but this time it wasn't with fear.

She opened the door, her heart pounding and her pulse racing. Since she had no intention of sending him away, there didn't seem any point in pretending to be annoyed that he'd woken her, even less in pretending that she wasn't glad to see him. He was breathing hard, as if he'd run almost to the point of exhaustion, so she smiled and held the door wide open. "Hello, Michael. Come in and catch your breath."

He didn't answer, but stared at her for a long, silent moment, seemingly hypnotized by the sight of her smile. His eyes, normally alight with self-mockery, appeared dark and unfathomable. Only minutes earlier, Julia had been groggy with sleep. Now, just looking at Michael, she felt aroused.

He stepped into the flat, kicking the door shut behind him. Still without speaking, he took her into his arms, tipping her head up as his descended, kissing her hungrily, claiming her mouth with a fierce, deep thrust of his tongue.

Julia arched against him, shivering as the cool dampness of his flesh pressed against hers. He was soaking wet, with rain as well as with sweat, but the chill of his touch had the strange effect of making her feverishly hot. She moved restlessly against him, letting out a tiny sigh of relief when he untied her robe and shoved it from her shoulders. His hands explored her body, skimming her breasts, sliding down her belly, making her throb. She clung to him, too uncoordinated to stand without his support. How odd it was that her body felt weak, when inside she felt strong, alive, vibrant—exhilarated by her power to arouse him, to make him want her. She was trembling, but so was Michael. The knowledge excited her.

He finally spoke, his mouth against hers. "Where's your bedroom?"

She pointed behind her, down the hallway, and he took her hand, pulling her along the corridor, kissing her as they went. Julia tumbled backward onto the bed, gasping and greedy, already on the brink of climax. Michael followed her down onto the bed, imprisoning her beneath the weight of his body, driving his tongue deep inside her mouth until she felt drugged and heavy with need. The gasp of her breath changed into a long, low moan, a primal sound that she would have controlled if she could.

Michael stared down at her, tense and unsmiling, his eyes glittering, the skin taut over his cheekbones. Then he bent down again, covering her mouth with his, drinking in the sounds of her desire. Her pleasure built and crested, teetering on the edge of pain, making her captive to his slightest movement, aching for his lightest touch.

She arched her hips off the bed in a silent plea for release, and he plunged into her, sending her soaring, setting her free. And capturing her heart more completely than before.

THE SILENCE HAD STRETCHED out much too long when Michael spoke to the ceiling of her bedroom. "I came to invite you to have breakfast with me. You owe me a breakfast."

Julia spoke to the same section of ceiling. "You have a…novel way of issuing breakfast invitations."

"I didn't want to phone." Michael rolled onto his side, resting his head on his hand so that he could look at her. "I was afraid you might refuse."

"I still might. Especially if you're planning to carry out your threats and make me eat syrup and sausages."

"Don't refuse," he said huskily. "Have breakfast with me, Julia. Let's spend the whole day together."

She pulled away from him and sat up, hugging her knees. "I thought you were supposed to go back to America today. We already said our goodbyes on Monday morning."

"I postponed my return to the States for one day."

"Why?" She finally turned and gave him a long, steady look. "Because of your work?"

"Because of you." Michael sounded almost angry. "I've missed you like hell these past two days."

"I've...missed you, too." Her voice softened. "We had a good time last weekend, didn't we?"

He drew in a harsh breath, linking his hand with hers. "Come back to Chicago with me, Julia. I want to show you my hotels, and hear what you think of the interior design. I want you to see how beautiful Lake Michigan looks from my living room window. I want to go to bed and wake up with you lying beside me. I want to know that I have to quit work at a reasonable hour because you're waiting to have dinner with me." His voice thickened. "Say you'll come, Jules. I really need you to stay with me for—a while."

For a while. In other words, until he got tired of her. Which might be next week, or not for several months if she was lucky. Desire and longing washed over her. Oh, God, she wanted to say yes! And knew that because she was a sensible woman she would have to say no.

Julia untangled her hand from his and gripped the sheet, forcing herself to speak calmly, to behave rationally. "Thanks for the offer, Michael, but I can't accept." She tried to smile. "I'm too demanding to make good mistress material."

He laughed at that. "Julia, honey, you're the least demanding woman I've ever met."

"In the little things, perhaps. But not in the big things."

"What do you define as the big things?"

She looked down at his hand resting possessively on her thigh. "Everything you're not willing to give to a relationship, Michael. I want love, faithfulness, commitment and enough freedom to spread my wings and fly, knowing that the man in my life will be proud of me if I succeed and supportive of me if I fail."

He looked at her broodingly. "I can give you creative freedom," he said. "I can give you more career opportunities than almost any other man, in fact. Our hotels would be the perfect place for you to start your career as an interior designer."

In some ways, he knew her too well, which meant that he understood exactly how to tempt her. Julia shivered with excitement as she contemplated the possibility of walking into a world-class hotel like the Chicago Carlisle Forrest, knowing that she had Michael's permission to redecorate the famous lobby or to refurbish a suite that had housed presidents and kings. She wanted the chance his offer represented so badly that she felt sick with anticipation. Her chest tightened and her stomach cramped. Did it really matter that Michael hadn't offered love or commitment if he was willing to provide her with such a fabulous chance to change the course of her life?

When Julia realized what she was thinking, she understood for the first time how fatally easy it could be for an honest person to succumb to a bribe. Anyone was vulnerable—providing the lure was tantalizing enough. She spoke quickly, before she could yield to his enticement. "It's tempting, Michael, but the answer is still no. People don't start their careers at hotels as prestigious as yours. Not unless they're on an inside track and sleeping their way to the top."

He scowled. "You're a damn good designer."

"Perhaps. But I have no experience that would justify your decision to hire me. If I'm going to sell my body in exchange for a job, at least let's be honest about what we're doing."

A trace of color flared along his cheekbones. "By all means, let's be honest. Does that mean you'll accept now?"

"No." She let out a shaky breath. "It means I'm not willing to turn into a whore, even for you, Michael."

His expression became shuttered. Then he made a quick, dismissive gesture. "All right, let's leave your career aside for the moment. There are other ways I'd make your stay memorable, Julia. Chicago is a fabulous city, much underrated in this country, and you wouldn't regret coming with me, I promise. We'd have...fun...together."

If she didn't go with him, she was throwing away the chance to discover how their relationship might develop. Was she crazy to believe that he might gradually come to understand that they shared something special? That beneath their superficial differences, they had a unique compatability?

Julia pushed away the beguiling temptation. She reminded herself to deal with reality, not fantasy. Michael had spent his entire adult life in a succession of short-term relationships with beautiful, brilliant, successful women. Women like Tate Herald and Cherie Lockwood. She would have to be delusional to imagine she could convince him to change the habits of a lifetime when those women had failed. After a week, or two weeks, or two months, Michael would inevitably become bored with her. He would move on to a new and more exciting mistress, and she'd be left to cope with the emotional devastation of her shattered dreams.

"What happens when you get tired of having me around?" she asked, the effort to keep her voice steady making her question sound caustic. "What's your standard severance package for mistresses, Michael? Do I get a gift certificate for a week at the Carlisle Forrest hotel of my choice and a plane ticket home to England?''

His eyes darkened with frustration, and perhaps with hurt. "You presumably don't expect me to make a serious response to that."

She sighed. "No, probably not. But I still can't come to Chicago with you, Michael."

"This is a no-risk proposition for you, Julia. I'm inviting you as a…friend, that's all. I'm not asking you to commit to anything serious or long-term."

She could tell him that far from being no-risk, from her point of view, his proposition was spring-loaded with hazards, chief among them the fact that he wasn't asking her to commit to anything serious. His feelings might be friendly, but hers were already something dangerously more. She could tell him that she wasn't quite foolish enough to put herself in a situation that guaranteed a major case of broken heart. Or she could tell him a half truth, and keep this conversation slightly less devastating to her ego.

She opted for the half truth. "Michael, I'm a schoolteacher brought up in a traditional family, with a strictly practical outlook on life. I can't throw away a solid career to fly halfway around the world on a whim."

"Why not?" he asked tersely. "You have no real obligations keeping you here. Isn't it time you stopped leading the life your parents want you to lead and let yourself do what you want? Have you ever even dared to sit down and ask yourself what your own goals might be?"

She hesitated. "If I had worthwhile ambitions, I think I'd have done something about them before now. Lianne and I are the same age, and look at what she's achieved—"

"Yes, she's achieved a lot—but with all the help and encouragement her parents could possibly provide! You, on the other hand, have heard nothing but warnings about the importance of keeping a steady job and finding yourself a husband and settling down. Why are you teaching French when you have more talent than ninety percent of the interior designers I've ever worked with? Why did you date a man like Edward Hillyard when you have nothing in common with him? No reason I can think of, except that your family thinks it's what you should be doing."

His assessment was too accurate for comfort. "Whatever influence my parents may have had in the past, I'm an adult now, and responsible for my own decisions."

"Then make your own decision, instead of letting your family decide for you. Come with me to Chicago tomorrow."

"Michael, we're not going to get anywhere with this discussion." She couldn't tell him that the reasons for her refusal had almost nothing to do with her family and almost everything to do with the fact that she was dangerously close to falling in love with him. She started to get off the bed, but he grabbed her wrist, pushing her down against the pillows, leaning over her, kissing the hollows of her throat, his body so close to hers that she could almost feel his simmering frustration.

"Julia, you're smart, fun to be with and stunningly attractive. If you really wanted nothing from life except to be married and a mother, you could have fulfilled that ambition ten times over by now—"

On the point of protesting, Julia was brought up short by the realization that Michael was right. Odd that he should have seen straight through to her restless core, even though it had been buried by years of submission to her parents' conservative views. Whatever it was she did want from life, Julia acknowledged that it was nothing as straightforward as marriage to a kind man, followed by the birth of 2.5 children and the purchase of a cocker spaniel. Edward was simply the last in a long line of worthy, honorable men whom she'd held at arm's length, refusing to allow them the chance to develop a closer relationship. In her own quiet way, she'd been running as hard and fast as she could from the future her family wanted to impose on her. In retrospect, Julia wondered if some of her attraction to Gabe might actually have been the subconscious knowledge that he didn't love her and wasn't going to marry her, so he was safe to get involved with.

When she married—if she married—it wasn't going to be because her husband was a worthy man who would make a reliable father. She wanted to marry a man she loved with all the passion she was capable of, a man who loved her just as passionately in return. She wanted a man who expanded her horizons, challenged her creativity, tantalized her with new possibilities, made love to her with a fire that burned away her inhibitions and sent her spirits flying.

What she wanted was to be married to Michael Forrest.

The recognition of her feelings for Michael brought almost no sense of shock in its wake. On the contrary, she felt as if she were acknowledging truths her subconscious had known for months. Pining over her abortive affair with Gabriel DeWilde had been an effective way to distract her attention from the fact that she was so attracted to Michael that it literally hurt to be in the same room with him. But nothing about her feelings for him fitted into the existing framework of her life, so it was small wonder she'd been terrified to admit to what she felt.

He framed her face with his hands. "What is it?" he said. "You're looking sad."

"Not sad," she lied. "I was only thinking that you were right. I'm not ready to settle into a house in the suburbs with a nice man and wait around to get pregnant."

Relief flared in his eyes. "I'm glad you understand that. So now we have that out of the way, say you'll come to Chicago with me. Take a chance, Julia, and let yourself live a little."

It was suddenly painful to breathe. "Michael, coming to the States with you isn't just taking a chance. It's the emotional equivalent of diving off the Golden Gate Bridge and hoping someone has remembered to tie the bungee cord."

"I promise to make sure the cord is secure," he said, lying down next to her and turning her to face him. "You can count on me, Julia."

"Can I? Like Cherie Lockwood and Storm counted on you, Michael?"

Julia realized that she'd tossed Cherie's name into the conversation more to remind herself that loving Michael was a high-risk proposition than for any other reason. But once she'd spoken, there was no way to call back her words. The sound of the two names vibrated in the space between them, impossible to ignore.

Michael eased himself away from her, barriers almost visibly falling into place. "I've told you before, Julia, that Cherie and I parted by mutual consent. And I keep away from Storm because Brad Stein prefers it that way."

"And did Storm sign onto this agreement?"

"No," he said tightly. "Storm got shafted for the convenience of the adults in his life. Children often do, as you pointed out to me not so long ago. I regret that."

She bit her lip. "I'm sorry, Michael. I have no right to question the custody arrangements you and Cherie have worked out for Storm."

Michael pulled on his shorts and shirt, then knelt to lace up his sneakers, his back turned to her. "My relationship with Cherie was finished three years ago, and it has nothing—absolutely nothing—to do with you and me. I asked you to come with me to Chicago. I'm still waiting for your answer, Julia."

She closed her eyes, unable to look at him when she refused. "My answer is no," she said. Strange that something she knew was right should feel so horribly wrong.

Michael finished tying his shoes. He straightened and started walking toward the front door, his reaction to her rejection masked behind an expression of slightly bored indifference. "Then I guess this really is goodbye."

At least she was no longer foolish enough to assume he felt nothing simply because his face betrayed no particular emotion. She swallowed over the outsize lump in her throat, fumbling to pull on her robe so that she could follow him to the door. "Yes, I guess so."

"Take care of yourself, Jules." He brushed his fist gently across her cheek, the merest flicker of emotion in his eyes. "Look me up if you're ever in Chicago."

"Yes, of course." Easy to promise, since she was unlikely ever to be within a thousand miles of Chicago.

"Quit your job, Jules. Have faith in your own talents. There's no point in being a second-rate teacher when you could be a first-rate designer." He kissed her, swiftly and with unexpected tenderness. "Lock the door after me."

"Yes, I will. Goodbye, Michael—"

But he was already gone.

CHAPTER ELEVEN

SMILING IN WELCOME, Grace opened the door to her hotel suite. "Hello, Michael, come in. I didn't expect you to get here for another twenty minutes or so."

"I took the tube—it was quicker than a taxi. Thanks for agreeing to see me on such short notice." Michael glanced across the room and saw the remains of a meal spread out on a table beside the window. "I'm sorry, Grace, have I arrived so early that I interrupted your lunch?"

"No, I'd already finished. Jeffrey's taking me out to dinner tonight, and somehow he always persuades me to have dessert, so I decided to eat lightly and save some calories."

Grace spoke with studied nonchalance, but even in his current mood, Michael wasn't quite self-absorbed enough to miss hearing the lilt of happiness in his cousin's voice. "Grace?" he said, spinning around to look at her. "Did it work, then? Are you and Jeffrey officially reconciled?"

Her blush deepened, but her eyes sparkled with merriment. "If you mean, did your outrageous ploy of locking Jeffrey into the bedroom with me at Briarwood Cottage have the desired effect...? Well, I would have to say the answer is a resounding yes. We're going to be married again, Michael. Quite soon, I think."

He swept her into his arms and whirled her around, before kissing her on both cheeks and setting her back on her feet. "That's wonderful news, Grace. Fantastic! Jeffrey doesn't deserve you, of course, but the poor guy's really been suffering these past few months. And I think you've endured a couple of fairly bleak patches yourself.''

"Too true," Grace said cheerfully. "I was so furious with Jeffrey that I couldn't stand to be near him, and I was so miserable without him that I could hardly bear my own company." She laughed. "It's amazing how difficult it can be to understand what we want out of life, isn't it?"

He'd never thought so, Michael reflected. He'd always believed his goals and desires were crystal clear, leaving no room for doubt and ambiguity. From the time he was an adolescent, he'd craved success in business, and the wealth and power that went with it. He realized that rage at his father's neglect fueled much of his ambition, but recognizing the lash that drove him did nothing to lessen the relentless, self-imposed pressure to succeed. Equally, he understood it was his parents' unhealthy relationship and his mother's constant adultery that had given him such an aversion to marriage. But understanding the cause of his feelings didn't change them. Love was a destructive emotion that Michael had no desire to experience. His relationship with Cherie Lockwood had merely reinforced every cynical, self-protective impulse he'd adopted as a teenager.

All of which made his current black mood difficult to explain. Julia fitted into none of his plans, so he ought to be delighted that she'd called a halt to their affair before they both ended up in a place where they didn't want to be. He ought to be rejoicing in his narrow escape from an entanglement that would only complicate his future. Instead, the knowledge that he might never see Julia again—that he would never again laugh with her, talk to her, make love with her—lodged in his gut like a throbbing wound. All in all, the way he felt right now was irrational, inexplicable—and downright disconcerting.

Grace led the way to two chairs, set on either side of a fireplace filled with fake logs. "May I get you something from the minibar?'' she asked. ''Or I could order a pot of coffee, if you like.''

''No, thanks, I'm fine.'' Michael sat down next to the fireplace, thinking that Julia would have a field day diagnosing all the problems with the Goreham's design schemes. Picturing Julia, he started to smile, then frowned with annoyance when he realized what he was doing. The reason he'd arranged this meeting with Grace was precisely so that he'd stop obsessing about Julia until his flight left tomorrow morning for Chicago.

He brought his attention back to his cousin. ''I'm really glad you and Jeffrey have worked things out,'' he said with complete sincerity. ''The two of you belong together, you really do.''

''We've both known that all along, I think. But human emotions are strange creatures, Michael, and I've come to the conclusion that the fear of being hurt by someone we love can be the most powerful emotion of all. From an outsider's point of view, my behavior over the past eighteen months must sometimes have seemed crazy, but there was always a horrible, twisted logic to what I was doing.''

Michael grinned. ''Okay, Grace, I'll admit you've got me stumped. If there was any logic to what you and Jeffrey were doing this past year, I'll be damned if I can see what it was. Unless you're about to tell me the pair of you were taken over by aliens and you've just now reclaimed possession of your bodies.''

''Trust me, I had moments when I wondered if that's what had happened. But in my saner moments, I knew I was lashing out at Jeffrey because I couldn't bear to give him the power to hurt me anymore. So every time he made a tentative gesture toward reconciliation, I'd sabotage his efforts.''

''You wanted to hurt him before he could hurt you,'' Michael suggested.

''Exactly. Once I realized he was probably doing the

precise same thing, it was relatively easy to find the way back to each other.''

Michael leaned forward and took her hands. ''Is it going to work this time, Grace? You and Jeffrey have both changed quite a bit. Are you going to be able to put the pieces back together again?'' He made an abrupt gesture, dropping her hands. ''I'm sorry—forget I asked that. It was way out of line.''

''Actually, it's a question I need to answer, at least to myself.'' Grace's gaze turned inward. ''I guess what I've learned from this debacle is that if a relationship is worth saving, you have to confront your fear of rejection and move past it. After the divorce was finalized, I realized life without Jeffrey was so miserable that the risk of laying my heart on the line and being rejected was no worse than the daily grind of carrying on without him. Sounds simple enough when you say it, but it's amazingly difficult to reach the point where you accept that you have nothing to lose except your pride. Jeffrey and I know now that we love each other, and we want to spend the rest of our lives together. We can build whatever partnership we want on that foundation.''

Nothing that she said should have been threatening, yet Michael felt an uncomfortable flash of self-awareness. The truth was that in thirty-six years of living, he'd never confronted his own fear of rejection. In fact, he'd constructed an entire life-style to minimize the chances of getting hurt. He chose to date women who weren't willing to commit to a serious relationship, and then, with cynical hypocrisy, turned around and claimed that love and long-term commitment were myths. Of course love and commitment were myths—for him. If he wasn't prepared to take any emotional risks, how could he ever hope to reap the rewards? For the first time, he found himself wondering if he was really willing to grant his parents such a stranglehold on his emotions that he allowed their failures to dominate his life. Okay, so Cherie Lockwood had screwed him over. That didn't mean every other woman in the world would do the same. And in all honesty, hadn't Cherie become involved with him in the first place precisely because his reputation and attitude suggested he wasn't likely to get hurt?

He got up and paced, too tense to sit. "You and Jeffrey had such a great relationship, Grace. You're both good people—wise people. What I don't understand is where it all went wrong in the first place." He tried to smile and found he couldn't. "My God, Grace, if the two of you couldn't make your marriage last, what hope is there for the rest of us messed-up folks?"

Grace's hands knotted in her lap. "Jeffrey and I made one big mistake," she said after a slight pause. "We tried to patch over a hole in our relationship without first acknowledging that the hole was there. Eventually the hole got bigger, and the patch strained at the seams, until it ripped wide open. Jeffrey and I found ourselves staring at this massive rent in the fabric of our marriage—knowing that neither of us had any idea how to mend it. We would never have found a path back to each other if we hadn't separated for a while and forced ourselves to decide what we truly wanted from our relationship. After thirty-two years of marriage, I'd forgotten how to think about myself as an individual person. When I finally crawled out of my depression and looked around at the shambles of my life, I knew I couldn't start to move forward until I found out who I was when I wasn't being Mrs. Jeffrey DeWilde. And it wasn't until I'd proved to myself that I could make it entirely on my own that I was ready to go back to Jeffrey. So simple once I realized it. So damn difficult to grasp when I was still floundering around in the dark." She smiled ruefully. "Does what I've just said make any sense at all, Michael?"

"Yes, of course it does." Michael astonished himself

by getting up and hugging her. "I love you, Grace," he said. "You know I wish you and Jeffrey every possible happiness. I sincerely hope I'm around to celebrate when they put your picture in the papers as the longest-married couple in England."

"Dear Michael." Grace touched him lightly on the cheek, her eyes misty. She sniffed. "Damn, we're about to find out if that new mascara I bought is really water-proof."

Michael's hug tightened momentarily. "You know, for two people who were supposed to be discussing a business proposition, we're becoming appallingly sentimental."

"You're right, we are." Grace drew back and searched her pockets for a tissue. "All right, Michael. Enough about my marriage, my remarriage and my ruminations on the meaning of life. Let's get back to business. Why was it that you wanted to see me? Something about a promotional scheme of benefit both to you and to my store?"

"Yes, although I may be approaching the wrong person at the wrong time. I assume if you and Jeffrey are getting together again, you won't be running Grace anymore?"

Grace raised an eyebrow. "You know, Michael, I find that there are certain depressing similarities in the func-tioning of the male brain. Or perhaps I should say the nonfunctioning of the male brain. For the past year, I've spent twelve hours a day, seven days a week, struggling to make Grace a success. I can't think of a single good reason why marrying Jeffrey should suddenly mean that I want to close the store, or sell it, or do anything except continue to run it. Preferably at a healthy profit. Did you listen to a single word I said just now about the difficult year I've spent learning to be an independent, self-sufficient person?"

Michael chuckled, genuinely amused for the first time since leaving Julia's apartment that morning. "Ah," he said. "Let me guess. I believe I've just stuck my finger smack bang on top of one of the sore spots you and Jeffrey have been attempting to resolve.''

Grace sighed. "Actually, it was a sore spot, but we've partially resolved the issue. I've agreed that it's only sensible for my store to become part of the DeWilde Corporation, subject to a suitable financial settlement, of course. But we're still debating exactly who is going to manage Grace, and how active a role I can play given that I'm not going to be living full-time in San Francisco anymore."

"Are you sure you want to listen to a promotional pitch at this point?"

Grace shot him a searching glance. "You're sounding unusually hesitant, Michael. Based on my past acquaintance with you where business is concerned, I'd have expected you to pitch a promotional idea at a funeral, if that was the only time you could get your quarry in your sights."

Michael winced. "I hope to God you're joking, Grace. I'm not quite that obsessive."

"Perhaps not quite. Anyway, relax, Michael, and tell me what you're proposing. Your ideas are always worth listening to."

"It's about Ashby Hall," he said. "I know the hotel has enormous potential, but we're struggling to establish a client base for overnight accommodations and losing money hand-over-fist while we wait for people to discover us."

Grace's forehead wrinkled in thought. "The location of the hotel isn't in its favor. You're not going to attract many people by chance. I'm assuming you've advertised in the obvious places and made some renovations so that the interior isn't quite so dreary?"

"Yes, that's all been taken care of. We've totally redesigned and reequipped the kitchens and offices, and we found a designer who did a magnificent job of refurbishing the main public rooms on the ground floor. Unfortunately, he died before he could complete the redecoration of the guest bedrooms, but I'm working on finding a replacement designer, so the bedrooms should soon be as appealing as the public rooms and the gardens.''

"It's an exciting project,'' Grace said. She smiled. ''I'm guessing you're having as much fun trying to make Ashby Hall a success as I've had with my store in San Francisco. There's something incredibly exciting about developing a business where your personal reputation is pinned right on the line. And the more success you've had in the past, the more closely you know everyone is watching and waiting for you to fail—and therefore the greater the challenge.''

"You're so right about that, but the truth is, I find the challenge energizing. Licking Ashby Hall into shape has been more fun than anything else I've worked on in a couple of years.''

"That surprises me, given how hard you've worked to restore the profitability of the Carlisle Forrest chain.''

"Don't get me wrong, I've enjoyed that, too. But the Chicago hotel was built in 1892, and the chain has been world-famous for at least three-quarters of a century, so I wasn't exactly starting from scratch. Then there were shareholders to answer to, as well as a very demanding board of directors and a dozen senior management members. That's not quite the same as working to build the reputation of a new hotel from the ground up, especially when the money that's at stake is your own.'' He grinned ruefully. "And the bank's, of course.''

"You can't tell me anything about the agony and the ecstasy of getting a financing package together,'' Grace said wryly. "So you're hoping I can help with a cross-promotional idea you have for Ashby Hall and Grace?''

Michael nodded. "Ashby Hall is ideally suited for wedding receptions, so I'd been thinking along the lines of advertising a wedding package in some of the trade journals—a reception in the Terrace Room or on the south lawn, accommodation for out-of-town guests who don't want to drive home after drinking too much champagne, and a suite for the bridal couple before they fly off on their honeymoon."

"It's a very workable concept."

He pulled a face. "Workable, but neither exciting nor in the least original. However, Julia came up with quite an intriguing proposal—"

Grace looked up. "Julia Dutton? Have you taken her to Ashby Hall?"

"Yes. We went there on Sunday, after our visit to the hospital." Michael had a dreadful suspicion that he might be blushing. Grace knew that he never took his dates to any of his hotels, let alone Ashby Hall, and she must be wondering why Julia was the exception. Michael kind of wondered that himself. He cleared his throat. "Anyway, Julia and I were tossing a few ideas around over lunch and she suggested expanding my wedding package concept to include anniversary celebrations. She pointed out that although newlyweds tend to want a beach and guaranteed sunshine for their honeymoon, a couple celebrating their wedding anniversary might be delighted to settle for a luxurious weekend at a hotel that promises excellent service, wonderful food and magnificent gardens."

"An anniversary package," Grace said, getting up and taking a notebook and pencil from the desk. "Interesting. It certainly seems an idea worth exploring. The great thing about the English climate is that a well-planned garden like Ashby Hall can support flowers and blooming shrubs nine months of the year, so you'd have something to serve as a focus—"

"And in December when there are no flowers, we can offer a nostalgia package that ties in with the Christmas holiday theme and plays up the idea of Ashby Hall as the local manor house," Michael concluded. "But here's where Grace comes in. I'm eager to publicize Ashby Hall in the States, and it occurred to me that this wedding anniversary concept could easily be linked to a promotion in your store. From the beginning, you've made sure that Grace carries products that meet the needs of nontraditional couples, so you already stock clothing and jewelry that's geared to older men and women. How about developing an advertising campaign that would target couples celebrating an anniversary as opposed to a wedding? You could announce that you've gathered together a collection of diamond eternity rings and other jewelry that's particularly suitable for anniversary gifts, and invite all your customers to participate in a draw for the Grand Anniversary Prize. Which would be two round-trip first-class plane tickets from San Francisco to London, and four nights, all expenses paid, at Ashby Hall.''

Grace stopped writing. "But no matter how massive an advertising blitz we ran, most of the customers coming into our store wouldn't be married couples celebrating an anniversary. They'd be engaged couples, or people shopping for wedding gifts for friends—''

"That's no problem, because we can make the prize transferable to family members. The only condition would be that the couple who actually comes to Ashby Hall would have to be celebrating their wedding anniversary.''

"It could work," Grace said cautiously.

"It will work. Handled right, this is something that could generate a lot of local media coverage—a bridal store that remembers there are years of marriage to come after the wedding day. For argument's sake, let's say that a young couple shopping for an engagement ring wins the prize. No problem. They can give it to her parents as an anniversary gift. Or his parents. Think of the positive publicity that could generate for Grace—not to mention my hotel.''

"I'm thinking," she said dryly. "I'm also imagining the family squabbles as our young couple tries to decide whether her parents or his get to go on vacation. I'm visualizing broken engagements and hurt feelings all around.''

''Don't be a cynic, Grace, that's my role. Think positively and visualize lots of human-interest media stories. You could have posters throughout the store displaying the full glory of the Ashby Hall gardens at different times of the year, which would benefit the hotel a great deal, but would also be a fabulous focal point for in-store displays if you chose to devote a month to the idea that couples can come to your store not just to plan a great wedding but also to arrange a wonderful anniversary celebration.''

Grace was scribbling furiously. ''You're setting off a whole chain of possibilities in my mind, Michael. We'd have to be very careful not to lose our focus and reputation as San Francisco's major upscale bridal store. On the other hand, I've been thinking for a while that we're missing out on a significant potential market. For all the marriages that end in divorce, there are far more that last a lifetime, and if we can come up with goods and services that are appealing to a couple celebrating a special anniversary, I believe we'd be tapping into an important new market.''

''Of course, my hotel would cover the full cost of the grand prize,'' Michael said. ''If you want to throw in a few consolation prizes of gold lapel pins or something, those costs would be up to you. We could split the promo budget.''

''What sort of timetable are you looking at?'' Grace asked. ''I can tell you that our plans are locked in tight for the next six months.''

''The sooner the better, obviously, but I'm flexible on timing. And we shouldn't get bogged down with the details, Grace. If you agree in principle, we both have competent people to work on the specifics. All I want is exposure for my hotel.''

Grace scribbled a few more notes, then closed the folder with a snap. ''You're right, Michael. I can see the scope here for a good deal of valuable cross-promotion. Send me a formal proposal, and if it lives up to my expectations, I'll hand it over to my marketing people with a strong recommendation to go ahead. You came up with such innovative ideas for the start-up of my store, I'm glad to know we might be able to return the favor."

"Great." Michael rose to his feet, conquering a ridiculous urge to take a cab straight to Julia's flat and share the news of how he'd implemented her suggestion. He reminded himself that she hadn't been willing to accompany him to Chicago, and that since there was nowhere for their relationship to go, he needed to forget her.

He took Grace's hand and kissed the tips of her fingers, not with any of his usual subtle mockery, but with respect and affection. "Goodbye, Grace. When you see Jeffrey tonight, don't forget to tell him that I think he's an exceptionally lucky man."

Grace chuckled. "I'll certainly tell him, since I feel on principle that it's wise to keep husbands properly humble, but at the moment, I confess I feel rather lucky myself. I'm in the sort of benevolent mood where I want to recommend love and marriage to everyone. Even you, Michael."

He flashed a practiced smile. "Grace, my sweet, I'm a hopeless case. I'll just have to resign myself to being a bachelor."

Instead of smiling, Grace scrutinized him with uncomfortable intensity. "You know, Michael, I've often remarked to myself that in many ways you remind me of Ian Stanley. You've met my friend Ian, haven't you?"

"Yes, several times." Michael wondered where this conversation was leading. "Ian's very entertaining company," he added.

"He is indeed. He's charming, good-looking, intelligent, hard-working and successful. He's the sort of man who gets invited to the most interesting parties, and no matter who else is there, he always seems to be escorting the most attractive woman in the room."

"Lucky man," Michael said.

"I wouldn't say so." Grace's gaze remained fixed on Michael's face. "Despite his amazing popularity, I've always suspected that Ian is one of the loneliest men I know."

"Are you trying to tell me something, Grace?"

"Yes, I am, and I'm not going to waste time being subtle. You're every bit as attractive, intelligent and hardworking as Ian Stanley. I hope that you're not going to wake up one day and realize that you're also every bit as lonely."

Michael forced himself to smile. "Not everyone is as lucky as you and Jeffrey. If I remember correctly, your friend Ian has been married three times. Seems to me he might have felt less lonely if he'd stayed single."

"Perhaps. But I had the impression when I saw you with Julia Dutton this weekend that the two of you felt something rather special for each other."

"Special?" Michael managed a shrug. "I find Julia attractive," he said curtly. "What man wouldn't? In a week or two, I'm sure I'll find some other woman equally attractive. You may think I'm like Ian Stanley, but I've always thought I take after my father. I find it a lot easier to commit to my work than to a woman."

"Don't make the mistake of comparing yourself to your father," Grace said. "I can't think of a father and son who had less in common than you two. And for God's sake, don't judge all marriages on the basis of what happened between your parents. They were one of the most tragically unsuited couples I've ever known."

Michael had no intention of prolonging a difficult conversation by pointing out the long and dreary roster of couples he knew whose marriages were every bit as gruesome as his parents'. "Send me an invitation to your wedding, Grace, and I promise to come and dance the night away. I think that's as close to marriage as I'm going to get this year."

Grace gave him a hug goodbye. "You never know what life holds around the corner," she said, then smiled sheepishly. "And you don't have to say it, Michael. I know that's one of those trite clichés people produce when they have nothing sensible to say."

He paused at the entrance to her room. "Stop over in Chicago on your way home from San Francisco," he said. "I'd like to take you and Jeffrey to my favorite restaurant for a celebratory dinner. Le Perroquet, do you know it?"

"It's one of my favorites, too," she said. "Thank you, Michael. If we can squeeze an extra night away from London, we'll definitely do that. Take care, and have a safe trip home."

There was no danger in flying across the Atlantic, Michael thought as he hailed a cab and gave the name of his hotel. The only danger he faced at this moment was the risk that he might extend his stay in London and see Julia again. The longing to do just that was fierce enough to keep him locked in his hotel room, drowning in papers, faxes, memos and phone calls until it was time to leave for the airport. Thank God for work. It was such a good way to avoid confronting disturbing feelings.

CHAPTER TWELVE

UNTIL GRACE LEFT HIM, Jeffrey had never appreciated how much of his enjoyment of life came from the pleasure of doing small, everyday things in the company of his wife. Driving to Kemberly after work on Friday evening, he was seized by a burst of happiness simply because she was there, in the seat next to him. They weren't discussing anything important in the grand scheme of things, just chatting about inconsequential snippets of news culled from Kate's latest phone call, Megan's plans for a trip to Hong Kong with Phillip, and Elizabeth Gabrielle's three-ounce weight gain in her first three days home from the hospital. In one way, Grace's presence at his side felt so absolutely right that it was as if she'd never been gone. In another way, it felt like several lifetimes since he'd been this content.

Overcome by a rush of emotion, he slowed the car and parked it on the side of the road, drawing Grace into his arms the moment he'd put on the brakes. He kissed her long and hard, only releasing her when another car drove past, honking loudly to indicate the driver's displeasure at finding half the narrow road blocked by a parked car.

"What was that all about?" Grace asked rather breathlessly, returning to her side of the car and adjusting her seat belt. "Not that I'm complaining, mind you."

"Making up for lost time, I think." Jeffrey squeezed her hand before resuming the drive. "Or maybe sheer unadulterated relief that you're here with me. The flat in London has felt empty without you, but visiting Kemberly has been like forcing myself to spend weekends in a barn built on a stretch of Arctic tundra. Your absence from Kemberly has been almost unendurable. I'm so glad we put off our trip to San Francisco so we could come here together.''

"You know, Jeffrey, you've become so eloquent at expressing your feelings since I left that I may have to fly away on an annual basis, just to inject some poetry back into your soul.''

His hands clenched the steering wheel. "Don't joke about leaving me, Gracie. That's one subject where I have absolutely no sense of humor.''

"I can only joke about it because I know it won't happen.'' She turned to look out of the window as they turned off the road and onto the lane that led to the house. "I thought I'd remembered how green the fields around Kemberly are, but I hadn't. Oh, Jeffrey, it feels so good to be coming home.''

"Nowhere near as good as it feels to have you here,'' he said. He managed to get the Rolls as far as the front courtyard before taking her into his arms again. "Welcome home, my love.''

He had no idea how many times the housekeeper coughed and cleared her throat before he finally noticed she was there. What was even more astonishing, Jeffrey decided he didn't care. "Good evening, Mrs. Milton,'' he said, getting out of the car and making no effort to smooth his ruffled hair. "And how are you on this fine summer night?''

"Very good, thank you, and all the better for seeing you here again, Mrs. DeWilde. We've missed you at Kemberly, and that's a fact.''

Grace gave the housekeeper a hug. "I've missed you, too, Mrs. M. Not to mention how much I've missed those wonderful dinners you always cooked for me. Nobody makes pastry like you.''

Mrs. Milton beamed. "Then you'll enjoy the rhubarb tart I made for dinner tonight. I made a salmon mousse, too, because I know that's one of your favorites."

"Thank you," Grace said. "It all sounds delicious, but you shouldn't have gone to so much trouble for the two of us. You're spoiling me."

"And happy to do it, Mrs. DeWilde. The meal's all ready, so I can serve it right away if you're hungry."

"Sorry, Mrs. M. I'm afraid I need to ask you to hold dinner for an hour. Grace and I have some important business to attend to first." Jeffrey held out his hand. "Coming, Gracie?" He ignored Mrs. Milton's scandalized expression and headed straight for the stairs—and the master bedroom.

Half an hour later, lying in his arms, Grace lay back against the pillows and chuckled. Jeffrey rested his hand possessively on her thigh. "A lesser man might find that giggle intimidating, my dear. What's so funny?"

"Mrs. Milton. You. I'm not sure which of you was more shocked when you instructed her to hold dinner and marched me upstairs."

"Definitely me," he said wryly. "She's intimidated me for years. It was quite astonishing to realize that if I wanted to make love to you, the housekeeper had no right to tell me that I couldn't."

Grace laughed again, then stretched lazily and got off the bed. "If we don't want to offend her for life, however, we'd better get dressed and go downstairs to eat. We'll have to lavish praise on her salmon mousse as compensation for keeping her waiting."

"That won't be a problem. At the moment, I'm feeling benevolent enough to lavish praise on boiled shoe leather."

As it turned out, Jeffrey had no need to be generous. Mrs. Milton's dinner was delicious, and had survived the delay without any noticeable damage. After they'd eaten, it was Grace who suggested they should skip their usual cups of coffee and take a stroll through the garden to see how her roses were doing.

They wandered through the grounds, taking a meandering route to the rose garden, holding hands but not talking very much. Jeffrey's thoughts drifted back to the first time he'd proposed to Grace. It had been in midafternoon, after church on a hot Sunday, when the air was filled with the scent of fallen rose petals and the bees buzzed drowsily among the blossoms. He'd been young, superficially sure of himself, and heady with the certainty of his love. Carried away on a flood of emotion—not to mention youthful hormones—he'd proposed in grand style. Grace had been seated on a white wooden bench in the arbor, and he had gone down on one knee to slip the heirloom DeWilde sapphire ring onto her finger.

During the dark days of his separation from Grace, he'd examined his memories of that scene with a mixture of contempt and self-pity. The rift between him and Grace—which had precipitated his affair and ultimately led to their divorce—had started when Grace had confessed to him that she had accepted his proposal that day without being truly in love with him.

Now he saw the scene in the rose garden from yet another perspective, not as a moment of deception on Grace's part and foolish romanticism on his, but rather as the start of a marriage that had united him with the woman he loved, brought him the gift of three wonderful children, and filled thirty-two years of his life with more happy moments than he would ever be able to count. The fact that Grace had not yet fallen in love with him when she agreed to marry him seemed supremely irrelevant in light of all that had since followed.

With her hand tucked into his arm, he led her across the flagstoned walkways of the rose garden to the same bench where he'd first proposed to her. In the moonlight, Grace looked impossibly young for a woman who'd just become a grandmother. Impossibly young, and impossibly beautiful. Jeffrey's heart swelled with quiet joy at the knowledge that she was his and they were together again, not just for a special occasion, but for every day. They sat without speaking for a few minutes, letting the nighttime scents and sounds of the garden fill their senses. A bird called out a brief song, and a breeze jousted with the leaves of a nearby beech tree.

"Do you think that's a nightingale?" Grace asked, leaning her head against Jeffrey's shoulder.

"I haven't the faintest idea." He smiled at her in the darkness. "You've only been gone a little over a year, Gracie. I haven't turned into a completely new man, you know. I still can't tell a starling from a cuckoo."

She closed her eyes, reaching up to stroke his face. "I'm glad. I'm kind of fond of the old tin-eared Jeffrey."

Since his conversation with his mother, he'd planned the moment when he would formally ask Grace to marry him a hundred times, but none of his plans had involved proposing to her when she was half asleep, drowsy from too much of Mrs. Milton's rhubarb tart. Somehow, though, it seemed easy and natural to disentangle himself from her arms and kneel in front of her, clasping her hands between his.

She looked down at him, and what she read in his eyes seemed to make the breath catch in her throat. "Jeffrey?" she whispered

"I love you, Grace," he said hoarsely. "A thousand times more today than I did when I first asked you to marry me. I want to share the rest of my life with you, waking and sleeping, the good times and the bad. You're my heart and soul, Gracie, everything that gives color and warmth to my life, but I realize now there's nothing I can offer you that you can't earn for yourself—except my love, and that's already yours. So I'm not sure why you'd say yes, but will you please do me the honor of becoming my wife?"

"Of course I will," she said. She leaned forward and kissed him, her eyes misty with tears. "I love you, Jeffrey DeWilde, and I can't imagine anything I want more than to be married to you again."

He reached into the pocket of his jacket and pulled out the worn leather box that contained the brooch his great-grandfather Maximilien had given to his wife, Anne Marie, on their first wedding anniversary. After the conversation with his mother, Jeffrey had grown curious about his great-grandmother's diaries, and he'd asked Mary to let him read the translation she'd commissioned. Shocking as he'd found the revelations in the diaries, he understood why Grace felt such an affinity for Anne Marie and why Mary believed that the brooch would be the perfect engagement gift.

"This is for you," he said, handing her the box. "It used to belong to Anne Marie DeWilde, and it's one of the few pieces of her personal jewelry that survived the Second World War. Maximilien gave it to her on their first wedding anniversary, way back in 1871. He wasn't very rich in those days, and he must have saved for months to be able to afford it. He gave it to her with love, Grace, and I pass it on to you with all that love, and my own, too."

Grace pressed the latch and the lid sprang open. She stared at the heart-shaped pin. A tear trickled from the corner of her eye and splashed onto the back of her hand, but she didn't seem to notice. "He loved her so much when they were first married," she said huskily.

"I know. I've read her diaries."

Startled, Grace turned to look at him. "You've read all of them?"

"Yes, just during the past few days. I know now that the DeWildes aren't really DeWildes at all, which I dare say would have been quite a scandalous piece of information if it had come to light seventy years ago. Today, it seems interesting but unimportant. We are who we are. From my personal point of view, I was more impressed by what a fool Maximilien DeWilde actually was beneath all that self-righteous bluster of his, and how he threw away his own chance for happiness."

"Anne Marie committed adultery," Grace pointed out. "Not once, but twice. In her day, everyone would have agreed she was the guilty party."

"She was wrong in what she did, whatever the justification, just as I was terribly wrong to betray our vows." Jeffrey was grateful when he felt Grace's hand tighten reassuringly around his. Thank God his sins had been judged by a loving, forgiving woman like Grace, and not a proud, intractable man like Maximilien.

"Anne Marie's diaries had a tremendous impact on me, Grace. Reading her outpourings, I realized that being proud and self-righteous is no compensation at all for being warm-hearted and forgiving. Anne Marie loved Maximilien, despite all his faults, and she waited an entire lifetime for him to see that by refusing to forgive her, he condemned both of them—and their children—to years and years of needless suffering."

He took the brooch and pressed it into Grace's hand, closing her fingers around the cherubs. "Take the brooch, Gracie, and when I get into one of my high-falutin' moods, remind me that I don't want to spend the rest of my life being a pompous ass like Maximilien DeWilde."

She pinned the brooch to her lapel, then cradled her hand against his cheek. "Trust me, Jeffrey, you may have moments when you're a touch pompous, but you're nothing like Maximilien. You're far more honorable and much too loving—more like your real ancestor, in fact."

"Thank you," Jeffrey said, and got up, brushing the dust from his trousers. He pulled a face. "I have to tell you, Gracie, my arthritic knee is killing me. If you ever want me to propose on bended knee again, we'll have to bring a cushion."

She laughed, tucking her arm through his. "Let's stroll for five minutes and then go back to the house. I've enjoyed my apartment in San Francisco, but I have to admit that I spent a lot of evenings this past year longing for the Kemberly gardens."

"Gracie, my dearest, try to remember that flattery will get you everywhere. You should have said that you've spent a lot of nights longing to walk with me in the Kemberly gardens."

Her eyes gleamed in the moonlight. "But of course! Isn't that what I said? It's definitely what I meant." She stopped to pick a spray of night-blooming jasmine and tucked it into his lapel. "We have to talk about when and how we're going to get married again, Jeffrey. Do you have any ideas at all about how you want to do this?"

"By special license, the day after tomorrow," he said promptly.

"In a way, that's what I'd like, too. But we have to think of the family, especially the children. Our separation was a devastating experience for them, and we might need to have a family celebration so that they can be convinced that we've truly managed to put our marriage together again."

Jeffrey sighed. "I see what you're saying, Grace, but it's a daunting prospect. I'm beginning to understand why Gabe and Lianne decided to elope. Between the two of us, we have an enormous family. Where do we draw the line? Do we invite just our three children and their spouses and Mother? But what about Ryder? In some ways, he's almost as close as a son. And if we invite Ryder and Natasha, how can we ignore Dev and Maxine? Lord knows, now that we've finally found Dirk's descendants, it seems a shame not to include them in major family get-togethers.

Then there's your brother, Leland, not to mention Mallory, who's your godchild as well as your niece, and her husband. And she might have had her baby by then—''

"Stop!" Grace laughed. "All right. I get the picture. Either we elope or we have an 'intimate' family wedding with a guest list that starts at two hundred and works its way up.''

Looking at her, Jeffrey knew there was no way in hell he was willing to wait while they put together a family wedding with a guest list two hundred strong. Even for the DeWildes, that meant a minimum of six weeks to allow time for guests to make travel arrangements, if for no other reason. Determined not to wait longer than a few days, he racked his brains for a compromise.

"I've got it!" he said, turning to her with a triumphant grin. "We'll get married as soon as we can in a small private ceremony at the church here in Kemberly. Then, sometime in September, we'll throw a huge party and invite the whole family and as many of our friends as want to come. We could really go to town, Gracie.''

"That's a wonderful idea," Grace said, her eyes lighting up. "And I know just the place to throw the party. At Michael's new hotel. It's a wonderful old mansion with beautiful gardens, and you know if Michael's in charge of arranging the catering, he'll do a bang-up job.''

If she'd wanted to throw the party in a submarine, Jeffrey would have said yes, just so long as she agreed not to delay their wedding ceremony more than a few days. "Ashby Hall sounds the perfect place. And I'll see if the vicar's willing to marry us next weekend. Since we're not inviting any guests, it shouldn't take more than fifteen or twenty minutes, so he can't claim he's too busy.''

She hesitated for a moment. "Even if we don't invite any guests, we'll need two witnesses for the actual wedding ceremony, Jeffrey.''

They might have been separated for a while, but after

thirty-two years he didn't have any trouble identifying the reason for her hesitation. "I guess I get to choose one witness, and you get to choose the other," he said. He stopped and turned her to face him. "My choice is easy. Ian Stanley was best man at our first wedding, and we've been friends ever since. I can't imagine anyone I'd rather have to stand beside us when we renew our vows."

Grace laid her head against his chest. "Thank you, Jeffrey," she whispered. She looked up, smiling again. "And my choice is easy, too. I would like to invite your mother to be our second witness. Maybe if she stands right next to us, some of her wisdom will brush off on us."

"More likely her bad habits," Jeffrey said, and grinned cheerfully. They turned and strolled at a leisurely pace toward the house. "Is that agreed, then? Next week we're going to San Francisco, but we'll fly home in time to be married on the weekend. Is Ian going to be in town, do you know?"

"He's not leaving for China until the end of the month, so we should just be able to squeeze in our wedding before he goes."

Jeffrey chuckled, and Grace turned to him. "What is it?"

"Mrs. Milton," he said in a low voice. "She's peeking at us from behind the drawing-room curtains."

Grace's expression became mischievous. "Then we should give her something worthwhile to look at, don't you think?"

"Definitely." Jeffrey folded Grace into his arms and tilted her head back, looking into the sparkling depths of her eyes. "Let's give her a real show," he said, and bent his head to kiss his once and soon-to-be wife with fierce, loving passion.

The drawing room curtains twitched and Mrs. Milton gasped, but by the time they finally walked back inside the house, they'd both forgotten all about the housekeeper.

CHAPTER THIRTEEN

JULIA HAD FELT pathetically sorry for herself when Gabe broke the news that he didn't love her. She'd moped around the flat, playing the role of brave but tragic heroine and generally indulging herself in a wallow of self-pity. In the wake of Michael's return to Chicago, her mood was radically different. She didn't feel in the least sorry for herself, and the pain of his absence was far too acute to be eased by role-playing. Instead of self-pity, what she felt was rage—at Michael for being such an idiot that he expected her to toss aside everything in order to become his mistress, and at herself for being such a hidebound fool that she'd lacked the courage to accept his offer and take a chance on love. She'd been brought up to believe that avoiding risk was always the prudent thing to do. More and more lately, she'd begun to wonder if avoiding risk wasn't a symptom of cowardice rather than good sense. What was life worth if you marched straight through it, never daring to explore any of the most enticing byways for fear of running into a patch of brambles?

The final two days of the school year kept her busy, and on Friday evening she celebrated eight weeks of upcoming vacation with some of her fellow teachers and managed not to think about Michael for three whole hours. But when Saturday afternoon rolled around and the household chores were done, she discovered that she couldn't knuckle down to sketching a design for the wall hanging she intended to embroider as a christening gift for Elizabeth Gabrielle. She'd found a wonderful reproduction of a Renaissance painting of the Archangel Gabriel at the National Gallery bookstore, but the fourth time she ruined the powerful line of Gabriel's arm, she gave up for the day.

Unable to settle, she wandered over to the old electric typewriter set up in a corner of her bedroom and scrolled in a sheet of heavy white bond paper. She'd typed her letter of resignation to the headmistress of Kensington Academy, effective immediately, before she had any conscious idea that this was what she'd spent the past several days planning to do.

Stunned, she stared at the letter for several minutes before she finally pulled out the page and read through the brief, formal paragraphs and the courteous tag line thanking the headmistress for her advice and encouragement over the past five years. Ignoring the slight tremor of her hands, she signed her name, folded the letter into an envelope and sealed it before she could change her mind.

In September, when school reconvened, she wouldn't be there. Her stomach lurched at the thought, but as much with excitement as with trepidation. Walking across the road to the corner pillar-box to post the letter, she could already hear the lectures her brothers would deliver at the next family gathering, and see the pitying looks she'd get from her sisters-in-law as they discussed this latest evidence of her failure to take life seriously. To her astonishment, she discovered that she didn't give a damn.

She knew her parents would be worried sick that she had done something so rash, but watching the letter slide down into the dark depths of the pillar-box, Julia felt as if she'd been released from an intolerable burden. Michael might have been wrong to expect her to give up everything at a moment's notice and fly to Chicago with him, but he'd been absolutely right to say that she needed to change her job. She was willing to work hard, and she had no dependents. If she couldn't afford to take a risk, who could? The mortgage on her flat was no good reason to put a mortgage on her soul, which was what she'd been doing for the past several years. It was time to stand up for herself and begin living the life she wanted to lead, instead of the life her well-meaning family had mapped out for her.

Julia's burst of self-confidence lasted until she got back into the house and began to read through the Situations Vacant column of the daily newspaper. Unfortunately, the four pages of job listings contained no mention of any company in need of an interior designer with no practical experience and a fascination with the techniques of antique fabric restoration. By the time she'd read the job listings for a second time, the old Julia would have been on the phone, begging the headmistress to pay no attention to her letter of resignation. The new Julia swallowed hard, wiped her sweating palms on her jeans and doggedly began to reread the list of openings. If she couldn't get a position as an interior designer, she'd work as a sales assistant in a home furnishings store or a paint-and-wallpaper shop. However limited the scope for exercising her creativity, she would be employing her talents more usefully than teaching French. She could match curtain material with carpets and bedspreads better than anyone she knew, whereas she'd met at least a dozen French teachers who were more inspiring at their jobs than she was. As for paying the mortgage on her flat out of a shop assistant's salary—well, she had some savings, and the rent from her flat mate, who would soon be returning from a short sabbatical in South Africa. If she lived economically, she could hold out for at least a year before she seriously depleted her small nest egg.

The phone rang, and she was tempted to ignore it. Her mother usually called at this time on a Saturday afternoon, and Julia didn't want to have to deflect questions about Edward Hillyard or risk letting it slip quite yet that she'd resigned from her job. Just as the answering machine was about to take the call, she screwed up her courage and grabbed the receiver. No use avoiding the inevitable.

"Hello," she said.

"Julia? This is Tate Herald. You sound busy, I hope I haven't called at a bad time."

"Not at all." Julia's spirits perked up at the unexpected call. "As a matter of fact, your timing's terrific, Tate. I was looking through the Situations Vacant columns and deciding that my skills are in terrifyingly short demand. I definitely needed the distraction."

Tate laughed sympathetically. "Believe me, I know the feeling. But I would have thought a teacher with your qualifications would have no trouble finding a job."

"I'm not looking for a teaching position," Julia said. "It's the end of the school year, so this seemed a good time to start a new career as an interior designer."

"How interesting. Michael mentioned that you had some very creative ideas for refurbishing some of the rooms at Ashby Hall."

Julia's grip tightened around the phone. "You've spoken to Michael since he went back to Chicago?"

"Mmm...yes, we're old friends, you know. He called me a couple of days ago. Your name came up in our conversation a few times."

Julia wanted to ask what Michael had said about her, but she couldn't find the words to form the question without sounding overeager. She hung on to the receiver and waited, hoping for she wasn't sure what.

"Do you have plans for tonight?" Tate said. "My date had to fly to L.A. for a last-minute audition, so I've been stood up. Would you be interested in joining me for dinner? If you wouldn't mind going somewhere quiet and out of the way, that is."

"I'd love to join you, Tate, and somewhere off the beaten track is fine."

"Thanks. You know, most of the time I love being recognized by my fans. Never believe an actor who tells you that he or she doesn't like fame—we're all hungry for it. But there are occasions when I really empathize with Greta Garbo, and tonight I'm having one of my 'I want to be alone' moods."

"Then why don't you come here to my flat so that you don't have to spend all evening signing autographs on paper napkins? I could cook us something simple. A cheese soufflé, maybe."

"Simple? A soufflé?" Tate gave an appreciative gurgle. "Julia, you're a marvel. I can be there by seven. Is that too early?"

"It's perfect timing," Julia said, relieved to have something to occupy her mind other than the twin problems of her nonexistent affair with Michael Forrest and her equally nonexistent job as an interior designer. "I'll look forward to seeing you in a couple of hours, Tate."

TATE ARRIVED PUNCTUALLY at seven. "What a lovely room," she said, following Julia into the living room. "The colors are so restful, and that sofa in front of the fireplace is gorgeous."

Julia smiled. "If I didn't know she's been too busy fussing over her baby to think of anything else, I'd suspect Lianne of coaching you on what to say. That sofa's my pride and joy. It's a 1920s piece that I bought from a junk shop on the Portobello Road, and then I spent weeks searching for material to reupholster it. I'm glad you like it."

Tate ran her hand along the back of the sofa. "Are you telling me that you recovered this yourself?"

Julia shrugged. "Well, yes, but it's easy to do once you know how. There's nothing skilled or high tech about it. Restoring the wood on the armrests was much harder than the actual upholstering."

"Lianne told me once that you were intimidatingly talented. Looking around this room, I realize that she wasn't exaggerating."

Julia blushed. "You know Lianne, she's much too generous about her friends. But thanks for saying all the right things, Tate. I'm still trying to convince myself that I'm not crazy to have thrown away a perfectly good teaching position in pursuit of a dream that may never succeed."

"You're not crazy, you're talented. There is a difference, although there will be plenty of days when you'll find yourself wondering. Trust me on this, Julia—I've been where you are now, and you're never going to be happy until your work reflects the woman you really are."

"When times get tough, I'll remind myself that you and Lianne both believe I can make it." Julia grimaced. "I suppose the worst that can happen is that I fall flat on my face and provide my family with endless opportunities to say they told me so."

"Then pick yourself up, dust yourself off and tell them to butt out." Tate gave the sofa a final appreciative stroke before sitting down. "You know, if I'd listened to my parents, I'd probably be slogging away at some desk job in a huge conglomerate, thoroughly miserable with life. But I'm lucky enough to have a grandmother who's my greatest fan. When I was starving my way through drama school—not to mention waiting tables for several years afterward—Gran would remind me that when you're born with a special talent, you have an obligation to develop it. She was more thrilled than I was when I finally landed a job as the model in an advert for women's underwear." Tate grinned. "To listen to Gran, you'd have thought I'd been signed for a world tour with the Royal Shakespeare Company instead of an agreement to be photographed in my bra and knickers."

Julia laughed, but she could hear a wistful note in her own laughter. Her parents were good people, so were her brothers, but they no more understood her hopes and dreams than they understood the motivations of a tribal chieftain in the Brazilian rain forest. She envied Tate her sympathetic grandmother. "She must be thrilled now that you're a genuine star."

"She is, but she helps me keep my success in perspective. As soon as I'd made it within sniffing range of the big time, she stopped telling me how wonderful I was and started to remind me that I can't afford to keep my nose stuck up so high in the air that I fall over my own feet. A wise woman, my gran."

"You're lucky to have her." Julia glanced at her watch. "The soufflé should be ready in a couple of minutes. Why don't you come into the kitchen while I check on it? The people who owned this flat before me knocked out the wall between the dining room and the kitchen, so it's one big room and you have to eat where you cook. Now that I'm used to the idea, I like it a lot better."

"Much more practical now that nobody has squads of servants to serve the meal," Tate agreed.

Dinner was a successful meal, and not only in terms of the soufflé and accompanying salad of baby greens. Tate turned out to be a fascinating guest, and Julia felt a genuine rapport growing between the two of them. If only she'd been able to find some tactful way to bring Michael's name into the conversation, she would have considered the evening almost perfect.

Finally, when they'd carried a tray of after-dinner coffee into the living room, Julia swallowed her pride and abandoned any pretense of subtlety. "How did you first get to know Michael Forrest?" she asked, pouring a cup of coffee and handing it to Tate.

"It was strictly an arranged match," Tate said. "We were hooked up by my PR consultant. I needed some publicity in the States to coincide with the launch of 'Grosvenor Square' on American network television. Michael and I both happened to be using the same PR firm, and they decided that pretending to have an affair with Michael was one of the easiest ways to get my name splashed across the front pages of the tabloids.''

"How did you manage to persuade Michael to cooperate?" Julia asked. "I'd have thought he generates enough affairs of his own, without needing a PR firm to set him up with dates."

"You'd be surprised at how many of Michael's dates are actually business arrangements," Tate said. "In my case, the PR firm brokered a deal between Michael and the producers of 'Grosvenor Square.' The cast of the show stayed at his hotels during our publicity tour, and the producers threw their launch parties at the Los Angeles Carlisle Forrest. In exchange, Michael agreed to partner me to enough high-profile events to generate a media buzz about our torrid romance. In reality, once the cameras turned off, our relationship was about as torrid as Ma and Pa Kettle's. Although, as it happened, we did become good friends."

Julia stirred her coffee, although she was too preoccupied to have put in any cream. "I can understand why the publicity might be valuable for you, since you're very photogenic, and getting your picture on TV, or in the tabloids, might persuade an American audience to watch your show. But I still don't understand why Michael would find the media attention worth his time. People don't choose a hotel because the company president leads a glamorous life."

"In fact, that's not entirely true. Michael's discovered that convention business can be influenced by adding an aura of glamour to a hotel's reputation. But Michael doesn't have the luxury of keeping out of the limelight, even if he wanted to. He became interesting to the media when he wrested control of the Carlisle Forrest empire from his father. He was still in his twenties at the time, his mother was already notorious for her succession of famous lovers, and his father chose to make a dramatic, public appeal to shareholders to side with him. When Michael won the battle and was appointed president, the media wouldn't leave him alone. His affair with Cherie Lockwood sealed his fate, because she chose to publicize their relationship in every way she could. After Storm was born, Michael learned the hard way that once you're in the spotlight, journalists will generate gossip about you, one way or another. He decided to make sure they generated the gossip he wanted people to read.''

Julia returned her cup to its saucer with special care. ''But Michael's affair with Cherie Lockwood wasn't a media invention, was it? Storm exists, and Michael's acknowledged he's the father.''

Tate took a few moments to answer. She finally looked up, her gaze locking with Julia's. ''Michael was royally screwed over by Cherie Lockwood, and I personally wish like hell that he hadn't allowed the story of their affair to be played out as if he were the bad guy. But my personal feelings don't give me the right to betray his secrets, or Cherie's, either, much as I despise the woman. If he hasn't told you the truth about his affair with Cherie, then it's not my place to do so. Besides, if you aren't smart enough to realize that Michael's the soul of honor, then you aren't the right woman for him. Which is a shame, because I thought when I saw you two together that he might finally have found the woman who would make him happy.''

It amazed Julia how calm her voice sounded when her stomach was turning cartwheels and her heart was hammering hard enough to burst. ''I first met Michael over a year ago,'' she said. ''Ever since then, I've used his relationship with Cherie and Storm as an excuse not to acknowledge how I feel about him.''

''Is it so difficult for you to admit that you've fallen in love?'' Tate asked quietly.

Julia didn't bother to deny that she was in love. ''I've always believed that people should be friends before they become lovers. With Michael, I seem to be doing everything backward. I fell in love first, now I'm trying to get to know him."

Tate shot an uncomfortably shrewd glance in Julia's direction. "It's pretty damn difficult to get to know a man when he's on one side of the Atlantic and you're on the other, wouldn't you say? Personally, I'd have thought it would be a hell of a lot easier to find out exactly how you feel about Michael if you were at least within shouting range."

TATE'S LOGIC WAS irrefutable, Julia thought after Tate had gone and she was alone again. There was no reason in the world for her to be sitting here in London, aching for Michael's company, when she could be with him. On Wednesday, when Michael had asked her to go to Chicago with him, she'd instinctively retreated into the habits of a lifetime. Instead of reaching for the chance of happiness and grabbing it with both hands, she'd drawn back in a futile attempt to protect herself from hurt. In retrospect, she wondered why in the world it had seemed sensible to send away the man she loved. How had she protected herself by turning her back on the most interesting, exciting and attractive man she'd ever met? How had she made herself less vulnerable to hurt by ignoring the fact that she was deeply in love?

It was suddenly so easy to see what she needed to do that Julia couldn't understand why it had taken her so long to work it out. She picked up the phone and called British Airways. Ever since Michael left, she'd felt incapable of performing routine tasks without a massive effort at concentration. All at once, with the decision made, her brain felt nimble again, her body light and coordinated. She tapped her fingers on the counter, doodling hearts on the message pad by the phone as she waited for someone to answer.

A clerk, sounding bored, asked how he could help her. Julia drew in a deep breath, calming her reckless sense of anticipation. "I'd like to book a ticket on your next direct flight to Chicago," she said. "How soon would that be?"

JULIA HAD TRAVELED throughout Europe, so she wasn't prepared for the sensation of foreignness that greeted her when she landed at O'Hare Airport on Sunday afternoon. Almost everyone around her was speaking English, but the unfamiliar accent and pitch of their voices meant that she had to focus all her attention just to understand what they were saying. The cavernous space of O'Hare struck her as profoundly alien. She knew that London's Heathrow airport was the busiest in the world, but its flights were divided among four separate terminals, so that the scale of each individual terminal appeared relatively cozy and intimate. By contrast, O'Hare gathered everything under one roof, as if flaunting its dominant position at the center of the vast North American continent. To Julia's eyes, its futuristic design, exposed pipes and shimmering laser lights all pulsed with the hurried beat of the twenty-first century.

The immigration officer viewed her passport with every appearance of intense suspicion, and Julia's confidence wasn't bolstered by having to ask him to repeat everything he said before she understood his questions. Whoever perpetrated the myth that Americans drawled had obviously never listened to the rapid-fire speech of the officials at O'Hare airport. Julia felt that she'd accomplished something major when she survived Customs inspection and managed to follow the overhead signs to a point outside the terminal building where she could get herself and her suitcase into a cab.

"The Carlisle Forrest, please," she instructed the driver, pushing her hair out of her eyes and wondering if she'd ever feel cool again. Her long-sleeved English summer dress was sticking to her all over. Thank God she hadn't worn panty hose!

"Carlisle Forrest? That's on Lake Shore Drive."

"Yes, that's what the address says."

The cabbie started his meter. "Humidity's a real killer today," he commented. "Heard on the radio it's ninety-four degrees, hundred percent humidity. That's Chicago for you. If it ain't freezin' you to death, it's fryin' you." He sounded rather proud of his city's demanding climate. He eased into the flow of traffic. "You gotta cute accent," he said. "Where did you fly in from?"

"London," Julia said, adjusting her mind to the interesting concept that she spoke with a foreign accent. "I'm English, and this is my first trip to America."

"I like the way you folks talk over there. My wife and me, we went to London last summer. Nice place. Expensive, though. That your hometown?"

When she nodded, he launched into a detailed account of his visit, during which he'd seen the changing of the guard at Buckingham Palace, visited the chamber of horrors at the Tower of London and enjoyed an afternoon at Madame Tussaud's. He was very upset that he'd been unable to catch a personal glimpse of either the queen or Princess Diana, and he informed Julia that the British royal family was missing out on a considerable source of profit by not agreeing to pose for photographs with visiting groups of tourists.

"My wife woulda paid fifty bucks, maybe more, to get her picture taken with one of the royals," he said. "Ten people at a time, that's five hundred bucks a pop, and it wouldn't take more'n a coupla minutes of their time. Diana wouldn't have to keep worrying about her divorce settlement, then, would she? She could earn plenty just posing for photos."

Amused by this evidence of the famed American entrepreneurial spirit, Julia agreed that this might be a good

way to make money, although she didn't hold out much
hope that the royal family would be jumping on the suggestion anytime soon.

The nine-hour flight had left her tired enough that she
was quite glad to have the cab driver do most of the talking, but when they reached downtown Chicago, her fatigue
vanished as she became lost in admiration of the spectacular architecture and spacious plazas. Most of what she
knew about the town was limited to gangster movies fea-
turing Al Capone, or documentaries recounting the horrors
of the blighted South Side. Nothing had prepared her for
the splendor of Lake Michigan or the magnificence of the
city's towering skyscrapers, aglow in the late-afternoon
sun.

The cab driver drew to a halt in front of an imposing
thirty-story building standing right by the lake. Michael
had mentioned that this flagship hotel of the Carlisle Forrest chain was more than a hundred years old. It was astonishing to think that in the 1890s, architects in Chicago had
already been able to safely design buildings as tall as this
one. Energized by the sheer vitality and elegance of her
surroundings, Julia paid the cab driver and walked into the
hotel.

The lobby was such a perfect example of art deco at its
best that she could only stare in silent awe at the sweeping
arches, the gleaming chrome fixtures and the polished wal-
nut counters. The very idea of her making suggestions on
how to improve the decor in a hotel this splendid would
have been funny if it hadn't been so absurd. It was mind-
boggling to realize that Michael was the president and
manager not only of this grand hotel, but of nine more just
like it. She'd recognized his leadership abilities and ambition from the first moment she met him, but having seen
him only when he was in the company of friends, or
against the relatively small-scale setting of Ashby Hall, she
hadn't begun to grasp the full size and scope of his position

as CEO of the Carlisle Forrest Corporation. Just standing in the lobby of his flagship hotel was enough to put his responsibilities into a whole new perspective.

A nagging voice, the legacy of her parents, warned Julia that she was about to make a first-class fool of herself. How was it possible that a man like Michael Forrest could have any lasting feelings for her? The two of them had been thrown together by force of circumstance, and they weren't in the least suited to each other. If Elizabeth Gabrielle hadn't decided to arrive a month early, they would never have discovered how many interests they shared. And from Michael's point of view, the lovemaking that she'd found so spectacular probably hadn't been anything out of the ordinary. Carried away by the heat of the moment, he had suggested she should fly back with him to Chicago. Now that she was here, he'd most likely be embarrassed that she'd taken his invitation seriously.

With a supreme effort of will, Julia shook off years of negative thinking. She knew what she was doing. God, she hoped she knew. The ache of yearning she felt for Michael made everything else irrelevant. In the last resort, what did it matter if Michael rejected her? If she didn't take this chance, she would always regret what might have been, and she was sick to death of leading a life based on avoidance of risk. Squaring her shoulders, she made her way to the registration counter.

"I'd like to speak to Michael Forrest if he's in the hotel," she said to the clerk. "I'm a personal friend of his and I've just arrived from London. My name's Julia Dutton."

The clerk's expression became simultaneously superpolite and totally inscrutable. "Is Mr. Forrest expecting you, miss?"

"Not exactly. Not today, at least."

If possible, the clerk's expression became even more

bland. "I'll dial his office number, Miss Dutton, but it is Sunday, and I doubt if he's in the hotel this afternoon."

"I have his home number, but somehow I expected him to be here."

The merest flicker of interest sparked in the clerk's eyes at the information that she had Michael's home phone number. "I'll call Mr. Forrest's office for you now, miss." He dialed a series of numbers and the phone was apparently answered almost at once, although Julia could only hear the clerk's side of the conversation.

"Mr. Forrest, this is David at the front desk. A friend of yours is downstairs at reception and would like to speak with you. Her name is Julia Dutton—"

The clerk got no further. "Yes, sir," he said, obviously in answer to a question. "She's right here at the check-in counter." He paused again. "Yes, sir. I'll make sure that she waits right here."

The clerk hung up the phone and looked at Julia again, this time with undisguised interest. "Mr. Forrest says he's coming down immediately. He asked you to wait for him here, Miss Dutton."

The elevators weren't visible from where she was standing, so Michael was only a few yards away from her when she saw him striding across the lobby, devastatingly handsome in a formal business suit. His gaze locked with hers, and suddenly she was running toward him, arms outstretched, the dozens of other people in the lobby entirely forgotten.

His arms clamped around her waist. Her hands clasped around his neck. "You told me to come and see you next time I was in the neighborhood," she said.

"Yeah, so I did." He pulled her against his chest, his smile crooked. "I'm glad you happened to be passing by."

"I came to pay off my debts," she said. "If you remember, I'm supposed to eat a real American breakfast. Something gross about pancakes, syrup and sausages."

Her fingers raced across his face, absorbing the shape and texture of him, reminding herself of how wonderful the stubble of his beard felt beneath her fingertips.

"I remember." His hands wound possessively in her hair, tilting her head back so that he could look deep into her eyes. His smile faded. "God, Jules, I've missed you. This has been a hell of a week."

His mouth came down on hers with passionate, seeking demand, and she surrendered herself to the kiss, sinking deeper and deeper, lost to the world until a polite male voice thrust her back to awareness of her surroundings. "Michael, sorry to intrude, but there was a photographer from the *National Investigator* here in the lobby just a few minutes ago. You might want to take your...friend...into my office so that you can both have some privacy."

Julia leaned against Michael, her breath coming fast and jagged, her legs too shaky to allow her to move. The man who'd spoken wore a dark suit and a discreet name tag bearing the inscription Thomas Burdine, Assistant Manager. She supposed she ought to feel ashamed of having made a spectacle of herself. How she actually felt was deliriously, gloriously happy.

Michael released his hold on her waist, but he kept his hand locked with hers. "Thanks for the warning, Tom." He grinned. "I'm sorry if we lowered the tone of the lobby."

The assistant manager permitted himself a small smile. "I'd say you raised the interest level rather than lowered the tone."

Julia glanced around and saw that, without exception, every employee in the place was staring at her and Michael with an identical expression of hypnotized fascination. She was just beginning to feel embarrassed when a uniformed bellman came in from the sidewalk. He looked at his fellow workers in puzzlement, then shrugged and made his way over to Michael's side.

"Your limo's here, sir. The driver says that traffic out to the airport is unusually heavy this afternoon, so you need to leave as soon as possible or you'll miss your flight."

Michael smiled. "Thanks, Ron, but I won't be going to the airport today, after all. Tell the limo driver to bill my personal account, will you?"

"Yes, sir. I'll let him know right away." The bellman was well trained, and he allowed himself only one quick glance at Michael and Julia's linked hands before turning smartly on his heel and returning to the canopied portico.

"You shouldn't have canceled your flight for me," Julia said. "I know how busy you are, Michael, and I could have gone with you wherever you were going. Or waited till you got back."

He looked at her, his eyes glinting. "I was going to London," he said.

"Oh." She felt a smile begin to play around her lips. "Not more problems at Ashby Hall, I hope?"

"No," he said. "I'd decided it was time to take care of some pressing personal problems."

"What a coincidence," she said. "That's exactly why I came to Chicago. What a good thing we didn't cross in mid-Atlantic."

"Julia." Her name came hoarsely from his throat. He moved toward her again, caught the eye of the hotel manager and stepped back, drawing in an unsteady breath. "You know, I'll bet if we went up to my suite, we'd be able to take care of each other's personal problems in a heartbeat."

She managed to keep a straight face. "You know, Michael, I'll bet you're right."

THEY LAY TOGETHER on the bed in Michael's private suite, their limbs tangled, breath gradually slowing to normal, hands stroking each other's backs in a sated, sleepy caress.

Julia only realized that she'd drifted into a light doze when she woke up and found Michael looking down at her, watching her intently in the encroaching dusk.

He saw that she was awake, and his hand reached out to splay against her rib cage in a gesture of mingled tenderness and possession. "What made you decide to come to Chicago?" he asked.

"I wanted to be with you."

His hand tightened over her breast. "Why?"

She wrapped her hand around his, feeling the heat of her own flesh beneath his fingers. "Because I love you and because everything else suddenly seemed trivial in comparison to that."

She was so accustomed to seeing his emotions shuttered behind a mask of self-mockery that it was almost shocking to see the naked relief and happiness that swept across his face.

"God, Julia, I love you." His voice cracked as if the words had been dragged out of him, the awkward confession of a man who'd been given too many reasons in the past to keep his emotions tightly guarded.

She brushed her lips over his before drawing back just enough to smile into his eyes. "If you practice saying that every day, I promise it'll soon be no more painful than having a root canal without anesthesia."

"I love you," he said again.

"See?" She cradled his face between her hands, her gaze tender. "That time you didn't even wince."

He smiled, but she could feel his tension. "We have a lot to talk about, Jules. We both know this isn't going to be an easy relationship to work out. And living on opposite sides of the Atlantic is almost the least of our problems."

"The best relationships are never easy. Look at Grace and Jeffrey DeWilde. I'm sure they love each other to distraction, but their marriage is still a work in progress thirty-three years after it started!"

He frowned, contemplating. "Grace gave me some advice last time I was in London. She said that you should never try to stitch a relationship together without acknowledging the problems that you're facing. So maybe that's what we should do. I want to give us a fighting chance, Jules, but it's hard for me to talk about commitment and marriage and happily ever after. My parents had the sort of marriage that gives divorce a good name, and the only time I fell in love before I met you, I got badly burned."

"By Cherie Lockwood," she said tentatively.

"Yes."

"You don't have to talk about her if you'd prefer not to." Julia leaned closer, holding his hand. "Is she really important to us? We're neither of us teenagers, Michael, and we'd be pretty boring people if we didn't have any relationships in our past."

"It's not as simple as that," Michael said. "I need to explain about Cherie so that you'll understand why, even though I love you, it's difficult for me to make the sort of commitment another man might find easy. I associate marriage more with broken promises and betrayals than with anything positive."

"But you were never married to Cherie, were you?"

"No, I've never been married, but from what I've seen, marriage has never been a beneficial partnership. My parents' marriage made me gun-shy until Cherie came into my life and I imagined myself deeply in love. I was already thirty-three years old when we met, and accustomed to thinking of myself as cynical and sophisticated and wise to all the angles, but in reality, I guess I was still naive enough to be an easy mark. Cherie seemed sweet and exotic and loving, a beautiful bundle of conflicting needs and temptations. She was also elusive, which had the immediate effect of sending me chasing after her in a big way. Which was exactly what Cherie had counted on, of course. She'd chosen her sucker well."

Julia looked up. "But why were you a sucker just because Cherie Lockwood chose to pursue you? She was attracted to you, presumably."

"Not in the least." Michael's smile contained no mirth. "Cherie arranged to meet me because she'd discovered she was three weeks pregnant and she was desperate to provide a father for her baby. She selected me because of my reputation as a bachelor who lived life in the fast lane, and also because I had approximately the same hair and eye coloring as her baby's real father. I'm sure the fact that I wasn't a Hollywood insider counted for a lot, too. I wasn't about to recognize great acting when I saw it up close and personal."

Julia frowned. "I'm not getting this. Why couldn't Cherie Lockwood name the true father of her child? Or if she didn't want to do that for some obscure reason, why did she need a father at all? She's an actress, not a nun or a candidate for public office. Lots of female stars in Hollywood have had babies without identifying the father. What did she need you for—or any father, for that matter?"

"Cherie was terrified that some enterprising journalist would put two and two together and come up with the name of her baby's real father, and that's what she was frantic to avoid. Storm's father was—is—a man who couldn't afford to be caught out in an adulterous affair. So to protect her lover, she had the most public and torrid love affair with me that she could manage to devise. What I really resent is that when she started to become visibly pregnant, she told me I was the father of her baby."

"Oh, no!"

Michael gave a cynical shrug. "I had no reason to disbelieve her, since at that stage, we'd been living in each other's pockets for almost four months. We'd used birth control, of course, but birth control fails, I knew that, and I was more than willing to take responsibility for my actions and learn to be the best parent I could. For the next two months, I kept asking her to marry me, and she kept inventing excuses as to why she couldn't say yes. Finally, she had the locks changed on her house and refused to meet with me or take my phone calls. She had her lawyers threaten me with a suit for harassment. It was only because a nurse called me anonymously to say that Cherie had gone into labor that I knew she was delivering the baby I still thought was mine. I flew back from New York, where I happened to be, and arrived at the hospital in L.A. a couple of hours after Storm was born.''

''My God, Michael, how could she do something as cruel as letting you think Storm was your son when he wasn't? And why did she do it?''

''I don't think she meant to be cruel. To be fair, I think Cherie misread me on the question of how I'd feel about having a child. Based on my reputation, she assumed I would dump her the minute she announced she was pregnant. She didn't expect me to keep insisting that I wanted to play a major role in Storm's upbringing.''

''The fact that she understood nothing about your character doesn't excuse what she did, Michael. In fact, it makes it worse that she could set out to use somebody she hadn't bothered to learn anything about.''

Michael smiled faintly. ''Thank you for sounding so indignant on my behalf.''

Julia flushed. ''I keep remembering all the times I needled you about your neglect of Storm. I feel so guilty, Michael.''

He took her hand and kissed the tip of her fingers. ''You have nothing to feel guilty for, Jules. You believed exactly what everyone else believed, and why wouldn't you? You'd never even met me when the stories about Storm's birth and my neglect of Cherie started to surface in the tabloids.''

''How long did it take Cherie before she finally got

around to telling you Storm wasn't your son? And once you knew the truth, why didn't you broadcast it to the world?''

"She told me right after he was born, when I came to the hospital in L.A. I threatened to take legal action to get access to Storm on a regular basis, and so Cherie delivered her ultimate zinger. She informed me Storm wasn't my son, that she'd already been pregnant when she met me, and that she was willing to have blood tests done to prove the baby wasn't mine.''

Julia rested her head against Michael's chest. "Did she tell you who the father was?''

"Yes, because I threatened to turn the tables on her and tell the media Storm wasn't mine. She begged and pleaded with me to let everyone continue believing that Storm was my son. And in the end, I agreed. Ironically, if she'd told me the truth in the first place, I might have agreed to help her out without any need for all the deception.''

"But why?'' Julia exclaimed. "Why would you agree to let yourself be used like that? Who in the world were you protecting?''

"Not Cherie,'' Michael said. "And certainly not her lover. I kept silent because of the other woman in the triangle. Terri was dying of muscular dystrophy, and she didn't need to hear that her husband had committed adultery and fathered the child with Cherie that she'd never been able to give him.''

"Oh, my God!'' Julia finally understood. "Storm's father is Brad Stein.''

"Yes,'' Michael confirmed. "The man famous throughout the movie industry for his devotion to his first wife, Terri. And now adding to his reputation as a good guy by marrying Cherie Lockwood and taking care of the son I supposedly walked out on.''

Julia shuddered. "How can you bear to know that Brad

Stein's so respected when he's got all the moral integrity of a cockroach?''

''I'd have destroyed Brad's legend in a heartbeat, but at the time Storm was born, Terri was in the terminal stages of her illness, and I didn't want to be responsible for hurting her when she was struggling to enjoy the last few months of her life. And much as I loathe the hypocrisy of what Brad and Cherie did, I honestly believe they were far more concerned about Terri than they were about anything else. Cherie genuinely liked Terri, and she was desperate to protect her from finding out the truth about Brad being Storm's father. She really needed to be able to point an accusing finger in my direction.''

''Cherie might have genuinely liked Terri, but she wasn't concerned enough about her to refrain from having an affair with her husband,'' Julia said hotly. ''And the same goes for Brad Stein. He didn't love his wife enough to remain faithful to her when she was dying. You're kinder to both of them than I would be, Michael, a lot kinder.''

He finally gave her a genuine smile. ''I've had three years to work on my charitable feelings. Besides, in retrospect, I keep thinking how damn grateful I am that Cherie Lockwood isn't the mother of my firstborn son. Because, you know, the kicker in all this is that by the time Storm was born, I realized that I'd never been in love with Cherie at all. She'd dangled an intriguing package in front of my nose, and I'd chased after it. I'd made no more of an attempt to get to know the real Cherie Lockwood than she did to get to know me.''

Julia moved closer, nuzzling her cheek against him. ''That sounds like the story of my relationship with Gabe,'' she said. ''He's good-looking, intelligent and the heir apparent to the DeWilde empire, so I convinced myself I was in love with him. The truth is, I never tried to get to know the real Gabriel DeWilde. I was too busy enjoying the image he projected to waste much time bothering about the fact that there was absolutely no spark between us, no genuine intimacy.''

Michael held her tight. ''I guess we have plenty of spark,'' he said.

She smiled. ''Yes, I guess we do. And even some excess sizzle.''

For a man who normally radiated self-confidence, he looked remarkably unsure of himself. ''When two people love each other, the logical next step is for them to get married,'' he mumbled.

Her laughter was tinged with a note of sadness. ''Well, yes, that's true as a general rule. But not when they look as terrified of the idea as you do, Michael.''

He drew in a shaky breath. ''The *idea* of marriage still terrifies me, but this past week I realized how crazy it was to throw away the chance of having something wonderful with you just because my parents were unhappy and Cherie Lockwood screwed me over. Ever since that morning in your flat when you sent me away, I've been trying to think of all the reasons why you were wrong to refuse to come and live with me. Last night, I finally quit blaming you and faced the fact that I was the one who'd behaved like an idiot.''

He stroked her hair away from her forehead, holding her gaze. ''I was flying to London to ask you to marry me. I know now that I want you to be the person who shares my life, the woman who'll be the mother of my children, my friend as well as my lover. Will you marry me, Julia? Please?''

She must have said yes, because next thing she knew, she was in Michael's arms and he was kissing her passionately, in between murmuring promises about how he was going to love and cherish her forever. When they finally broke apart, he held her head cradled against his chest.

"Did I mention that I'll expect you to sign a pre-nuptial agreement?" he said casually.

She jerked away, but he tightened his hold and pushed her head back against his chest. "There are only a couple of clauses in the agreement," he said. "The first is that you have to guarantee that all our children will look like you."

She blinked. "*All* our children? How many do you plan on having?"

"The precise number is subject to negotiation. The pre-nup will merely state that they all have to look like you."

She let out a tiny breath of laughter. "Well, that sounds entirely reasonable. I agree."

"There's one other clause. You must offer your services as an interior designer exclusively to corporations run by me."

"Mmm...I don't know, Michael. That might be a deal breaker. I already promised Tate Herald that I'd act as her decorator for the house she's just bought in London."

"You did?" Michael looked delighted rather than chagrined. "Congratulations," he said softly. "I'm sure you'll do a great job for Tate."

"Thanks, I hope so. I've taken your advice, Michael, and resigned from Kensington Academy, so I have plenty of time on my hands." She sent him a provocative glance. "In fact, for the right sort of fee, I'm sure I could be persuaded to work two design jobs at once. Say, refurbishing the bedrooms at Ashby Hall at the same time as I do Tate Herald's house."

"It's an interesting offer. What sort of a fee did you have in mind?"

She waved an airy hand. "Oh, several million pounds at least."

His eyes gleamed. "I'm a tough negotiator, sweetie. How about giving me a hundred thousand pounds' discount for every night we spend together in Mr. and Mrs. Blodget's bedroom?''

''A hundred thousand a night?'' Julia collapsed against the pillows, laughing. ''Good Lord, Michael, you place a pretty high value on your services.''

''And I'm worth every penny.'' He leaned over her, arms braced on either side of her body. ''Do you want me to show you how I'll earn my hundred thousand?''

Desire burned suddenly in her throat. ''Yes,'' she said huskily. ''Show me now, Michael.''

His smile contained tenderness along with predatory male satisfaction. ''My pleasure, sweetheart,'' he said, and closed his mouth over hers.

CHAPTER FOURTEEN

FOR THE PAST SEVERAL DAYS, relatives, friends, colleagues and well-wishers had been arriving at Ashby Hall from all over the world, and, finally, the gala dinner celebrating the remarriage of Grace and Jeffrey DeWilde was about to begin. Outside, the October night was cold and dark, but inside, the hotel reverberated with warmth, light and the hum of voices. Waiters circulated carrying trays of champagne and hors d'oeuvres, and guests admired the attractive table settings and the superb arrangements of chrysanthemums and dahlias plucked from the hotel's famous gardens.

In the Salisbury Suite, Jeffrey paced up and down, elegant in black tie and dinner jacket. He tried not to watch the ormolu clock, ticking reproachfully on the mantelpiece. Many things had changed over the past months, he reflected wryly, but one thing had remained the same. Grace—who was never so much as a minute late for a business appointment—still couldn't manage to get ready on time for her own parties.

She hurried out of the bedroom, breathless, flushed and ravishingly attractive in a strapless gown of midnight blue satin. The Dancing Waters necklace shimmered at her throat, the only jewelry she wore tonight other than her engagement and wedding rings. She sent him a smile that was both shy and rueful. "I know I'm late, but you're not to scold me, Jeffrey. I wanted to look beautiful for you tonight. Unfortunately, that takes considerably longer to achieve these days than it did the first time we celebrated our marriage.''

Jeffrey remembered how beautiful he'd thought Grace was thirty-three years ago when she'd floated down the aisle in her white bridal gown embroidered with pearls, her features misty and enticing beneath her fluttering lace veil. He knew beyond any possibility of a doubt that she was a hundred times more beautiful to him tonight than she'd been then, just as he knew that the love he had felt for her that day was no more than a flickering shadow of the love he felt for her now.

"You look breathtaking, definitely worth waiting for, and I love you to distraction. Your dress is perfect with that necklace.'' He took her into his arms and kissed her, taking care not to muss her hair or ruin her lipstick. Along with all the big lessons, years of marriage had taught him some of the little things, too. He held out his arm. "Well, Mrs. DeWilde, shall we go downstairs and greet our guests?''

Over the past year, she had never expected her son to look as happy as he did tonight, Mary thought as Grace and Jeffrey came downstairs to the accompaniment of a round of applause. Grace looked radiant, too, and—as usual—more elegant than any other woman in the room, her sense of style impeccable, and her happiness adding a soft glow to her complexion.

"Hello, Mother.'' Jeffrey bent to kiss her cheek, and Mary hugged Grace before falling into step at her son's side. Ian Stanley, recently returned from a trip to China, excused himself from a conversation with Sloan DeWilde and came to bow low over Grace's hand. Mary was saddened to see that the tan Ian had picked up during his travels couldn't disguise either his underlying pallor or his continuing weight loss. He'd definitely lost ground since the last time she'd seen him, when she and Ian had been the witnesses at Grace and Jeffrey's remarriage.

But the smile he gave Grace and Jeffrey was vintage Ian—dashing, debonair and faintly wicked. He bowed to Mary with a flourish and kissed the tips of Grace's fingers. "Darling Grace, you really ought to take pity on the rest of the women in the room and try not to look quite so stunningly beautiful. No wonder Jeffrey is wearing that infuriating look of smug self-satisfaction."

"You're misinterpreting my expression," Jeffrey said, giving his friend's arm a gentle squeeze. "I'm merely displaying delight that you decided to bring all three of your ex-wives to our party. That was certainly an unexpected pleasure."

Ian grinned. "Thought you might appreciate a graphic reminder that it's much simpler to keep marrying the same woman."

"Thank you for your thoughtfulness," Jeffrey said dryly. "But Grace and I have already decided that two weddings in a lifetime are about all we can handle."

"Grace! Jeffrey!" Leland Powell hurried across the room and kissed his sister's cheek, then turned and shook Jeffrey's hand. "I only wish Liam and Mallory could be here to celebrate such a joyous occasion with the family. But the baby's too small to travel. Did I tell you they're calling her Catherine? Isn't that a lovely name? Mallory decided to name her after our mother, you know."

Grace hugged him, obviously delighted to see how thrilled her brother was about his new granddaughter. "I love the name Catherine!"

"Now we're both grandparents," he said, beaming smugly.

"Welcome to the club," Grace replied, smiling. "How are Mallory and Liam coping?"

"Mallory's fine, and Liam's over the moon." Leland sobered for a moment. "I'm glad they had a girl. This way, Liam will be able to fall in love with his new daughter without feeling disloyal to the memory of the son he lost.''

Michael Forrest came up and asked Jeffrey a question about the wine being served with the first course of the dinner, and Grace left to circulate among her guests. Michael was a handsome devil, Mary thought. Good-looking in any circumstances, he was almost lethally attractive in evening dress. He reminded her in some ways of her late husband. They both had that aura of intense, controlled sexuality that women found so compelling. Mary smothered a spurt of silent laughter. By Jupiter, if she were forty years younger, she'd give Julia Dutton a run for her money.

She tapped Michael on the arm, snagging his attention. ''Jeffrey tells me your fiancée is responsible for the way the bedrooms in this hotel have been redecorated.''

''Well, yes, that's right—''

''She's a talented gel.'' Mary looked across the room to where Julia was talking and laughing with Lianne and Gabe. ''She's pretty, too. You should marry her before she has a chance to slip through your fingers, Michael.''

He smiled. ''Don't worry, Mrs. DeWilde, I intend to marry her as soon as possible. Her family wants a traditional ceremony, though, so we're going to have to wait until Christmas.''

''Christmas weddings can be delightful. Where are you going to have the ceremony?''

''Here in England, probably London, because Julia's family are all here, and she has two little nieces that are going to be flower girls. And you'll have to excuse me, Mrs. DeWilde. I see my manager over there, trying to send me signals. I believe he's anxious to start serving dinner.''

''Of course, you must go to him. We don't want to ruin the meal.'' Mary walked through the crowded lounge, avoiding people she knew, content to be an observer. That couple in the corner with Ryder Blake must be DeWilde

Cutter and his wife, Maxine. She'd have to meet them later and get to know them. One of the compensations of getting old was that one could ask questions that cut right to the heart of things without being told that one was being impertinent. Cutter didn't look much like a DeWilde, but Mary detected a definite hint of the family arrogance in the thrust of his jaw and the way he carried himself, shoulders squared, spine straight, ready to take on the world. Ryder's wife, Natasha, had exactly the same bearing and the same proud tilt to her head—a more compelling and enduring legacy from Dirk DeWilde than the stolen jewelry she'd inherited.

Megan and Phillip Villeneuve were talking to Kate and her new husband, Nick Santos. Kate still looked all fine-drawn lines and bundled energy, but Mary was pleased to see how close she stood to her husband, and how willingly she accepted the touch of his hand on her shoulder. She smiled to herself when she saw Nick's hand slide up and down his wife's bare back. Even across the room, Mary could feel the sexual tension between the two of them. And the same was true of Megan and Phillip, who were having a hard time keeping their hands away from each other.

Of all her grandchildren, Mary considered that Megan had undergone the greatest transformation in the last year. For some reason, despite her achievements, Megan had always been unsure of herself and her place in the world, but once she realized that Phillip was willing to give up everything in order to make her his wife, she'd blossomed with self-confidence. For that, if for nothing else, Mary would have been more than willing to bury the decades-old feud with Phillip's father. She smiled to herself as Megan emphasized the point she was making to Nick Santos with an expressive and uniquely French gesture. The DeWildes had always been international mongrels, despite the fact that Charles had struggled to perpetuate the myth that they were solid British citizens. Mary found it oddly satisfying to know that Anne Marie's descendants were scattered on three continents and in five different countries. Megan and Phillip's children would undoubtedly be intriguing people to know.

The crowd was thinning as Michael Forrest, with Julia Dutton at his side, ushered the hundred or so guests into the dining room. This seemed to be the year for weddings, Mary mused, making her way to the table where Grace and Jeffrey were already sitting with their children and spouses. She hoped with all her heart that this generation of newlyweds would find as much joy in their lives as she had found with Charles.

Mary waited until the guests were all seated, then she rose to her feet and held up a glass of champagne. "I claim the dubious privilege of being the oldest person in the room," she said. "Which gives me the right to make a speech, giving you the benefit of my wisdom, whether you want it or not." She smiled and waited for the ripple of laughter to die down.

"Fortunately for all of us, I have only a few words to say, but they come from my heart. This has been an amazing year for the DeWilde family. My three grandchildren have married, we've welcomed Elizabeth Gabrielle, the first member of the next generation, into the world. We've discovered a new branch of the family in Australia and New Zealand, and reconciled long-standing feuds that had their origins in events that took place before most of the people in this room were born. Best of all, Jeffrey and Grace have found their way back to each other. The path may have been twisted at times, but I believe the two of them have discovered how sweet love is when it's finally reclaimed. And now, before I'm overcome with embarrassing sentimentality, I ask all of you to join with me in drinking a toast to my son and his wife, Mr. and Mrs. Jeffrey DeWilde. Grace, Jeffrey, may the next thirty-two years of your marriage be even happier than the first thirty-two.''

Mary sat down to a thunderous burst of applause and hugs from her grandchildren. Jeffrey lifted his glass and touched it to his wife's. "Welcome home, Grace. It's wonderful to have you back.''

"It's wonderful to be home again." Grace touched her glass to her husband's. "Here's to us, Jeffrey," she said softly. "Here's to us.''

Weddings by DeWilde

Since the turn of the century the elegant and fashionable
DeWilde stores have helped brides around the world
turn the fantasy of their "Special Day" into reality. But now the
store and three generations of family are torn apart by the
separation of Grace and Jeffrey DeWilde. Family members
face new challenges and loves in this fast-paced, glamorous,
internationally set series. For weddings and romance, glamour
and fun-filled entertainment, enter the world of DeWilde...

Watch for *TERMS OF SURRENDER*,
by Kate Hoffmann
Coming to you in November 1996

Merchandising manager Megan DeWilde had major
plans for the expansion of DeWildes' Paris operation.
But Phillip Villeneuve, scion of a rival retailing family,
was after the same piece of real estate Megan had her eye
on. Caught in the middle of a feud neither understood, they
were powerless against the sizzling chemistry that overrode
property, family and every shred of common sense.

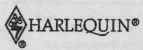

HARLEQUIN®

Look us up on-line at: http://www.romance.net

WBD8

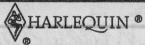

HARLEQUIN ®

Don't miss these Harlequin favorites by some of our
most distinguished authors! And now you can receive a
discount by ordering two or more titles!

HT#25657	PASSION AND SCANDAL by Candace Schuler	$3.25 U.S $3.75 CAN.	☐
HP#11787	TO HAVE AND TO HOLD by Sally Wentworth	$3.25 U.S. $3.75 CAN.	☐
HR#03385	THE SISTER SECRET by Jessica Steele	$2.99 U.S. $3.50 CAN	☐
HS#70634	CRY UNCLE by Judith Arnold	$3.75 U.S. $4.25 CAN.	☐
HI#22346	THE DESPERADO by Patricia Rosemoor	$3.50 U.S. $3.99 CAN	☐
HAR#16610	MERRY CHRISTMAS, MOMMY by Muriel Jensen	$3.50 U.S. $3.99 CAN	☐
HH#28895	THE WELSHMAN'S WAY by Margaret Moore	$4.50 U.S. $4.99 CAN.	☐

(limited quantities available on certain titles)

AMOUNT	$
DEDUCT: 10% DISCOUNT FOR 2+ BOOKS	$
POSTAGE & HANDLING ($1.00 for one book, 50¢ for each additional)	$
APPLICABLE TAXES*	$_____
TOTAL PAYABLE	$_____

(check or money order—please do not send cash)

To order, complete this form and send it, along with a check or money order
for the total above, payable to Harlequin Books, to: **In the U.S.:** 3010 Walden
Avenue, P.O. Box 9047, Buffalo, NY 14269-9047; **In Canada:** P.O. Box 613,
Fort Erie, Ontario, L2A 5X3.

Name: _____

Address: _____ City: _____

State/Prov.: _____ Zip/Postal Code: _____

*New York residents remit applicable sales taxes.
 Canadian residents remit applicable GST and provincial taxes.

Look us up on-line at: http://www.romance.net

HBACK-OD3

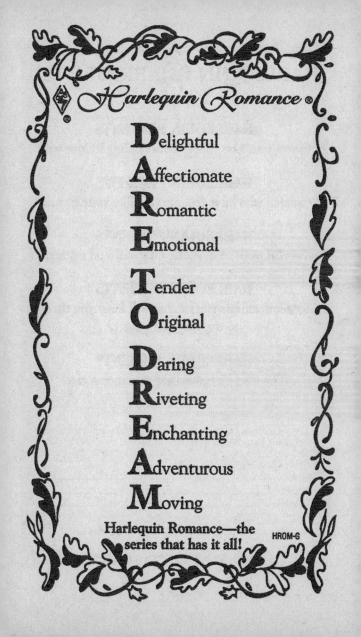

Harlequin Romance ®

Delightful

Affectionate

Romantic

Emotional

Tender

Original

Daring

Riveting

Enchanting

Adventurous

Moving

Harlequin Romance—the
series that has it all!

HROM-G

HARLEQUIN PRESENTS®

HARLEQUIN PRESENTS
men you won't be able to resist falling in love with...

HARLEQUIN PRESENTS
women who have feelings just like your own...

HARLEQUIN PRESENTS
powerful passion in exotic international settings...

HARLEQUIN PRESENTS
intense, dramatic stories that will keep you turning
to the very last page...

HARLEQUIN PRESENTS
The world's bestselling romance series!

Harlequin® Historical

If you're a serious fan of historical romance,
then you're in luck!

Harlequin Historicals brings you
stories by bestselling authors, rising new stars
and talented first-timers.

Ruth Langan & Theresa Michaels
Mary McBride & Cheryl St.John
Margaret Moore & Merline Lovelace
Julie Tetel & Nina Beaumont
Susan Amarillas & Ana Seymour
Deborah Simmons & Linda Castle
Cassandra Austin & Emily French
Miranda Jarrett & Suzanne Barclay
DeLoras Scott & Laurie Grant...

You'll never run out of favorites.

Harlequin Historicals...they're too good to miss!

HARLEQUIN®

I N T R I G U E®

THAT'S INTRIGUE—DYNAMIC ROMANCE AT ITS BEST!

Harlequin Intrigue is now bringing you more—more men and mystery, more desire and danger. If you've been looking for thrilling tales of contemporary passion and sensuous love stories with taut, edge-of-the-seat suspense—then you'll *love* Harlequin Intrigue!

Every month, you'll meet four new heroes who are guaranteed to make your spine tingle and your pulse pound. With them you'll enter into the exciting world of Harlequin Intrigue—where your life is on the line and so is your heart!

Harlequin Intrigue—we'll leave you breathless!

INT-GEN

HARLEQUIN ®

Scandals

A passionate story of romance, where bold, daring characters set out to defy their world of propriety and strict social codes.

"Scandals—a story that will make your heart race and your pulse pound. Spectacular!"
—Suzanne Forster

"Devon is daring, dangerous and altogether delicious."
—Amanda Quick

Don't miss this wonderful full-length novel from Regency favorite Georgina Devon.

Available in December, wherever Harlequin books are sold.

Look us up on-line at: http://www.romance.net

SCAN

1997
Reader's Engagement Book
A calendar of important dates
and anniversaries for readers to use!

Informative and entertaining—with notable
dates and trivia highlighted throughout the year.

Handy, convenient, pocketbook size to help you
keep track of your own personal important dates.

Added bonus—contains $5.00 worth of coupons
for upcoming Harlequin and Silhouette books.
This calendar more than pays for itself!

Available beginning in November at
your favorite retail outlet.

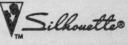